Also by Lance C Wilson

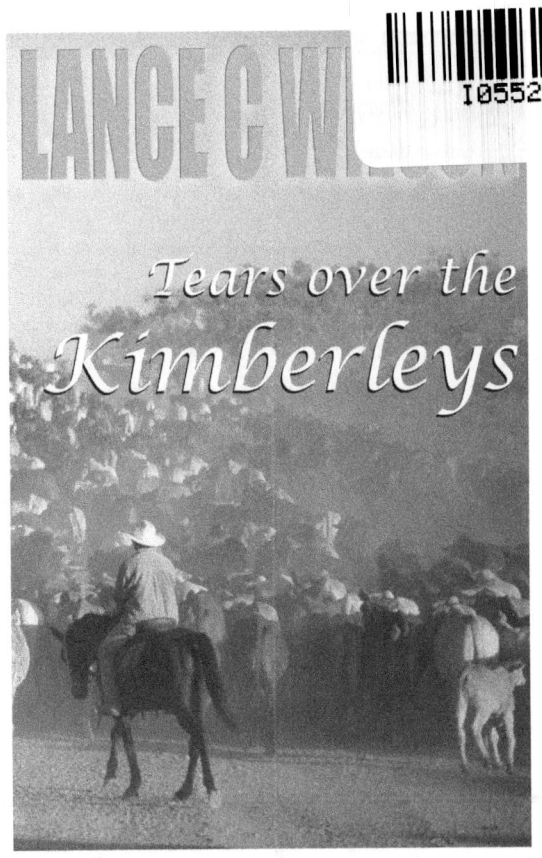

ISBN 9780977550524

Other published books
The Laird of Braidwood

www.lancecwilson.com

DARE TO LIVE
THE DREAM

A novel that will change your life

by

Lance C. Wilson

Printed and published by Kimberley Cottage Press in
Chinese
German
English

National library of Australia
Cataloguing-in-publication data:

Wilson, Lance C., 1945- .
Dare To Live The Dream.

ISBN 9780977550517 (pbk.).

I. Title.

A823.4

Edited by
Book and cover design
Typeset in 12 Times New Roman by

Made in Ink - Tasmania Australia

Acknowledgements

To Jo Grant my graphic designer who worked tirelessly assisting in the publishing of my novels. Jo's inspiration and encouragement has driven me on to finish my first two adult fiction attempts. Without her encouragement and hard work putting both together I honestly believe neither would have reached the printers.

The greatest thank you goes to my wife Cynthia who through good and bad times has put up with my eccentricities and dark periods. Cynthia has survived being chased by irate cows, stranded in crocodile infested rivers and a myriad of other adventures following her mad husband on his many escapades around Australia.
I have been inspired to write both my novels published to date by the wonderful characters and places we have traveled to and worked in over the years.
A special mention to my great mate Jacky Russell, a true character and loyal friend, who has traveled the highways and byways of our fantastic country and he has inspired me to use him in the latest novel.
Thanks to our friends Wayne and Lorraine, especially Wayne for his assistance with the adventures of the Matilda at Port Davey; his knowledge is appreciated.

Lastly to my family which I am so proud of, it has always been my opinion not much else matters in life but your health and family, without either nothing else really is of any significance.

I hope you enjoy my books. I have had a lot of satisfaction writing both to date and have three more in various stages which I intend to publish soon.

Foreword

Monica Spielberg agrees to go on a holiday to Broome in West Australia with two friends from her retirement village. Pushed into the village by her overpowering daughter Celia after the death of her womanising and overpowering husband, Monica makes a mad decision fuelled by too many wines and the exotic atmosphere of Broome.

After four decades of verbal abuse and repressed sexuality, Monica meets Sam Stewart, a widower, traveling alone in his caravan. Sam is visiting places he and his wife lived and worked, visiting old friends and reliving old memories.

Sam rescues Monica and her two friends from an embarrassing situation and what follows is totally unexpected, something that would change the lives of four elderly people forever. A novel that proves no matter what the age, adventure and romance are possible.

This story proves that no matter how old we are it is possible to completely change our life forever by daring to dream. Our hopes, dreams and sexuality never fade.

Chapter 1

Squalls of intermittent rain driven by freezing winds ran in from the sea over the Harbour Bridge enveloping Sydney. Tracy Brown cursed as she negotiated traffic on the way to work, already late due to a row with her husband William. The inclement weather and traffic did not help her temper and she was in disgust at her weakness.

Tracy, a cook at one of the north shore's leading old age villages, a supposedly 'up market establishment', had spoken with her husband about the disgusting food she was forced to prepare and serve to the village residents and she told him of her plan to complain to the authorities about it. To make matters worse, the families and residents had paid considerable amounts of money to gain entry to the village, with ongoing monthly payments that should have guaranteed those in the care of the managing company excellent service and care.

Instead greed and corporate profits, along with uncaring management interested in profit only, cut corners in all aspects of the running of the establishment. Tracy was forced to use food long out of date and reuse leftovers to save money. Today was soup and sandwiches for lunch; the soup a disgusting brew of cabbage leaves and leftovers, followed by sandwiches from out of date ham purchased cheaply along with yesterday's bread.

Her husband, afraid she may lose her job if she complained,

forbade her to speak out to the authorities. With two small children the couple would lose the house they had recently purchased without two wages coming in. Even so, it was a constant grind and struggle to survive. Aware of the hopeless scenario Tracy cursed her weakness and the position she, like thousands of fellow workers, found herself in. Another interest rate rise would put the family in serious financial trouble. As she parked her old Holden in the staff car park she looked through the dining room window and recognised her three favorite occupants, each gave her a cheery wave as she hunched against the sleeting rain and ran towards the kitchen.

She immediately set to work preparing lunch for the forty three permanent residents. To save money the manager had informed the cooks that no assistant cooks would be employed; the head cook and one waiting staff would in future manage all meals as well as cleaning up and serving.

Tracy busied herself trying not to think about the food she found herself preparing and instead thought of the three ladies with whom she had struck up a deep friendship and adored. She felt that none of the three really belonged in this place.

The eldest, being the leader of the group, Victoria Plumstead, aged seventy eight, was with no doubt the feistiest and more determined of the three. She had been a high profile public servant until the age of forty six when she met and married Harry Plumstead, the love of her life. Leaving her career she had sailed off into the sunset with her love for the next twenty years until the sudden death of Harry as they cruised aboard their yacht around the Pacific. Shattered she returned to Sydney with no family and terribly lonely. She had purchased a unit in the complex mainly for company and not a day went past, however, that she did not think of the great love she found late in life with Harry and the carefree life and adventure he introduced her to. Victoria was bored, frustrated and aware she had been taken in by the glitzy advertising by the corporation that owned the facility. She was quite aware when she purchased the unit that the company representative seemed more concerned with her financial position so she had deliberately misled them into believing she had far less money than she actually had. Every month she met with her accountant and with careful investment, was doing very well in the share market.

Mary Canning, aged seventy two, a born follower, had been happily married to husband Ken for fifty years and had four children. When Ken died two years previously, Mary's children, with her blessing, had sold the family home and business thinking they had the best interest of their adored mother at heart and purchased a unit in the best facility available in Sydney. Of the three women Mary was perhaps more content than her two confidants. Married to Ken while young, they had initially struggled but he was hard working and soon built up a large transport business while Mary raised the children, making sure all had a good education. Ken had handled the business side of the couple's union and made all decisions. A very content Mary had experienced a happy marriage raising their children, now all married with their own families, she waited for the visits of her grandchildren, which became less and less as they grew up and started work.

The youngest of the trio, and most reserved, was Monica Spielberg, aged only sixty two. Her philandering husband had died only a year or so previously in the arms of a young secretary who worked for his firm of solicitors. Monica had met her husband at university and quickly fallen for the charms of the overpowering Nigel, soon becoming pregnant; the two had married within a few months of meeting. Nigel was a bully and treated Monica as a slave, verbally abusing her from the start. Being beautiful, he kept her for show only and he soon climbed the corporate ladder; he had his own firm of solicitors at the age of forty. The union produced two children:

the son left home at a young age and joined the army, much to the disgust of his father, to be stationed in Darwin, and still there to this very day. Monica saw him only once or so a year.

The daughter Celia, a social climber, admired her father and classed her mother as weak and a nuisance, so when her father died, she immediately moved her husband and family into the family home and shoved her mother into the retirement village.

Victoria had been shocked at the treatment dished out to the compliant Monica by the overbearing daughter. A few weeks previously when Celia had turned up for the purpose of getting a signature from her mother, to access money held in trust for Monica, Victoria had intervened much to the ire of Celia and told her to fuck off and leave her mother alone. Squeaking and shaking at the onslaught from Victoria, Celia had left the facility and had not returned since.

Now, as the three unlikely friends sat at the table looking out at the dismal weather, waiting for the midday meal of unknown quantity and quality, Victoria turned to her friends and said, "Listen you two. I cannot stand another day here. Who is for one last big adventure?"

"*Really* Victoria what do you mean?" asked Mary looking surprised.

"We are all sitting here waiting for a meal of crap, bored senseless, we all have good health for our age, no one visits any of us. I for one am not going to sit here and wait to die," replied Victoria.

"Well why not?" Mary again broke in. "I am in for anything. Never done much in my life apart from raise and worry about the kids. Hell yes, what do you have in mind?"

"Victoria, what would my daughter say dear? And I really do not know if I have any money?" said Monica.

"I only mean let's go to Broome in West Australia to get some sunshine for fuck sakes Monica," said Victoria irritably staring at her two friends. "Harry and I cruised the coast there once, Cable Beach was beautiful, and as for money you have bloody heaps. Anyway it is my shout, can't take it with me."

Like three school children, the stirring of adventure excited them. They huddled together whispering quietly so as not to alert the other residents as Victoria outlined her plans. In the morning, all three would grab a cab into town, find a travel agent and book three glorious weeks at the resort opposite Cable Beach.

Perhaps for the first time since arriving at the village, to quietly spend what was to be the last remaining years of their lives, all three seemed to take on a new lease on life.

Drinking the warm coffee they retired to Monica's unit to dine on food they had purchased on the trips into the city; they had plans to make for their one last adventure. Victoria called at the manager's office and informed staff that the trio had decided to go on a holiday for three weeks. The management had, in fact, relished the thought of the money saved by the absence of the three. They were also relieved they wouldn't have to listen to complaints from Victoria about the crap food and a myriad of other complaints.

Perhaps no one was more thrilled and shocked at the announcement than Tracy. Hugging the women in turn she told them of her dilemma and Victoria agreed that her husband was right, it was not worth losing her job over.

"Might will always beat right," said Victoria. "We now live in a great period of greed and unfortunately in many instances, one must go with the flow in order to survive."

High with excitement they sat in the Flight Centre the following afternoon as Victoria informed the agent of the holiday they wanted. A very helpful assistant soon booked the trio on their adventure. With tickets and itinerary in hand the three returned to the village to pack and prepare for departure the following Monday.

Chapter 2

The clear blue Kimberley sky rose above the shimmering white sands of Cable Beach as the three women dropped their towels in the sand and entered the warm, aqua blue waters that sparkled along the Kimberley coast. They had arrived the previous evening and feeling tired had retired early with none having slept much the previous few nights, excited at the thoughts of the forthcoming trip. Now refreshed and having had an excellent breakfast of tropical fruit, the three friends enjoyed the beautiful warm waters of Broome.

"Thank you both of you. I never realised such a place existed. I would have loved to have travelled when I was young but unfortunately circumstances made it impossible," said Monica as she turned to her two friends.

"Same here, so thank Victoria, it was her idea. God this feels great, I feel alive for the first time in a long time and I want this feeling never to end," replied Mary.

"Okay, both of you, perhaps we should not class this as our last adventure but the start of a new direction for us all," said Victoria.

Splashing each other like excited schoolgirls the trio spent as much time in the water as they dared, thanks to Victoria, who had informed them of sunburn if they did not gradually acclimatise to the warm sun.

Over the next few days they visited the market, the Staircase to the Moon, and all the other local attractions as well as swimming daily, enjoying the service and excellent food served at the resort.

A few days passed and Victoria suggested a sunset camel ride on one of the camel trains that operated on Cable Beach. Enthused, they booked at the resort and that evening made their way to the starting point for the adventure.

Laughing and chiding each other as a patient camel train operator helped them onto the protesting animals, they whooped with delight and held on as the groaning beasts lurched to their feet at the command of the cameleer.

As the camel train lurched along with the rhythm of the beasts, it all seemed surreal, so removed from the lives Monica and Mary had experienced; they now realised the life Victoria had led was so different from their own.

The train had gone just a few metres when Monica realised that all those on the beach, in fact, were nude. Turning to Victoria she exclaimed, "Victoria, no one has clothes on."

"Oh, I forgot to tell you two ladies it's nude north of the line of rocks. We will see plenty of flesh on the trip up the beach, some good and most not so great," answered Victoria casually.

Several of the other riders, hearing the conversation, burst into laughter. Monica looked at Victoria, all so casual, then at the wide-eyed Mary and burst into fits of laughter herself causing Mary to break into uncontrollable laughter and nearly falling off the camel.

Somehow, with the sun setting and the camels loping along, it all seemed so natural. *Strange,* Monica thought, *perhaps these people live in the real world and we are the aliens.* It all seemed to excite her as if her life had made a complete change, all the new experiences and surrounds and smells fascinating.

After the ride ended in the darkness of the balmy evening, they made their way back to the resort, excitedly talking about the day's adventures and looking forward to the meal waiting back at the resort. Since starting the holiday their appetites seemed to have improved and they gained a zest for life that now coursed through their veins.

Enjoying a shower and changing into loose fitting frocks they had purchased at the market, they entered the dining room, beaming in anticipation at the upcoming feast of lobster and excellent wines stocked by the resort. The dining area was a buzz with sounds of talking and laughter; the atmosphere exhilarating as the trio chatted over the sumptuous feast. All three drank more wine than usual, caught up in the tropical paradise that is Broome.

A slightly tipsy Monica, usually shy and reserved, turned to her companions and taking them completely by surprise said, "Listen girls, I have a wish and that is to swim bloody naked as a plucked chicken with the nudies. What says youse?"

Victoria, usually unshakable, coughed and spluttered into her wine and turning to Monica, as Mary looked wide-eyed with a stupid grin on her face, replied, "Why the hell not? Harry and I did all over the Pacific and even here. Tomorrow afternoon, after the market and lunch, we will drop the gear and plunge into the water, a la nude!"

So caught up in the moment, the trio drank far too much and giggling like teenagers, later staggered off to their beds, laughing and hugging each other at the madness they seemed caught up in.

At breakfast the following morning, all seemed more subdued and admitted to more than feeling a little seedy. Having a coffee only, the decision was made to miss the market and retire for a few more hours rest, and yes, the nude swim was still on the agenda; none wanted to chicken out of the plan.

Meeting for lunch they ate a small chicken salad and then decided to go for a long walk before picking up the towels and heading to the beach.

Finding a deserted part of the beach after a short walk, excitedly like children, they dropped the sarongs each wore at the water's edge and ran into the sanctity of the warm water. The feeling of elation and freedom that overcame them, as they lay submerged in the warm water, was something they all felt and openly told each other of.

Never had Monica and Mary ever had such fun; again they appreciated the life Victoria had experienced and understood their friend even more, glad she had talked them into this magnificent adventure. Even the quiet Mary admitted that never in her life had she felt such freedom, she informed the others she even felt young again, the experience being so exhilarating.

So immersed in their own feelings, they laid back in the water, looking at the birds soaring overhead in the clear blue sky, talking to each other about their naked states and how each felt the act would change their life.

None were aware that the tide had crept over their clothes and towels, and in fact, having moved from their entrance point, did not notice them float out to sea.

It was Victoria who first saw a male person wearing shorts, walking up the beach with a small Jack Russell scooting along in front of him. It had been at this point that she'd also realised their apparel and towels had indeed disappeared.

Sam Stewart was in his mid sixties, having lost his beloved wife of forty five years two years previous. He now lived with his single daughter in Hobart in a unit under a house they had purchased after the death of his wife. Having worked and lived in the Kimberleys over the years, he was now on a pilgrimage visiting the friends and places he and his beloved had met and worked with over the years. Traveling in a caravan towed by his old land cruiser, he had been in Broome for a week and intended leaving in a few days. His best mate was 'Jacky', his faithful dog, aged twelve, who loved a run on the beach. Parking the cruiser on the nude section of the beach, he and Jacky had walked a short distance when he heard a yell.

"Excuse me sir, we seem to be in a spot of trouble here. Our clothes seem to have been taken or washed away. Can you please find us something to hide our saggy tits and let us leave the water with a bit of modesty?" yelled Victoria.

"Dear lady, may I suggest you stay ensconced in the position you're in and I will bring my vehicle and rescue all three of you fine looking damsels?" replied Sam with a wry smile.

"Thank you kind sir, and please hurry as my friends are quite alarmed at the predicament we damsels find ourselves in," said Victoria, now with a sense of the theatrical.

Scurrying off, Sam could not help the smile that came over his face. Aware the three had hoped to enjoy a skinny dip alone, he was amused at what had apparently happened.

Monica looked fearfully at Victoria and asked, "How in the hell do we get to his vehicle with some modesty?"

"Well girls, it is a nude beach and I guess our rescuer, having made it here, has seen the odd fanny and tits and no doubt more alluring than ours," replied Victoria.

All three burst into laughter, finding the situation somewhat exciting as well as totally unbelievable; what a story they would have to laugh about this evening over a few wines.

It was Monica who rose out of the water and informed the others, "Well, it was I who suggested this mad escapade, the first time in my life I have done anything totally unpredictable and outlandish. As a matter of fact, I cannot believe I have been drinking more than in my entire life and now find myself skinny dipping. Thank you Victoria for showing me a life I never knew existed. I feel alive for the first time in my life."

Striding unashamedly to the water's edge, followed by her giggling companions as they waited for the land cruiser, now approaching down the beach, Victoria mused, *Here is a woman who, until this trip, hardly spoke, sat quietly and timidly in the retirement village waiting to die and having absolutely no confidence; the change in such a short time has been amazing.*

The youngest of the trio, Monica, still maintained her beauty and until here and now, she had sensed in her friend some hidden and terrible secrets being held back. Even in the most confidential discussions about their past lives, those secrets had never been revealed.

Victoria suddenly realised they did not even know the rescuer's name, as he came powering down the beach with his dog looking out of the front window, caught up in the excitement. Pulling up next to his passengers, all three piled into the rear seat.

Without turning around the driver said, "Firstly, may I introduce myself, Sam Stewart at your service and secondly, where to my fair damsels?"

"To the resort opposite the entrance thank you Sam. Thankfully we left the keys at the front desk," replied Monica.

"No problem," Sam replied. "Where are you ladies from?"

"From Sydney on our last big adventure. Where are you from?" asked Victoria.

"Well, I live in Hobart in Tassy now, but worked all over the north here over the years, since I lost my wife, god bless her, I have lived with my daughter. Now I suppose you would say I am on a pilgrimage visiting our old friends and the places we worked at," said Sam.

They made their way up the beach, now mid afternoon, the beach packed with bathers. As they neared the end, Sam stopped as a couple recognised him and pulled him over, much to the alarm of his passengers.

Sam spoke to the man and woman who approached, "Hi Bill, how's things?"

"Great Sam, good to see you back in the Kimberleys," his friend Bill replied.

His companion, a small petite woman in her late fifties,

leant on the back door and spoke to the three nude women in the back seat. "Hi, I am Merle, Bills wife. We work in Broome. Are you coming down for a few drinks on the beach at sunset? We would love to have you join us, it will only be a couple of hours before sunset."

Sam, who was in conversation with Bill, and the only one with any clothes on, turned around and spoke to all three.

"I have some chairs back at the park and if you want I'll drop you off to change and then pick the three of you up in a hour or so to watch the sunset from the beach; its a must in Broome!"

"So kind of you Sam and thank you Merle and Bill, why not? But Sam, only if you allow us to shout you a meal back at the resort after," said Victoria.

"Done deal then. See you back here shortly folks," said Sam to his two friends. He drove off up the beach, stopping outside the resort and volunteering to go into reception to borrow three towels for his passengers so they could cover themselves up to retrieve the keys and retire to their bungalows.

With his passengers now wrapped in towels, carefully alighting from the vehicle, Victoria introduced herself and her companions to Sam and thanked him for the assistance he had given them. With a cheery wave Sam and his little dog drove off, promising to return to pick them up for a beach sunset.

Back at the caravan park Sam placed three chairs in the rear of his land cruiser, gathered some fresh clothes and showered. He had been terribly lonely so far on the trip, missing his wife terribly. Many times in the long lonely hours of darkness, on the road, tears came to his eyes as he remembered her. He wished he had told her he loved her more often and perhaps been more kindly and thoughtful towards her; in hard times and good she had stuck with him, been a faithful and good companion.

Looking at the Jack Russell - whom she adored - he felt that somehow, through him, she still traveled with them. Leaning down he patted his little companion and placed some food in his dish. Only the best for Jacky who refused to eat anything that was not cooked and it had to be good quality.

For the first time on the long trip north, having crossed the Nullabor and then wound his way through the Pilbara to Broome, Sam had a spring in his step. He thought of the three women and found them an interesting group. Victoria seemed to be the spokesperson for the group while Mary was more a follower, but Monica who was apparently much younger, closer to his age, was the dark horse. He found difficulty placing her in any category.

He was about to leave when the caravan couple next to him, also with a little dog, came out and in a friendly conversation asked Sam what sort of day he'd had. Sam answered it had been fine and explained that he was off with Jacky and some companions to watch the sunset on the beach. They offered Sam some extra chairs if he wanted them and Sam gratefully accepted an additional one. They waved to him as he left the park.

Both neighbors felt sorry for the quiet older man and his faithful dog. Not wishing to intrude, they could only guess at his loneliness. Being of the older school Sam was refined and kept to himself.

Chapter 3

On the way Sam called at the bottle shop and collected a couple of bottles of wine, not being sure as to his guest's tastes he purchased a mild wine. As he was leaving the drive-through, he stopped and jumped back out laughing, he had forgotten glasses. Purchasing four he placed them in the esky and drove off feeling elated at the coming event.

As he neared the resort even Jacky was caught up in the excitement jumping from the front seat to the back. As Sam approached the resort he was surprised to see all three in nice colorful dresses waiting on the footpath for his arrival, smiling and waving as he pulled over opposite to pick them up.

Victoria jumped into the front and her two companions in the back before Sam was able to get out to open the doors. Chatting away like old friends the four drove onto the beach, heading north to the nude section to park as parking was not allowed on the clothed section.

Jacky immediately sat on Victoria's knee. Sam had to apologise and warn her it was his usual position when he and his late wife traveled. The three ladies replied that Jacky would be welcome on any of their knees.

It was amazing how quickly all four became friends.

Jumping out of the vehicle next to several other four wheel drives, one belonging to Merle and Bill, now clothed and sitting out front in their chair, Sam placed more chairs in a row and the women were seated ready for the sunset.

The camels had already started up the beach, altogether they could see three camel trains. Jacky insisted sitting on

Monica's knee, quite content and happy to have a selection of people ready to pamper to his needs.

Giving each of his guests a glass, Sam poured wine and they sat chatting with the gathering, waiting for the event that was the sunset over Cable Beach.

Nobody ever seemed to tire of the sight. They watched the old Pearl Lugars and their tourist customers sail down the bay with camel trains passing in front of them as the sun slowly sank into the ocean in a huge red ball; somehow it seemed biblical. It was an event, as they discussed later, that is hard to explain: something one must experience first hand, an event one never forgets in their lifetime, something that makes one feel insignificant in the universe, an event money cannot buy, free to all.

Sitting in the twilight it was Mary who spoke to Victoria and Sam, "Well, thank you both for bringing me here tonight and especially Victoria. I never knew this all existed. I pray every night that it will never end. I nearly didn't come at all, having never left Sydney in my entire life. You have opened up a new world to me and I somehow feel I could die happy. I have done things I've never even dreamt. Victoria and Sam, I know you both have led a life of travel and adventure, thank you so much for sharing a little with me."

"Same here. I wanted to go nude bathing to do something wild for once. I've led a terribly lonely life and now I realise it was my own fault. Like Mary, I never want this to end, but I realise it must sadly. My son always told me it was up to me to change my life, now I realise what he meant. I was too weak to do anything," said Monica.

Sam noticed a tear trailing down Monica's face. He and Victoria took her by the hands and sat silently, all remembering past times in their lives: some good, and for one, some bad experiences. Perhaps it was the atmosphere and unaccustomed wine that brought the truth out of humans at a time like this. It was Mary who broke the trance and springing to her feet she said, "Lets not get morbid, I am starving. Don't forget we owe our good, new friend Sam a meal."

Clinging to Jacky Monica sat in the vehicle rather ashamed at her outburst but relieved it was off her chest. Somehow the past abuse that made her feel stupid and unworthy had just been lifted and it dawned on her that one must make decisions in life to change the situation, that no one else can do it for you. Thanks to Victoria and Sam she now felt empowered to take her own life back.

As they drove back to the resort none spoke. It seemed there was no need to. Victoria suggested that Sam park the vehicle in the guest's car park behind her bungalow so that Jacky may be checked on during the meal. Using her security key, Victoria let the vehicle in and guided Sam to the space behind her room.

Spirits were again lifted as they made their way to the dining room. Sitting down, all three insisted Sam order whatever he wanted, cost was not an option. He had been their knight in shining armor in perhaps what may have turned out to be an embarrassing situation. All three took a shine to Sam, he was a natural, no pretence. He wasn't that good-looking but inside beat a heart of gold.

Seated at the table they waited until Sam made his choice. They were all amused when he chose a T-bone and chips. His decision sparked interest and when ordering Victoria said, "Make that four and bring us a round of beer."

The decision delighted the girls and Sam smiled in satisfaction. Over the meal, set amongst the tropical atmosphere, they all chatted like long, lost, old friends, with even Sam caught up in the moment, drinking far more than he had for years.

Victoria asked Sam what his plans were and he replied that he was heading to Cape Leveque to see an old aboriginal friend and perhaps catch a few muddies. Asked what muddies were, Sam replied crabs, and that they were delicious. Calling the waiter over he ordered one for the girls to try. Like three teenagers the women sampled the crab meat exclaiming how it was a shame they were unable to go crabbing and visit Cape Leveque that they had heard so much about since arriving.

"Ladies," Sam replied, "it would be my privilege for you to accompany me and Jacky on the trip. Perhaps I can show you a few other local delights on the way."

Looking at each other in surprise, again it was Monica, to the surprise of the other two who replied, "Sam, I can only speak for myself but I would love to go. What do you say my fellow adventurers?"

Both Victoria and Mary nodded in agreement, unable to believe their luck.

"The only thing is," Sam informed them, "I have a room booked, the only one available and it only has four bunks."

"Well Sam, if it's okay with you, we have nothing to hide that you have not already seen and safety in numbers puts you at the disadvantage." Victoria replied.

All four roared with laughter. Victoria certainly was not backwards in coming forward. The conversation then turned to the trip: what to take and how much to pack, the excitement from all was electric. Victoria even suggested Sam bunk in her room in the spare single as he had obviously drank too much and they would call at his caravan on the way to collect his clothes for the trip.

"Thanks but no thanks. Old Jacky likes his bed and I'd better head back,' Sam replied.

Monica, half sloshed replied, "Bloody old Jacky can sleep in my room. I'll slip him in no worries and you can wake me up early and I'll put him back in the car."

Knowing Jacky liked Monica Sam agreed. Then out of the blue Monica said, "Sam you sleep in my room with old Jacky.

I have a spare bed too and if we get turfed out then we can go together."

Victoria agreed that Jacky liked Monica and the arrangement seemed to work for everyone, however, she was amazed that sitting here before her was a woman who would sit for hours back in the village and say nothing, never drank, swore or even talked to a strange man, let alone asking one she had known for a only a day into her bedroom. *Life sure can be full of surprises,* she mused.

It seemed in no time at all that the dining room had emptied, so tied up in their little group, none had realised until the waiter informed them they had ten minutes before closing time as it was twelve o'clock.

It was, in fact, a strange sight as the four, all rather inebriated, left, assisting each other out the door into the dim light that guided their way down the frangipani lined path to the bungalows. Amused staff immediately cleaned up the table littered with bottles and cans, amazed at the capacity of the group of oldies who seemed to be enjoying themselves so much.

As they made their way to the bungalows, Monica, leading the way, in her enthusiasm turned to signal to the others she was turning right to collect Jacky and went head first into the fish pond. Sam immediately went to her aid and grasping his hand Monica pulled him in head first. Bursting into fits of laughter, Mary and Victoria just about split their sides uncontrollably as the two, looking like drowned rats, tried to extricate themselves from the pond.

"Bloody hell!" Mary exclaimed. "I just peed my bloody pants."

This caused all four to completely break down and lights came on in several of the adjoining bungalows as guests came out to see what all the noise was about. The foursome sheepishly tried to control their laughter and disappeared into the night.

Letting themselves into the bungalow, Monica and Sam went for a shower, while Victoria retrieved a happy Jacky from the land cruiser and placed him in the room. Then she and Mary quickly headed to their bungalows to try to regain some composure.

Sam looked in the mirror and saw the two of them covered in vegetation, finding it hard to believe that in one day, three naked women had jumped into his vehicle and now he was sharing a room with one after drinking more than he had for years.

Coming out of the shower, a happy Monica, still laughing, bid Sam a good night and pulling the sheets back, jumped into bed with Jacky laying on the end quite content. After showering, Sam climbed into the spare single and dropped off to sleep; it had been an eventful day.

Chapter 4

Small streaks of sunshine burst into the room. Startled, Monica feeling something on her leg bolted upright in bed. Looking at her with his tail wagging sat Jacky ready for his morning walk. Memories of the previous day came flooding back as she looked across the room at Sam slumbering away in the bed opposite.

Feeling nauseous and with a headache, she cradled her head in her hands, coming to realise the previous day's happenings. She found it hard to believe what had transpired. And now she was waking up with a dog on her bed and a man in the spare bed on the other side of the room. At that moment Sam swung out of bed stroking his hand through his grey hair as he spoke to Monica.

"Thank you old girl for letting me share your room. Better take Jacky for his morning walk. Would you like to come? It sort of blows the cobwebs out, a nice walk on the beach."

Monica thought for a minute and said, "Thanks Sam. Yep, I feel rat shit, it might help. God I have to stop this decadent lifestyle, I am too old to keep up the pressure."

Quickly dressing, the pair checked outside in the early morning rays to see that no one was present and with Jacky in tow they left by the rear gate and headed to the beach. It did not take Monica long to start feeling better. It was magical walking on the beach at that early hour. Cutting through the sand dunes, Sam led them onto a track which was the return back street to the resort. Taking Monica by the hand, he helped her over the dunes. Never in her life had she felt so comfortable and safe than with this quiet, unassuming man and his beloved dog. Even after only knowing him for only a day she felt at ease in his presence.

Returning to the resort and placing Jacky in the vehicle, she knocked on the door of Mary and Victoria's bungalows, then she and Sam headed to the dining room for breakfast. Sitting in the empty room Monica looked at Sam for the first time and studied him. She really liked him, he was someone whose presence she really felt safe in. He noticed her studying him and looking into her beautiful face, thinking of the previous night, he grinned and said, "Listen here Monica, if you and I are going to be friends you must stop running around naked and pulling me into fish ponds."

"Done deal Sam," laughed Monica. " I am looking forward to our trip. I hope we won't be too much of an inconvenience to you."

Sam sighed and said, "Before I met you ladies I was lonely. It will be my privilege to be accompanied by three lovely people."

The coffee arrived and Monica realised how much she really needed it. As Sam tucked into bacon and eggs, the two chatted away. They were soon joined by Victoria and Mary looking a bit worse for wear.

"I think these two are teaching us bad habits Monica, running around naked and getting drunk, but I wouldn't miss a minute of it, what a blast eh?" said Mary.

Finishing breakfast the little group collected the luggage and set out for the caravan park to collect Sam's gear. Arriving, they were surprised at the neatness of Sam's caravan as they checked it out at Sam's invitation. All seemed in place and in order. Sam collected his belongings and drove out of the park quietly. Few had stirred and it was still only seven in the morning.

Just north of Broome Sam swung left onto the road that led

to Cape Leveque. The first stop was at Two Wells, a beach north of Broome, then onto Willy Creek Pearls where Sam waited with the dog while the girls enjoyed a tour of the farm.

Two things the trio learnt that day was the enjoyment of the music that Sam loved. He had quite a selection of Isla Grant, The Pigrim Brothers and Ollie Austin, all whom they had never heard before; it was easy listening music. The other thing was his amazing knowledge of the area. Driving inland off the main road he took them to a gate and finding it open, drove to an abandoned shack surrounded by the most beautiful flowering plants, palms and fruit trees.

Sam told them the story of how years previously he and his wife had been fishing off the coast and noticed the palms. Intrigued, they had landed and found a Dutch man and his Indonesian wife living there; they had been sailing round the world and chose this piece of the world to settle. After getting a mining lease they had settled in the homemade shack, separated from the world's troubles. Two children were born there and home schooled. Both later left home to finish their education and eventually the couple separated. The last time he saw them the man had joined Medicines Sans Frontiers and was working in Africa somewhere while the wife lived in Broome. *A sad ending to a beautiful story,* Sam reflected.

Standing in this place of paradise, the group felt sadness that such a beautiful story had such an ending. Climbing back into the vehicle, Sam negotiated the overgrown track back to the road then onto the main track heading to Cape Leveque. Before doing so Sam had called into Quondong Point to show his fellow travelers a spot where he and his wife had camped and fished years before. Victoria noted the sadness in his voice as he stood there as if on sacred ground. Monica placed her hand in his and gave it a squeeze, fully aware of his grief at old and beautiful memories, while being grateful to share such feelings.

Sam deviated several times to explore a beautiful shell altar built by monks in a church in the early part of last century at Beagle Bay. His stories fascinated them as much as the conviction he spoke with. They stopped for lunch at Middle Lagoon, an absolutely magic spot. Victoria vaguely remembered that she and Harry had passed there years ago, sailing totally carefree, in total freedom. Like Sam, a tear ran down her cheek as she stood looking out to sea.

At Lombadina Sam pulled in to buy some bread from the locals. They were amazed how the occupants kept the town in such clean condition. Sam informed them that the traditional owners took great pride in keeping their town clean.

It was late in the afternoon when they arrived at Cape Leveque and they immediately placed their bags in the room. Sam then drove to the beach just out of town for Jacky to have a run. Monica and Mary, along with Jacky, decided to walk the beach while Victoria and Sam sat contentedly chatting. Victoria remembered the island off Cape Leveque that she had passed long ago and thanked Sam for bringing them with him. She had enjoyed herself, they all had, it had been a magical day.

As the others in the distance turned to walk back, Victoria said, "Sam please don't misunderstand me but I have been watching Monica and I am sure she is falling for you. With all the hurt she has experienced in her life I feel another disappointment may destroy her."

"Victoria who would fall for the likes of me? An ugly old man. I was privileged to have the love of one beautiful woman, my luck would never extend to two," Sam softly chuckled.

"Don't under estimate yourself Sam, you are a bit of a gem and its what's in in the heart that matters. You and your old dog are indeed two gems."

"I have no intention of leading Monica on, she is a beautiful lady, as are all of you. You have certainly made my trip a new experience. I had never intended starting a new relationship after Carol died but loneliness is a terrible master. Perhaps let us see what transpires."

As the others approached Sam and Victoria walked to meet them. Driving back to camp Sam suggested they prepare for the evening meal; he would catch up with his friend and arrange the crabbing expedition in the morning.

There was no shower so the three women took it in turns to use the camp shower. The room was sparse with only the four beds and a table. After the showers, as they sat on the bed, the discussion hinged on the magnificent trip they had just experienced and how Sam made it so special.

Monica said, "I wish I had met Sam years ago. One can only imagine the life his wife had, it must have been one long adventure, I suppose like yours Victoria, I envy you both."

"Well Monica, you are still reasonably young and have good looks still, in fact, both of you have good health so why not go for it? Sam is lonely and I am sure he likes you," said Victoria.

Startled, Monica replied, "Really Victoria, such an idea is ridiculous, we are too old, it's preposterous!"

"I was only a few years younger than you when Harry unfortunately died. Until the end we retained passion. I am sure if he was still alive our love would still be insatiable."

Mary intervened. "Monica if you have a chance at love, please dear, dare to live the dream. The alternative to return to the life we have been living in the retirement village is unthinkable after this greatest of adventures, I dread the return. It seems to be coming to an end all so quickly. I intend making the most of every minute, today was one of the greatest of my life."

At that moment they heard the return of Sam as he knocked gently on the door. All three called for him to come in, happy to see their guide return. In his presence, something always seemed to be happening, his grasp of life seemed insatiable and infectious.

"Billy will be ready to take us out crabbing at about eight o'clock and I met another friend who runs the sight seeing trips by light aircraft from the strip; he will take us out to the islands for a trip on our return about lunchtime," said Sam as he burst in full of excitement.

Looking at each other the trio could not contain their smiles. The adventure seemed to be getting better all the time.

"What can I say Sam? We are in your debt already. If we surpass today I will be surprised. I hope I can sleep tonight," Mary said.

"Yes, thank you for a wonderful day Sam. Well, I expect we're all hungry. Would you like to shower first? We'll wait for you," said Victoria.

"No problems. You three go on ahead, the restaurant is not far. I'll shower and come on straight over. Jacky is dead tired and asleep in the vehicle. He's got water and his bed in the back looks to be softer than ours," said Sam.

Grabbing a towel, Sam picked up a clean shirt and left. Closing the doors, the three made their way to the restaurant; the evening was warm and the palms swayed in the gentle breeze as they made their way down towards the beach. The gentle crashing of the waves on the sandy beach and the lamps sitting around the outdoor eating area, made for an enchanting and romantic setting. They were surprised they had hardly sat down when Sam appeared.

"Must have been a quick shower Sam," said Monica.

"Well yes. A queue was lined up at the showers so I kept it short and I did not wish to hold you nice ladies up."

Mary replied, "We would have started without you Sam. It has been a long day and we are famished."

The four chose seafood and salad. Victoria suggested cold

beer to drink as it was so warm and everyone hastily agreed.

Over dinner they talked about the day and the next day's big plans, well aware that by the time they returned to Broome, it would be late and they would be exhausted. Sam had a full schedule planned; even he reckoned they would not leave Cape Leveque before four in the afternoon if all went to plan.

After the meal they returned to the room. They were all glad to escape the onslaught of mosquitoes that zoomed in after dark. The only thing to cool the room was a fan; they all felt hot and sticky. Sam suggested stripping to the bare necessities after lights out; Victoria agreed, having slept in the tropics on many occasions. Turning off the lights, all four did strip to the bare necessities and lay on their beds. If sleep was to be hoped for, all would have be disappointed as enthusiastic talk lasted for hours, until exhaustion finally overcome them and they drifted off to sleep.

Chapter 5

Sam was awakened by Victoria gently tapping on his shoulder. "What's wrong?" he asked.

"I need a wee. Is it safe to go out on my own?"

"We need to go too Sam, " whispered Monica and Mary in the darkness.

"Pull on a top girls and I'll escort you. As a matter of fact I need to go too, bloody beer."

Much giggling and bumping in to each other occurred as they prepared to go to the toilet block

"Don't turn on the lights," Sam warned them, "or the place will fill with mozzies."

Taking each other by the hand, Sam led them to the door, seemingly the only one with a sense of direction.

"Good god," Victoria exclaimed, "even doing a pee turns into an adventure," and they all burst into laughter.

The air was cooler as they made their way to the toilet block and the night was enchanting. Sam stood by the door as the women entered the block and when they had all come back out, he slipped into the mens."

On the way back, Monica placed her hand into Sam's; she felt safe next to him as they made their way back to the room. The move was noted by Victoria and Mary though Monica did not even think of what she had done, it was just the feeling of security while being next to Sam, someone who she knew genuinely cared for her.

Sam checked on Jacky who was sound asleep and then he returned to the room.

"Is Jacky alright Sam?" whispered Monica.

"Okay."

With that he lent over without thinking and gently kissed her on the forehead. Without realising it, a bond of strong affection was growing between the pair.

Morning soon dawned and after quickly packing bags into the vehicle, all four ate a hearty breakfast. The three girls anxious to begin the day's adventure. Driving the short distance to the meeting point, Billy, an amicable aboriginal, greeted Sam and gave a low whistle.

"Gee Sam," he said, "for an old bloke you sure have a lot of women."

Sam laughed. "My good friends only Billy. Would not have the luck to snare three such fine women."

Helping the three into the boat Sam and Billy hopped in. Jacky was already in his position at the front of the vessel going wild with excitement. Sam sat up forward with Jacky as Billy started the outboard and slowly motored out to sea.

The ride down the coast was exhilarating. Jacky excitedly barked at fish jumping and birds taking off from the Mangroves. Sam could see all three women were really enjoying the experience; the trip brought back memories for Victoria, while being a totally new experience for Mary and Monica.

The tide was nearly full as Billy swung the boat up a creek with Mangroves thick on either side. Baiting the crab pots, Sam set a string of them up the river. They then showed the girls a few crocodiles further up stream before returning to the sea to catch a few fish while the traps did their work catching the mud crabs.

Victoria let Mary and Monica fish either side as she helped bait the hand held lines. Both squealed with excitement as the bait hit the bottom and giant Trevally grabbed the bait. In an hour or so, with the help of Billy and Sam, the two excited women had landed ten fish; a feast for Billy's family and a couple to take back to Broome for tea that evening for the four friends.

Much excitement was had hauling in the pots and removing the huge mud crabs. Billy and Sam, both capable of the job, dropped the crabs into a huge esky and stored the pots forward. Jacky yapped and carried on amusing the women with his enthusiasm.

It was midday when all four piled into the land cruiser, thanking Billy for the wonderful morning, along with the four crabs and two fish they had tucked in the esky. Sam bid a fond farewell to Billy; it appeared they had known each other for years and both knew perhaps it would be their last meeting.

All three women felt sadness at the scene before them. It was a fact they all knew well, good times and good friends can be fleeting and that life must go on.

The trip to the airstrip was only twenty minutes and true to his word the pilot was waiting. He even had sandwiches and fruit juice prepared for the four as he knew the schedule his passengers had.

Jacky was the first one into the plane, taking up the front passenger seat ready to hop onto the knee of the occupant. Sam helped the three into the back seats and hopped in the front with his friend.

As everybody strapped themselves in the pilot started the engine and while taxiing down the airstrip gave his nervous passengers a briefing on safety in case of emergency and this made the three women even more fearful of the coming flight. Turning at the end of the strip, Phillip, the pilot, poured on the power and the little plane shot into the clear blue Kimberley sky. The view that opened before them caused all to go quiet. Never had they seen such magnificent scenery from the air although Victoria recognised several islands in the Buccaneer Archipelago. Philip gave an excellent commentary and the passengers soaked up the moment.

Monica felt tired and wondered how her older friends were coping. Running on adrenaline and excitement since meeting Sam, the three women started to unwind as the fairy tale scenery passed under the plane. Sitting in one of the rear seats, Monica reflected on the past two weeks of her life. With the gentle swish of the wind passing under the wings, she had a feeling of total freedom, of soaring with the birds. She stared out at the magnificent scenery passing under them as the pilot switched off the intercom and allowed them to take in the landscape.

Looking at Sam, with Jacky perched on his knee, talking to the pilot, she was amazed at the people he seemed to know wherever he went. She guessed the two men knew each other from past meetings. She reflected on her life. Here was a man who loved nature and the country, his enthusiasm and lust for life was infectious.

Her own life, like a fog, passed before her. Being the prettiest girl in the school she had been pursued by Nigel. He was both the most successful sportsman and student at college. She now realised he never loved her nor she him and he had simply classed her as a trophy. Caught up herself in the adulation others showered on him, she soon became pregnant. After marriage, he had started to despise her and treat her with disdain.

After the birth of their daughter she knew he started affairs, but for appearance and for their daughter, she never did anything about it and continued to perform her duties as a wife, entertaining his friends while the conversation was always about shares, the economy and always money; conversation she never joined in. Over the next two years he only had intercourse with her only when he was drunk and always roughly, often trying to do unthinkable things to her. She realised now that it was intended to make her feel worthless, like a chattel to do with as he pleased. When she became pregnant the second time he was furious and moved to the spare room, From that time he never touched her again.

For many dark years, she threw herself into caring for her two children. Being terribly lonely she blamed herself for the position she found herself in and an inground feeling of worthlessness descended on her very soul. When Nigel eventually died in the arms of a lover, god forgive her, she thought it was a great day in her life, as if the shackles had been released from her very being. Nights had been long as she lay in bed wishing someone would care for her, hold her hand and be her friend.

Now, as she looked at Victoria and Mary, she realised she not only had two beautiful friends sitting there with Sam, but there was Sam himself. A single tear ran down her face as she reflected there may have been many Sam's in her school years but she had been too vain to even consider a union with an ordinary boy. *Well,* she reflected, *I have paid my penance.*

Monica also thought of the return to Sydney. It was distasteful as it seemed as if she had been born again. After all this, how could she return to the village? She reflected on Mary's words *'Dare to live the dream'.* Looking at Sam with his weather beaten appearance and the strength it reflected, she made a decision. *If Sam makes a move I will go for it, for once in my life, if someone wants to love me. What a fool I would be to deny myself one last chance at love.* It was then she realised, blushing, that she was already head over heels and totally infatuated with Sam.

Monica was abruptly snapped out of her thoughts by the pilot informing them he was landing on an island that had once had a mine on it in the past, for afternoon tea. As they came gliding in for the landing, Sam turned and looked at her; she blushed like a teenager and gave him a wave, the warmth of his smile made her feel weak. Monica thought *life in the future without you Sam seems unthinkable, even after just a few days.*

The plane seemed to ghost down onto the little strip. Half the island had been eaten away by mining, only a few houses still remained and it was now a small tourist venture.

After being helped out of the plane the group made their way to a small restaurant for coffee. Unable to contain herself Victoria questioned Phillip about how he knew Sam.

Phillip explained that many years ago he and his girlfriend, now his wife, had been traveling on the Nullabor coming from Melbourne to try and get work flying up north in the tourist season for the purpose of getting hours up and to also make a few dollars. Their car had broken down and Sam and his wife had pulled up to help them. The gearbox had disintegrated and Sam towed them for two days behind his caravan; illegal, but in those days the Nullabor had sections not sealed and no-one cared.

Arriving at Norseman, he managed to get a secondhand gearbox from Perth but had insufficient money to pay for repairs to make it to Broome. Sam and his wife lent them five hundred dollars, which in those days, was a lot of money. Phillip suspected Sam and his wife did not have a great deal of money anyway. Leaving Phillip to wait on repairs, Sam left to work seasonally in Kununurra with his wife, giving Philip his address to post on the money when he was able to. Phillip did send the money to Sam and they had been good friends ever since. That is why, Philip informed them, that he was only too grateful to give Sam a free afternoon in his plane as he believed one must never forget old friends and past favors.

All three found it a wonderful story and then Victoria said, "I just knew old Sam was a gem when we first met him. Monica my girl, if you don't go for Sam, he is welcome in my bed anytime."

Monica blushed, "Victoria you are outrageous sometimes. But yes, I can assure you that Monica is no fool. I have the hots for him I must admit and well, as Mary advised me, I'm going to dare to live the dream."

Sam came wandering back to the table after having tied Jacky up outside after his little run. Joining the group, he listened as they chatted about the trip. As they were about to get up and leave, a young lass of perhaps thirty approached Phillip asking for a ride back to Broome. Philip was heading to Broome after dropping off his passengers as he and his wife lived there, he only stayed at the strip on Cape Leveque sometimes, in a donga, when business was brisk. The new passenger informed them that unfortunately would they have to wait an hour till her relief came on. Not wishing to offend, all three women agreed and it gave them a chance to check out the island.

In fact the past few days had began to sap the strength of the three women. They relished the chance to relax for a time on the cliff top, looking out to sea, chatting away while Sam and Philip, followed by Jacky, went off to visit another acquaintance. They all commented on the change in their outlook on life, the change that this trip had made.

Although exhausted, they now had a new lease on life. They found it impossible to contemplate, even at their ages, returning to the life they had been living. The terrible feeling of lethargy that their unfit bodies were tuned to at the retirement village was becoming a distant and unwelcome memory

Chapter 6

The hour passed very quickly for the three friends, soaking up the view, so far isolated from the madness that is Sydney; this other world made them feel wild and free. Even Victoria commented she found it difficult to comprehend what had transpired since her frustrated and mad decision to come to Broome.

"Imagine if Monica had not made the mad decision to go nude on Cable Beach? Certainly no Sam. Just one decision can change the lives of so many: meeting new friends and enjoying new directions and adventure. Look," gestured Victoria pointing out to sea, "I once sailed that wild and fancy free.

"Why Harry chose me god only knows why? I was not that good looking, tall and awkward, men avoided me really. I threw myself into work, then Harry came along and for some reason I drove him wild. We made love for hours; he was insatiable. Roaming the blue Pacific, madly in love, I was blessed," she said crying softly, as if reliving her past.

"You know," she went on, "in many ways Sam reminds me of him: in touch with nature; unfazed about money and wealth. What he enjoys is free, a free spirit and soul; his type are truly blessed.

"Well ladies, now we're in our last days. I may be old and weary but my spirit still remains. I have led an amazing life. Thank you for being my friends and putting up with my temper and eccentricities. You must be sick of hearing about my past life, but when I die, who will know, or care? Perhaps Harry is waiting for me on his yacht. God," she laughed, "I had better stock up on lubricant."

Mary and Monica stood beside her, the three holding hands. Mary told her they never tired of her stories. As a matter of fact, they often felt a bit of jealousy at her passion for living and her honesty and frankness with which she approached life. Lastly Monica told her if it had not been for her they would be sitting back in Sydney vegetating. It was she who showed them the wider world and something neither she nor Mary had ever envisaged was out there. In fact, she went on to say that they would always be eternally grateful for her bringing them to Broome and changing their lives, and whatever the future, they were sisters in arms and friends forever; they hugged passionately.

Jacky came bounding up and launched himself at Monica. He had chosen her as his new mistress. Following the dog was Sam and Philip with the passenger carrying a backpack. She was bubbly and friendly. "Cynthia," she informed them shaking hands. "Really appreciate you waiting for me."

Climbing into the plane they took off into the heavens for the trip back to Cape Leveque. The afternoon had quickly passed and evening was fast approaching. They landed at Cape Leveque where lights had already started to twinkle and it looked almost magical; again it all seemed surreal as the plane drifted down and taxied to Sam's land cruiser. As they were about to unload, Phillip suggested that the three women fly back to Broome and he would take them to their resort. Sam would stay in his donga and drive back to Broome in the morning.

The women eagerly agreed without hesitation but there was no way they would leave Sam on his own. Monica suggested she stay and she and Sam would leave early the next day. Both Victoria and Mary were tired. Monica was eager to spend time with Sam alone. Mary started to protest until receiving a dig in the ribs from Victoria when she immediately feigned a headache and said, "What an excellent idea."

As the little plane rose steadily into the air, Victoria and Mary watched the small, petite Monica and the much taller Sam, with Jacky sitting patiently in front of them, disappear from sight.

Turning to Mary, Victoria whispered, "We have done well Mary, I think a relationship may be consummated tonight."

As they waved the plane off, Sam suggested they go to the resort for tea, but Monica insisted they stay in as they had some cold beer in the esky and had kept one fish that she could cook up in the donga. Entering the small building they found a small kitchen, shower and toilet and at the end a double bed. Sam glanced nervously at Monica and smiled.

Sensing his unease, Monica squeezed his hand and said, "Don't worry Sam, I will share it with you."

Both showered and enjoyed a cold beer. Sam filleted the fish as Monica found a pan and lit the gas stove. Jacky had already retired to bed and was sound asleep. They enjoyed the fresh fish, it was delicious. Now totally dark, Monica felt exhausted and slipping off her dress, slid into bed holding up the sheet and waving Sam seductively towards her. Sam undressed and slid in beside her. Monica snuggled into his arms. Neither spoke, they did not have to. Exhausted and unsure, Sam pulled her to him and she snuggled closer into his embrace.

Kissing her gently, he felt that old feeling of passion start to rise, it was not missed by Monica. Slipping out of her panties, she opened her legs as Sam gently spread them with his and feeling the rising passion as he entered her with slow and easy strokes, she closed her eyes and gave small gasps of pain and delight. He seemed huge and not having had intimacy for decades, it initially hurt briefly, until she felt unbridled and the repressed passion gripped her body. She begged Sam to take her and satisfy her lust. Sam held her closely and thrust deep into her until both came, pent up in an explosion of ecstasy. Collapsing, Sam rolled off her panting. He held her hand and kissed her with passion. Monica lay back against Sam satisfied, totally in love, and within minutes, both drifted off to sleep.

Sam woke early feeling the sleeping Monica close to him. He reflected on the previous evening and was quite surprised that he had performed so well. The thought had crossed his mind that not having had much experience and after only really having had one woman in his life, he wouldn't be able to have sex, not only with someone else but at this stage of his life.

The bed was comfortable and Monica's small but firm body lay close to him. Sam was pleasantly surprised as he felt his member start to rise against the cheeks of her firm buttocks. Monica stirred and turning over, she became aware of Sam's lust rising. Smiling, she pulled him down onto her as she wrapped her legs around him and what followed was totally raunchy and exciting. Now the ice had been broken, both entered into the encounter with wild enthusiasm. They were surprised by the tenacity of each other as they pleasured the other in vigorous thrusting, with Monica riding Sam in total abandonment. Both collapsed, sweating, in a powerful climax.

The attraction between them had been immediate and total. Perfectly matched, even their age did not detract from the bonding that occurred. Laying on the bed, panting with exertion, beads of sweat trickling down their bodies and feeling totally sated, Sam kissed her gently.

"We had better get married old girl," he said to her.

"Sam please, don't feel you have to marry me. I would never wish that you felt that way."

"Monica my love," he replied. "If you will have me, please

marry me. To consider life now without you is unthinkable."

"Really Sam," Monica asked, "are you really sure? I am in love and lust for the first time in my life. I can't believe at my age, and yours, that such passion can still exist. It is like a dream."

"I feel the same way," Sam replied. "I can't believe my luck in finding you. When my dear wife died I was prepared to live out the rest of my days alone, but loneliness is terrible. Now I have you and I really can't believe my luck."

Both showered together then had coffee and toast. Packing the bags in the land cruiser, they took a photo of the donga.

"For memories," Monica chuckled.

With Jacky perched on her knee and Sam driving, they headed south to Broome. It would take about three hours, she calculated, with the road being unsealed and corrugated. Looking at Sam, she felt a rush of love and warmth, finding it hard to believe her new found happiness.

Sam looked over to her and seeing her in deep thought asked, "Monica dear, how does this sound? You come on with me in the caravan, we'll visit your son and then get married in Darwin, I know just the perfect place.

"After that we'll go on to Sydney and I'll drop you off and return home while you tidy up affairs and then come on to Tassy. I think I can last a couple of weeks without you."

"Yes, thanks Sam, that sounds fine, but what about my two dear friends? I'd hate to abandon them."

"You know I thought about that. I'm going to ask them to come on with us to attend the wedding. I have a double and two singles in the van. What do you think?"

"Oh Sam that would be wonderful. I feel I owe them, but what about our lovemaking?"

With a cheeky grin Sam said, "Thought about that too: we are all adult, I have a curtain for privacy and as for noise, don't think it would worry those two ladies."

Monica laughed, "Okay, why not? It would make it even more exciting."

"I think they would also like to see the rest of the Kimberleys. I would love to show them as a thank you gift for bringing you to me."

"Oh Sam, you are so considerate, I am so happy. I do look forward to seeing my son Allan and the rest of the family," beamed Monica.

The two chatted away and before long they had reached the highway that led into Broome where they pulled up outside the resort at lunch time. Victoria and Mary had gone into town leaving a message for the pair to wait so they could join them for lunch.

In the meantime, Monica packed her bags ready to move into Sam's caravan. She only had two nights to go before checkout anyway. She decided to wait for her companions before canceling tickets and to hear what their decision was.

Sam loaded Monica's cases into the vehicle and decided to take them back to the caravan while Monica waited for her friends. Sam wanted to inform the caravan park owners and pay for the extra person he now was to share his van with.

Monica realised that Sam wanted to make sure all was in order for his new bride. She smiled as Sam and Jacky drove off, thinking of Sam putting up some form of privacy for them. It felt great that she had someone who really cared for her.

Victoria and Mary came into the restaurant shortly after Sam's departure. Plonking down next to Monica, Victoria was almost breathless.

"Okay," she said, "tell us every gory detail. By the way, where is Sam, hope you haven't killed him?"

"Well girls, Sam has asked me to marry him," said Monica.

Mary let out a low whistle. "God that was quick," she exclaimed.

Victoria quickly said, "At our age dear, a day is too bloody long. Hell Monica that is not what I meant. Come on, give."

Monica blushing, blurted out, "I know what you want Victoria, you evil woman! Well, we bonked our brains out, never had so much sex in one night ever, as a matter of fact, I feel sore and peeing bloody hurts."

Victoria clapped and burst out laughing. "See Mary, I told you they would consummate the relationship." Passing Monica a parcel she went on. "Here is some lubricant, I knew you would have honeymoon soreness."

"What is honeymoon soreness?" Monica asked alarmed.

"God you're naive Monica. It means sore pussy from too much screwing, " said Victoria.

The conversation suddenly ceased as Sam entered the restaurant and seating himself next to Monica said, "Have you told the girls the news dear?"

"Well some Sam, they have just arrived."

"Okay. We've decided that Monica is coming on with me and we are getting married in Darwin. I have moved her gear into my caravan."

"Sam that is wonderful; both of us leftovers are jealous. Congratulations to two wonderful people," said Victoria.

"Ditto," said Mary. "I am so proud of you both. Pity us two back in Sydney."

Sam looked at both. "We are quite genuine in what we say now girls and have talked it over. One, we want you at our wedding, and two, you started your adventure together and you shall finish it together."

Victoria looked perplexed, "What do you mean Sam?"

"You are coming with us girls. I have two spare bunks in the caravan and besides, I want to show you the Kimberleys and the Northern Territory. Also, to be married without our two best friends would be unthinkable."

"Do you two really understand what you are saying? You'll want your privacy now, well especially the physical side of the relationship and all that," sobbed Victoria.

"Girls we are all adults and we insist. If you hear a bit of hanky panky, so what? I can assure you I will not miss out on anything; thanks to you two mad mates I am here," said Monica laughing.

"I know you are genuine but we will pay our own way. You see Victoria, no way am I turning down this offer to go back to an absolute shit hole. We will give you all the privacy you need and I thank you from the bottom of my heart, both of you," said Mary.

"That's settled then. I cannot think of any other people who would ever put up with us two old farts. I'm very grateful to you, you are a pair of absolute gems, I love you both," Victoria gushed.

Sam then suggested that they stay the last two days. He would service the land cruiser and a rest would do them all the world of good until departure.

Victoria, in her glee, raced off to contact the retirement village to inform them of their delay and cancel the air tickets home. Monica worried about her daughter and Victoria informed her she would still be pissed off and would not know she had even gone. Mary phoned her family; they were happy she was having a great time and wished her well.

Monica phoned her son in Darwin and he was amazed when he heard she was in Broome and even more amazed when she informed him she was in a caravan traveling to Darwin to be married. He was thrilled for his mother although speechless for a time. His surprise soon turned to happiness and Monica was elated when all he could say was, "Well done Mum," which he kept repeating.

His wife grabbed the phone and insisted the wedding reception be held at their house, no if's or buts.

Monica and Sam returned to the caravan and without hesitation, stripped and climbed into bed. It was a magical time for them both, entwined in each others arms they soaked up the love they felt for each other. Feeling more exhausted than they had ever known, they both drifted off to a contented sleep.

Chapter 7

Monica awoke unaware that they has slept in. Glancing at the clock she was surprised to see it was nine. Warm and content, snuggled next to Sam, she was disappointed that she needed to go to the toilet.

Lifting Sam's arm off her she slid out of bed completely naked. She picked up the bottle of lubricant off the floor and placed it in the cupboard. *Thank god for helpful friends,* she mused.

Dressing, she looked at Sam sleeping peacefully and found it hard to believe she was so happy, yet living in a caravan. *With Sam,* she thought, *I would be happy in a tent. What great adventures and loving I will now have in my life? How lucky am I?*

Grabbing a towel and some personal items she opened the door and closed it quietly, making sure Jacky didn't follow as she made her way to the amenities block; after a shower she felt refreshed. Placing her wet towel on the line she opened the caravan door letting Jacky out and decided to take him for a walk.

On her return she smelt bacon and eggs. Sam, having showered and dressed had started to cook breakfast. Coffee already brewed as he kissed her and gave Jacky a pat. Monica was surprised how easy it was to fit into virtual marital bliss so easily with Sam. Her situation was simple and uncomplicated, making her realise that humans do not really need all the modern goods they are told they need. Sam's caravan had very few items but he seemed to have everything they required. He did, however, inform her they would go shopping and get a couple more plates and cups for the girls before they departed for the north.

Dropping her off at the shopping centre where she was to meet Victoria and Mary, who had taken a bus into town earlier, Monica gave Sam a peck on the cheek as he drove off to have the vehicle serviced.

Monica had a list of the few items they needed. Sam reckoned the the caravan fridge was so small that fresh items would need to be purchased each day on the coming trip. Apart from utensils and cups very little needed to be bought. The pair had decided that Monica would go back to the resort with the girls so they could spend the afternoon relaxing on Cable Beach while Sam finished waiting for his vehicle to be serviced.

Monica soon found her two friends waiting on a seat in the air-conditioned shopping centre, both enthused about the forthcoming trip and positively glowing with excitement. Victoria firmly insisted on buying the other necessities required and if let go, she would have purchased half the supermarket, so excited was she about the coming trip. With the shopping finished they sat having a coffee and chatting.

Victoria looked at Monica and shook her head. "I can hardly believe you are the same woman I knew for well over a year back at the retirement home. You look absolutely radiant Monica. The lust for life has definitely bloomed since we arrived here, I just cannot believe it."

Smiling, Monica replied, "Yes, it all seems like a dream. I am so happy it makes me afraid it will all end."

"Monica enjoy the moment, every second. I am so happy for you, and for me too," laughed Mary.

Gathering up their shopping bags they left the centre and went outside into the brilliant sun. Again it was a balmy day:

thirty two degrees. The bus arrived within a few minutes and they wound their way back to the resort.

Sam arrived before lunch with Victoria insisting on shouting lunch for at the resort. After a leisurely meal they drove down onto the beach. Now well accustomed to the nudity Sam found a quiet spot while Jacky scampered about the beach.

Laying towels on the sand they stripped to their bathers and lay down, enjoying the warm sun and the beautiful scenery. The four had become good friends and laughed about many of their adventures to date, especially Monica's fall into the fish pond.

Sam had a few cold drinks in the esky and standing up he opened a can of soft drink for each of them.

"Anyone for a swim?" he asked.

"Yep, you know this is our last day in Broome? Let's do something special. Who's game for our last swim, a la nude?" asked Victoria as she sat up.

"Only if Sam is comfortable," said Mary.

"Hell Sam has seen us all anyway. Come on, one last wild idea, and we will leave the gear up here by the vehicle, and walk heads held high to the water," chortled Victoria.

Sam looked at Monica and she shrugged. "Let's do it Sam, I talked them into it the first time and that's how I met you."

Sam shrugged, dropped his bathers while the three women threw theirs off, and started walking to the water, laughing madly.

"Lucky bugger, no wonder you were a bit sore, he is hung like a horse," whispered Victoria as she sidled up to Monica.

Plunging into the water, a mad water fight started. All three women focused on Sam, absolutely covering him with water. Sam took great delight in dunking the three of them to high pitched screams and then watching them spluttering as they surfaced.

The mayhem lasted an hour or so. The exhausted foursome made their way back to the vehicle and even little Jacky was drenched after swimming out repeatedly trying to join in. Drying themselves and putting their cozzies back on they again lay on the towels to bask in the sun.

Monica was the first to speak. "I find it impossible to believe what we just did and if you had suggested we do it even one month ago, I would have been shocked and found it unthinkable."

"You know most of Australia would think that way perhaps, but be envious of us for doing it, what harm did we do?" said Sam.

"You are right Sam, I enjoyed it myself. Perhaps once in our life we need to do something classed as outrageous, in fact I found it quite natural and exhilarating, I am in for it anytime," said Mary.

Victoria laughed. "I cannot believe you two girls, back at the centre you never laughed, always so prim and proper. Since arriving here you have been drunk, swam nude and in one case, much to the jealousy of the others, started a sexual relationship. Now we are off in a bloody caravan for god knows how long and loving it all."

"You ladies have certainly given me a new lease on life. I hope I can repay you all by showing you a good slice of Australia. We really do live in paradise but many don't know it as they're too busy raping the country to make money," said Sam.

"You have strong views on some matters don't you Sam?" said Victoria.

"No, not really, but we live in a time of great greed. No-one is happy yet what we just did was free and gave us a lot of pleasure. Many people own dozens of houses and are held up as icons yet thousands cannot afford a home."

"Sam is so right, we spend our lives chasing the great god

money, yet this last two or so weeks have given me an insight into a different Australia, one I never knew. I feel I have really lived the last few days, it is hard to explain but I feel free," said Mary.

"Well," Sam went on, "when you come to Tasmania and you all will, or else, I will take you south in my old fishing boat and show you some really wild scenery."

Victoria sat bolt upright. "Sam, what the hell other secrets do you have? How big is the old fishing boat?"

"No big deal Victoria. It's fifty or so feet long, an old steel fishing boat. Myself and a very good friend, now deceased, done it up. It's my pride and joy," replied Sam casually.

"Bloody hell, we sure will come to Tassy Sam, never been there, they tell me it is beautiful. And I will keep you to the promise of the boat trip, you will make an old girl happy Sam, believe me," exclaimed Victoria.

Monica realised there was much to Sam that she did not know but decided to let matters take their own course. She realised Sam was not a material person like most and that he had no need to boast about his possessions. Monica also thought about money for the first time. Sam was far from tight with money, he had already given her a few hundred dollars although she protested that she had plenty of her own. In his old fashioned way she knew he thought the man must support his wife, or in her case, intended wife.

"Can we all fit into your unit Sam? Perhaps when we come down we could stay in the caravan," suggested Victoria.

Monica knew Victoria was hell bent on the boat trip and would never cease to press until the invitation came to fruition, it would become a part of her search for a return to the past.

"No, I only have one bedroom, but we can all stay on the farm when you visit. Monica and I will stay with you also," said Sam.

This was too much for Victoria, she gave up. Monica lay back looking at the sky and noticed Mary looking casually at Sam shaking her head. She was also perplexed at the casual way this simple man seemed to mention his affairs. Others would have soon spoken out without the questioning, hoping to impress.

Monica looked at Mary who smiled and shook her head. *What a turn our life and our Monica is in for*, thought Mary.

They were still feeling tired and decided not to watch the sunset but leave it for tomorrow night which was to be their last night in Broome. Monica wanted to be alone with Sam; she intended making up for lost time and she was aware the next two nights would be the last with privacy for some time. Although she was determined to participate in as much lovemaking as possible, she had let her intentions be known to her two friends and both agreed, insisting that this be the case.

"We are adults," said Victoria seriously, "and it is Sam's caravan."

Dropping her friends off at the resort, Monica and Sam made their way back to the caravan park, showered and returned to the van in the darkening evening light. Monica asked Sam why he did not watch TV much.

"Well, the news is all bad and besides there's not much to watch anyway."

She agrees and preferred talking to Sam. Her days had become so full that any spare time was needed for sleeping, and now, she grinned, lovemaking.

Monica noticed Sam had a few books in his van and picking one up, she flicked through a few pages. The title was 'Tears of the Moon', the author Di Morrissey. Having never been a reader she went to return the book but Sam stopped her saying, "I think you would find this a great read, it's based in Broome; a magnificent novel by an excellent author who really does her research."

Laying on the bed, now interested, Monica started to read. Sam was outside talking to his neighbors who were interested in the new, smart looking woman Sam had turned up with. Overhearing the conversation, she heard Sam casually say that Monica was his wife to be and how lucky he felt having such a wonderful companion. Monica felt a glow at the feeling someone really cared for her, it gave her a feeling of absolute satisfaction.

Sam stuck his head around the caravan door. "Monica dear, next door insist on shouting me a drink on my good fortune. I told them you were in bed, is that alright with you?"

Monica smiled. "Of course Sam, please take your time. I am engrossed already with the book. You have opened another new world to me."

When Sam drank his glass, even though they tried to refill it, he declined and returned to the caravan. Monica was asleep, the book still open at the page she was reading. He gently removed it, marking the page, quite surprised at how far she had read. Climbing into bed he felt her snuggle up to him and switching off the light he closed his eyes and soon fell asleep.

The next morning they made love again with a passion so intense, it seemed that Monica felt it would never end. She was passionately making the most of every opportunity, unable to comprehend not having Sam in her life and feeling almost fanatical for physical contact. For some reason she needed intimacy strongly, maybe after being shunned and made to feel unwanted for so long. She now relished her new role, determined to please Sam and make him happy.

They took Jacky for a long walk, a practice they both looked forward to. Sam prepared the caravan for an early departure and they went into the resort for lunch with the girls, all going later for one last long walk on Cable Beach. That evening, they again sat on the beach, gazing at their last sunset in that particular spot. As she sat on Sam's knee, arm around his shoulder enjoying the remarkable sight, she wondered if it would be the last sunset for all of them at Cable Beach.

Returning to the restaurant they enjoyed a beautiful seafood meal. Victoria suggested an early night as she and Mary would be up early packing. They wanted to leave in good time to begin the start of the next phase of the adventure and Monica's wedding.

Sam and Monica bid farewell, promising to pick the others up about seven thirty in the morning. They both went straight to bed. Monica read for a short time, totally engrossed in the book. *Indeed Sam had great reading tastes,* she thought. Sam dozed off to sleep and Monica placed the book on the shelf. She switched off the light and pushed herself against Sam; it made her feel secure and content.

She lay awake for a short time wishing that the Broome adventure would last forever, but practicality intervened and she realised everything must come to an end, sooner or later, as she dozed off to sleep.

Chapter 8

Monica stirred and opening her eyes she glanced at the time, it was only five in the morning. She felt Sam next to her, the smell of him and of the sex that permeated throughout the caravan heightened her senses. Laying next to him she thought of her life. She realised now that she had always been highly sexual and had fought hard to suppress her desires because if she made any move towards Nigel, he called her a slut. All their encounters had been brief, lasting only a minute or so. He used her for sexual relief only, but that left her longing for satisfaction.

She thought of the hundreds of nights she lay awake in frustration believing there was something indeed wrong with her. Having only her sexual fantasies, she had suppressed little groans of delight as she played with herself, always feeling ashamed afterwards..

She and Sam had retired early the previous evening and both had woken at about eleven that evening to go to the toilet. On their return, she had apologised to Sam for being sexually aggressive and spilled her most inner thoughts and desires out to him. Surprised, Sam responded by telling her he had the hots for her and that he and his wife Carol had experienced a highly charged sexual relationship and that intimacy was one of the things he missed most.

He also informed her that Broome, with its exotic location and surrounds, had an unexplained impact on a great number of people. Many succumbed to the inhibition of the place and it had the ability to bring out suppressed desires. He understood it was a coming out for her, it was no surprise to him, he loved her and his desire for her had no limits.

Sam then confessed that Carol had even shaved her pubic hairs to heighten their lovemaking. Monica, now relaxed after the open conversation, suggested she would like to try it. Like teenagers, using Sam's hair clippers to remove the vaginal hair, then the lubricant and a razor to shave the area, Sam gently helped her and they both became incredibly turned on, as she lay with legs wide apart, until the area was smooth; the atmosphere became sexually charged.

Monica's last inhibitions were removed and she felt more in charge of her sexuality than she had in her whole life. Perhaps, she thought, that is what Victoria and Harry had been like, she always spoke of the hours of uninhibited lovemaking. Monica had the same feelings for Sam, even though she groaned in pain sometimes as his huge member stretched her to bursting point. Still, it was somehow erotic and she always had an insatiable urge for more, the wilder the better.

Sam, unable to control himself, mounted her and after a few wild thrusts ejaculated, his desire out of control. As she now felt his penis against her buttocks - he always slept naked - she started to practice enjoying the raw encounter, it was a feeling of freedom. Wild thoughts entered her mind as she applied lubricant to her smooth pubic area and gently started rubbing some onto Sam's penis, causing him to stir and his member to rise. As he rolled onto his back she grabbed his rising organ and mounted him.

She felt him grow even more inside her and wildly she pounded up and down. Sam responded by grabbing her buttocks and thrusting into her, both soon dripping with sweat and sliding deeper into each other. Sam rolled over and spreading her legs wider, slammed into her. Monica was groaning with uncontrollable ecstasy.

He became so caught up in the wild lust, he felt he could not get enough of her. Both bounced up and down on the bed as he rammed in and out of her, unable to feel a climax coming or bring one on. He rode her like a wild animal and after what seemed an eternity he pulled out of her. Rolling her roughly over he pulled her buttocks to him and spread her legs wide apart and rammed his pulsating cock deep into her, the position and depth of his thrusting made her cry out in gasps of pain and pleasure.

Harder and harder he rammed into her buttocks feeling a climax approaching. He slammed into her so hard her head drove up against the end of the bed. The slapping sound of the two bodies, as he slammed uncontrollably into her, filled the caravan. Finally he exploded into her and then stopped, shaking, and with sweat pouring from him, he held her buttocks to him as his cock shrunk and slid out of her. Letting her go, she collapsed onto the bed, legs wide apart, flat on her stomach gasping for air. Sam rolled over beside her. The episode had been frightening with such strong, insatiable desire and lust that he felt ashamed.

"Monica I cannot believe what I have just done to you. I was overcome with passion and if I hurt you, I am sorry," he said softly.

Without moving, Monica said breathlessly, "Sam, our love is insatiable, take me again if you wish. I will never get enough of you, the harder and wilder you take me the better, I feel totally satisfied for once in my life. I cannot believe that at our age such passion can exist."

Sam lent over and kissed her. "Well my girl, I don't know how many more rounds like that I can go, but it was unbelievable."

Looking at the clock Monica jumped out of bed. "God Sam," she cried. "We've been at it for over an hour and a half, we'll be late to pick up the girls."

"Don't panic," said Sam. "Lets shower and it will only take a minute to hook up the van."

Grabbing towels and fresh clothes they raced to the showers. When Monica returned Sam was hooked up ready to go with Jacky waiting on the front seat.

"How about Jacky's walk?" Monica asked.

"Jacky had a pee while I was hooking up. When we stop for morning tea I'll take him for a run."

The decision to have breakfast with Victoria and Mary had been made the previous day to save time and washing up in the caravan. It was nearly on seven thirty when they rolled up outside the resort.

Jacky started going wild so Sam decided to take him for a short walk before meeting the trio inside for breakfast.

Entering the resort, Monica spied the luggage stacked by reception and went through to the dining area where Victoria and Mary sat smiling as she approached.

"What have you been up to my girl," Victoria asked. "You look a bit jaded."

"Well actually," Monica replied, "I have a job to walk. We've been bonking for and hour and a half."

"Good lord," Mary exclaimed. "Are you for real?"

"Told you he was like Harry, I knew old Sam would be a stud, " said Victoria.

Sam arrived and they enjoyed their final meal at the resort. Later while Sam loaded the cases, Victoria and Mary finalised the account at reception,

Sam let them choose which bunk they wanted and set their luggage underneath each. He did one final check of the caravan as the trio piled happily into the land cruiser.

"Yep, can tell by aroma in caravan some serious hanky panky has been going on," whispered Victoria.

Monica smiled and absolutely beamed. Both Mary and Victoria knew she was madly in love with Sam. He pulled out with all the women chatting excitedly for the start of a new adventure and the many good times to come.

Chapter 9

Again it was a typical day in the Kimberley dry season. The weather had already started to warm up as the little group drove out of Broome past Blue Haze and all felt a little remorseful that the wonderful time in Broome had came to an end. Passing the turnoff to Cape Leveque, they all recognised it and thanked Sam for the wonderful time they had exploring this special part of the world.

"Especially me Sam, it was the start of a new life for me. I will always adore you for it," said Monica.

Victoria looked at Monica thinking she seemed so small and fragile next to Sam, her magnificent obsession. Sam was over six feet tall in the old measurement, dwarfing Monica at only five feet at the most. *Indeed,* she thought, *an odd couple but so infatuated with each other.*

A sense of foreboding came over Victoria as to what would happen should something unforeseen occur to either one. So madly in love, neither would stand another heartbreak. When Harry died, she had at the time, considered ending it all. It had taken years before she realised life must persevere and continue. Now she watched as the glow of love shone from her friend's face and she hoped with all her being that lady luck would allow these two special people at least several years of happiness.

She found it amusing that when she had used the word bonking back at the retirement home, Monica had looked a little shocked. Yet in the last few days she had used the term herself with such excitement. Victoria knew Monica was extending herself sexually because of a lifetime of sexual suppression and a burning desire to make Sam want her and in fact Victoria knew her plan was working as Sam could hardly take his eyes off her.

Watching out the window with the cool air rushing through they passed the turnoff to Crab Creek. Sam pointed out the little holdings on the left hand side that produced much of the fresh fruit for the area. It did not take long before they arrived at the Roebuck Roadhouse and the Great Western Highway that snaked north and right through to Perth eventually if one turned south.

It now seemed as if a new adventure was about to begin and even Jacky was excited as he visited the two back seat passengers at every opportunity. Sam informed them that the area was perhaps one of the best for raising cattle in Australia and that by evening, they would be in the great Fitzroy River flood plains which was the best land for producing the best beef in northern Australia. By mid-morning they pulled into Willare Bridge Roadhouse.

Sam advised them to use the time for a toilet stop while he topped up with diesel. All three took the advice and chatting excitedly made their way to the rest rooms. As they left the toilets, Victoria went to the cashier and waited till Sam hung up the fuel hose and requesting the amount, paid for it.

On the way back she met Sam and told him the amount had been paid. Sam started to protest before a stern Victoria, in front of Mary and Monica said, "Now listen here our most precious Sam, you are outnumbered. So the ladies who have the upper hand have decided and passed the following rules: I, Victoria will pay for fuel, Mary will buy food and as she loves cooking and will cook also, while your good-self and magnificent lover shall pay for camping fees."

Sam started to protest but realised it was futile.

"My dear Sam, if you can put up with all of your harem and maintain your great sense of fair play and humor, that is more than sufficient," said Mary who was having the best time of her life.

Monica squeezed Sam's hand. "Just take care of us all Sam. Show us the sights and delights we never dreamed of our lifetime and make our dreams continue my most precious darling."

Giving Jacky a little run the adventurers pulled back onto the highway and headed north. A short time later, Sam deviated left heading to Derby. He explained that the area there experienced the world's second highest tidal flow, nearly twelve metres in height. They would check it out at the Derby wharf and have some Barramundi for lunch at a small café in the car park there.

On the way they saw many Boab trees. Sam told them as he pointed out the nuts growing on the trees that the aboriginals carved them and sold them to the tourists, in fact, he had several at his home.

At one point, Sam turned off the road and as always, with delight, showed them the world's longest stock trough where drovers watered their cattle on the way to Derby to load onto waiting ships. He also walked them to a Boab tree which was used by the early mounted police as a prison tree.

They were surprised when he pointed to the Gibb River Road, showing them the map and pointing to where it came out south of Wyndham, it was mainly unsealed and not suitable for caravans he told them. The Air Force had a base in the area also. Again he was proving to be an exceptional and informed guide.

Arriving in Derby they drove slowly through town and crossed a mud flat to the wharf. Alighting, they were able to walk on to the wharf as the tide was out. Sam agreed the tide was in fact out as large ships usually loaded here when it was full. They found it unbelievable that large ships actually entered and loaded in what was now virtually mud flats. A large mining operation had only a few years previously built the sheds and conveyer belt at the site to load the ships. The operation used to take place at Wyndham.

Enjoying their lunch in the gazebo built for tourists, all four relished the flavor of the delicious Barramundi. The three women all seemed to be having a magnificent time enjoying Sam's knowledge and stories of the area. Mary told them she was now able to understand why so many older Australians chose to travel by caravan or motor home. She never imagined herself doing it but now she found the experience exhilarating and loved it.

"It is all so amazing," said Victoria. "I feel young again. It's great to be back on the road."

Monica looked at Sam. "Since I met you I feel I have been born again. I've made up my mind for good and buggered if I am staying in Sydney. We'll call and put my unit up for sale. I'm on my way home with my husband," she smiled and embraced Sam.

Sam seemed more than enthused with the idea and hugged her. The big man lifted her off the ground in a warm embrace, their love was infectious.

After lunch they drove back through Derby and Sam deviated to give them a tour of the town. Most of the occupants seemed aboriginal. Sam told them that was the case as it now boasted excellent facilities. He suggested they would probably be into Fitzroy Crossing later that day and to purchase something fresh for the evening meal.

Mary was inspired as the three friends entered the supermarket while Sam gave Jacky a run. Monica placed the shopping in the caravan and when Sam returned, all three were waiting by the vehicle. By now it was hot inside the car and Sam ran the air-conditioning to cool them down.

By the time they reached Fitzroy Crossing the lights had begun to twinkle against the darkening sky. The two back seat passengers dozed during the last hour of the trip; it had been a long day and it was taking a toll on the two older women. After being inactive for so long at the retirement village they were feeling the events of the last three weeks. Sam decided to rest at the resort in Fitzroy Crossing for a couple of days to unwind and recharge.

Passing through the town they observed a large number of aboriginal inhabitants walking about in the twilight crossing over the Fitzroy River Bridge. Sam pulled into the Fitzroy River Lodge and he and Monica went in to book a caravan space while Victoria and Mary sat in the vehicle.

Returning to the car Sam was relieved that they still had a few vacancies as it was usually pretty hectic at this time of year. Driving down into the flat camping area, Victoria exclaimed at the scene before them. "Looks like a huge Bedouin camp."

Dozens of caravans, campers and tents littered the area, the smell of food cooking permeated the still air, dozens sat around in chairs drinking and chatting.

"Looks like an army on the move, this is unbelievable," said Monica excitedly.

"It is an army on the move," Sam informed them. "The grey nomads, over three hundred thousand at any given time."

Finding the numbered site allocated to them, Sam backed the caravan in and getting out from the vehicle he soon unhitched and wound the stabilisers down. He suggested the three women shower first as he pointed to the large building on raised ground behind them while he wound the awning out and set up the chairs and table outside so they could dine in the cooler evening air outside the caravan.

Returning from the showers the trio found Sam had indeed set everything up. Mary suggested Sam go for a shower while she prepared the evening meal. Monica and Victoria felt like a walk so they took Jacky on his lead and headed off amongst the huge gathering of travelers and their various forms of traveling accommodation.

Walking along, Monica and Victoria were surprised by the friendliness of their fellow travelers. All waved and in many cases spoke to them, asking where they had been and where they were heading. Everyone seemed so full of enthusiasm.

"We are spending our children's inheritance," one elderly lady informed them.

As they reached the end of the huge camp both looked in awe as they saw several camels tied up next to the perimeter. Unable to contain herself Victoria asked the young man attending them where had they came from. To their absolute surprise he told them that he and a companion had just crossed the Tanami from Alice Springs and were taking the beasts to Broome to sell to the camel operators on Cable Beach.

When they returned to the caravan, both excitedly told Sam and Mary of the camels and the meeting with one of the young men walking them so far across desert to Broome.

"It is a Bedouin camp," laughed Victoria.

Sitting in their chairs enjoying a drink of wine before the evening meal, the group again discussed what a magical day Sam had led them on. Here now, sitting amongst a sea of elderly adventurers, indeed their great adventure was continuing and each day brought new sounds, scenery and aromas.

Mary not only liked cooking but was an efficient chef. They hungrily ate her grilled steak and vegetables followed by fruit salad.

Sam recommended to them that the next the morning they should have a lie in, then do the washing. In the afternoon he would take them on a cruise down Gieke Gorge; he was sure they would be impressed. They murmured that everything

Sam did impressed them. Chatting away Monica turned to Sam, anxious to feel as close as possible to him; she loved being cradled in his arms, so safe and secure. Fatigue took over as they bade each other goodnight after a long day of travel.

Chapter 10

Victoria was quite surprised at how comfortable the beds were that she and Mary were to sleep on in the van. Events had happened so fast and the excitement had been so great they were all thoroughly exhausted. Sam and Monica retired behind the curtain Sam had erected. In a short while everyone had fallen soundly asleep.

Victoria sat bolt upright awakened by a loud crash and something ripping the sheet off her bed. It had always been her practice to sleep naked, especially in the warm climate she found herself in. Jacky started barking excitedly as she and Mary, now also awake and alarmed, turned on the light above their beds. Monica at the same time turned on her light and there was Sam lying on the floor tangled in the curtain he had so carefully put up for privacy for himself and Monica.

Leaving the bed quietly to go to the toilet, it seemed that Sam had forgotten the curtain and stepped onto the bottom of it, causing him to lose balance and fall forward, taking the curtain with him; at the same time he grabbed at Victoria's bed tearing the sheet off her. The caravan was absolute mayhem with Jacky caught up in the raucous barking madly. Monica and Victoria sprung out of their beds, totally naked, alarmed that Sam might be hurt. Mary sat up wild-eyed, surveying the scene before her in utter disbelief.

Seeing the absolute absurdity of the situation Sam burst into laughter as the two women assisted him to his feet. Monica grabbed Jacky to settle him down as Sam apologised for causing such a disturbance. It was only then that they looked at the nakedness of Victoria and Monica and burst into uncontrolled laughter.

Taking control, Mary suggested that Sam go to the toilet if he was alright and the girls would clean up the mess to gain some composure. She would then boil the jug as a cup of warm Milo might help calm things down again.

Sam said he was fine. He felt a right fool for forgetting the bloody curtain, he laughed as he left the van.

Mary and Victoria could not help but notice Monica's smooth shaven vagina as she stood holding Jacky. Victoria pointed out she had followed the practice too, men seemed to like the idea. To their complete and utter surprise, Mary spoke up to say that it was a nuisance sometimes shaving every day to stop the prickling feeling of new growth.

Mary also suggested throwing the stupid curtain into the rubbish bin, it would not stop any noise in the confined space, and that the outlines of Sam and Monica could easily be seen through the curtain with the light on in their section anyway.

"Perhaps," said Mary. "If all agreed to lights out first, allowing everyone to hop into bed at the same time, the curtain isn't at all necessary." On reflection she added, "Not that it affects me, I wear a nightdress, but we have nothing to hide that all of us haven't seen anyway."

They all agreed that it was a good idea if they were to share the confined space. It was silly to try and practice modesty when they did not really care anyway.

When Sam returned they told him of the decision. He agreed to throw out the curtain and dropped the torn item into the rubbish bin. While drinking their Milo, Victoria with her sense of humor joked to Sam that she thought her luck had changed and she was disappointed someone was not tearing off her sheets to ravish her to make wild passionate love.

Now fully awake they laughed and chatted for hours before

snuggling back into their beds. It all seemed so natural as they pulled back the sheets and hopped into bed; it was three in the morning before they settled into a sound sleep.

To their surprise it was well past nine that morning before anyone stirred.

Mary prepared breakfast while Sam and Monica, helped by Victoria, changed sheets and gathered up any dirty laundry. Sam took Jacky for a walk while Monica and Victoria started the washing in the laundry behind the caravan. Mary had cooked bacon and eggs which was Sam's favorite and all four enjoyed a hearty breakfast. Sam helped Monica hang out the washing while Victoria and Mary washed the breakfast dishes and cleaned the caravan. The four already worked as a team in harmony. Sam was beaming, unable to control his happiness at the recent turn of events in his life.

As the tour he had arranged of Gieke Gorge was in the evening, Sam suggested they check out the town and buy a few supplies for the night's meal.

They all piled into the vehicle and drove back to Fitzroy Crossing. Sam pulled up outside the clothing store next to to the supermarket and suggested to Monica he buy her a pair of boots and some shorts, more suitable clothing for traveling in the north than what she had. The four excitedly entered the shop for a look.

Coming out a short time later Monica was proud as punch and looking great in a pair of Rossi boots, khaki shorts, leather belt and a check shirt tied at the waist, looking absolutely fabulous. Sam stood beside her grinning from ear to ear.

"What a great pair you are. Monica, I think you look another ten years younger," said Victoria with Mary nodding in agreement.

Mary and Victoria held up the new clothing they too had bought, suitable for their travels. Placing the shopping in the vehicle, the group locked the car and walked across to the supermarket.

Sam stopped at the entrance talking to a large group of aboriginals who seemed to know him well. The trio of women entered the shop and purchased sufficient food for the evening meal. On the way back Sam filled the car with fuel and again Victoria shot out of the vehicle determined to pay her share as agreed. Arriving back at the park they decided to rest and read some of Sam's books until it was time to go on the cruise.

Sam struck up a conversation with the couple next door and apologised for the noise the night before though was surprised to learn that his neighbors had slept through it.

They told him they had done the boat tour of the gorge the previous day and were heading off in the morning. As they had a small female Jack Russell, they asked if Sam would like them to take care of Jacky while they did the cruise. He agreed, thankful he did not have to leave Jacky alone as the gorge was in a national park and no dogs were allowed.

Monica finished reading the book that Sam had talked her into reading as they sat quietly enjoying the beautiful Kimberley climate.

"What a wonderful story," Monica said to Sam. "One of much love and compassion which is oh so familiar to me now."

Later in the afternoon all four left for the boat cruise. Climbing down onto the vessel, the operator, a C.A.L.M. employee, gave an excellent commentary of the river and the area as they cruised between the magnificent cliffs of the Gorge. Monica held Sam's hand as she looked mesmerized at the huge cliffs, the experience was breathtaking and she had no idea that places she had vaguely heard of were so inspiring.

As the guide pointed out a mark indicating the height of the water in the wet season on the walls of the gorge, she was hardly able to conceive such a volume of water passing through.

It all ended too soon as darkness crept over the boat as it cruised back for the passengers to disembark. On the way they chatted to others and a get together for a few drinks was planned on arrival back at the park.

As they disembarked back at the jetty, Mary hugged Sam and said, "Once again Sam, thank you for showing us something I would never imagine so stark, raw and beautiful. I'm simply unable to describe properly how I feel."

She then gave Sam a peck on the cheek. Victoria had never seen Mary so happy and content. *Mary*, she thought, *is having the time of her life, she really likes Sam; he inspires her, as well as the rest of us and he is a special person.*

On the way back Sam deviated giving them a tour around the Old Crossing Inn, while telling them this was, in fact, one of the first buildings in the area and now a rest place for travelers going north on the old highway.

Dozens of aboriginals sat around drinking as Sam pulled up and invited the women for a drink in one of Australia's highest turnover, drinking establishments. Mary seemed alarmed as Sam stepped out of the car. He informed her that basically aboriginals are decent people who would not harm anyone, though sadly, they are killing themselves with alcohol. Standing amongst a sea of aboriginals Sam was recognised by many of them, it appears he had worked in the area.

After drinking their beers, which did not take long as they were all parched, they jumped back into the vehicle with their new aboriginal friends waving excitedly as they drove off.

On the way back Sam drove over the original crossing; only a little water still ran over it. They arrived back at the park on a dirt road that ran parallel to the park.

Back at the park they grabbed chairs and made their way to the designated area where they had agreed, on the tour, to meet to have a few pre-dinner drinks. Jacky was happy to see them, along with his new girl friend, and her owners.

Surprised to see at least twenty couples in the circle around a small camp fire, they placed their chairs amongst the group. Sam opened the esky and poured his three female companions a glass of wine. Victoria looked around the circle and saw that many of the women sat on their husband's or partner's knees, as did Monica. *After lives of child raising, mortgages and hard work, old loves are being revitalised* she mused. Great adventures and life long dreams were being played out. The atmosphere was exciting, almost unreal.

In what seemed to be no time at all, the woman who had joked with them about spending their children's inheritance, announced to the crowd that it was 'time for tea' as she pulled her husband from his chair. "We should all return to our caravans and take our medications," she laughed. "Make sure the men don't forget their Viagra."

This was the cue for the group to disintegrate and everyone, carrying chairs and eskies, returned to their camps.

After taking showers, Mary and Victoria found Sam and Monica had already returned to start preparations for Mary to cook the evening meal; a small salad with crumbed fish.

The evening was late as they retired after the meal. Victoria had just started to drift into sleep when she heard small ecstatic cries from Monica. Drifting off, she smiled, happy for her little friend who had found her knight in shining armor.

Chapter 11

Sam woke the others as he dressed, letting an excited Jacky out as he departed for his morning walk. Monica did not accompany him as they wished to leave early before the day heated up too much. The women busied themselves preparing breakfast and arranging the caravan for travel, placing cold drinks in the esky to have on the way.

Sam returned and after a leisurely breakfast, hitched up the caravan after Victoria helped to guide him back under the tow bar.

It was a good feeling to be on the road again, all looking forward with anticipation to the next leg of the journey north. The landscape was wild, open and devoid of any human population. Sam pointed out that although it seemed the case, several mines and aboriginal communities existed off the many tracks that snaked from the main highway.

Sam turned off the road at a sign that read 'Mary Pool'. Driving over a concrete causeway he pulled up on the bank of the river. The women were amazed at the small city of people camped by the river. "It's a free camp," Sam informed them. "Some call camps like these PCA's."

"What is a PCA?" Mary requested.

Sam chuckled. "Pensioners' catch up area. Many stay at these places until the next cheque arrives in the bank and then move on."

Sam and Monica wandered off with Jacky as Mary and Victoria boiled the jug to prepare morning tea. After an hour or so of chatting to the other campers, enjoying their drinks, Sam drove his charges back onto the highway. The day had turned very warm and humid, hotter than any day they had experienced so far.

Victoria started to feel slightly faint with the heat even though the open windows let fresh air into the vehicle. Sam turned on the air-conditioning but it just made the air even dryer.

The sun was fiercely at its peak by two that afternoon when Sam decided to call it a day. He realised Victoria had a bad headache and although not complaining, even though painkillers had failed to check it, she was looking quite unwell. Slowing down, Sam turned off the highway at a creek signed 'Spring Creek'. He drove off down a track and came to a small clearing by the river. The temperature was now thirty eight degrees and humid. He pointed out it was indeed rare weather for the time of year.

Informing his passengers that they would camp there for the night, Sam told them that a nice clear pool of running water lay over the bank, just near the spot where he had parked. He decided not to unhook the van but simply wind down the stabiliser legs. Removing their clothes, they pulled on their bathers, by now sticky, sweating and uncomfortable. They gratefully followed Sam down the small track to the river.

The water still flowed slowly and was absolutely crystal clear with small fish darting about; apart from several large boulders the creek had a sandy bottom. Sinking into the inviting water they felt relieved at the immediate effect the cool water had on them, it felt so invigorating. Above them a large canopy of trees gave excellent shade over the creek.

Sitting on the soft, sandy bottom, propped against the large rocks, they all felt much better and spirits again rose. An animated and happy conversation started, all relieved that Sam had found such an excellent stopover.

While sitting in this isolated and beautiful surrounding, Victoria in her usual inquiring way, looked at Sam and said, "Now Sam isn't it time you told us your fascinating life story. You've heard ours but we know very little of yours."

To everyone's surprise, Mary quickly chastised Victoria and said, "Sam's life is private if he so wishes, we have no right to be snooping into his past."

Sam looked at them all, especially at Monica and in a slow but steady voice replied, "No Mary it is perfectly proper. I should tell you, especially Monica, she has a right to know who she intends to marry."

Drawing a deep breath Sam began slowly, as if he was unloading a great weight from his shoulders.

"Well I can't remember my father as he was killed in the war in New Guinea. My mother was beautiful once but the death of my father had a terrible impact on her. We lived in a small flat in Melbourne at the time." Sam's voice began to waver as he exposed his very soul for the first time in his life.

"Times were hard. Mum worked in a factory long hours to support us, her health suffered as the flat was always damp and cold; *now* I know she could not afford coal for heating. I was working part-time and going to school mornings. I was twelve when mum took ill, within two weeks she died."

Monica looked at Sam spellbound as did the others. Tears began to run down her face as her heart went out to him, her magnificent obsession.

Sam continued, driven by the want to get this awful sadness off his chest. "I don't know what happened to Mum. We had no money to bury her and no one helped us. I've tried to find her grave for years but haven't found it. It's my greatest heartbreak, not being able to find her.

"Anyway I packed my few belongings and left our flat as the landlord had let it to new tenants. I remember walking out of Melbourne into the country and near Geelong. I stopped at a small farm to ask for work. It was a small dairy and the couple were perhaps our age, had no work but feeling sorry for me took me in and gave me a home.

"I lived and worked the farm with John and Agnes Smith for several years. They gave me a few pounds now and again that I managed to save. I was eighteen when they decided to sell the farm and move into town. It was a sad farewell and although both are now dead I still miss them greatly. Their generosity and kindness shaped my life."

Drawing breath Sam looked beaten and sad as he continued. The women were enthralled by the story he was telling with so much feeling and heartbreak.

"I went north into New South Wales and started in the shearing sheds for a contractor who was kind enough to teach me to shear and it seemed at last, through hard work, I was able to start making money, which I hoarded perhaps because of my difficult life up till that time.

"I purchased my first car at that time, it was my prized possession, an old Holden. It held all my worldly possessions and at last I felt I had a base, some form of belonging strangely, in a bloody old car. I settled into my new life and I loved it, wandering from shed to shed, it was a great life. I registered for National Service and was called up. After basic training and jungle warfare instruction in Queensland I was stationed in Darwin for three months.

"One weekend, with three companions, we had a pass from the Friday until Monday and went into the city for a few drinks. I didn't drink as much as others but after a few beers we went into Kentucky Fried for a meal. Behind the counter was a young girl, she was nineteen at the time.

"I had never even been out with a girl though I was enthralled with her. She was small and angelic, like Monica, and I was tall, awkward and gangly with no looks. She introduced herself to us as Carol. My two companions tried to crack onto her as I stood back watching her beautiful face and she just rebuffed their clumsy advances with good humor. She looked at me standing there like a goose.

"I shall never forget when she whispered to me, ""Hello shy one. Would you like to walk me home after work? I knock off in ten minutes."

""Sure if that is okay with you?"" I remember stammering.

"I remember she nodded and smiled at me and my legs went weak. I felt such a fool and my two companions left me to wait and went back to the barracks in absolute disgust shaking their heads.

"I sat sweating in fear until she finished and came bouncing out of the store smiling and grabbing my hand she talked to me, asking about my life and I told her what I have told you.

"When we got to her flat about three blocks away she stood on tiptoes and gave me a peck on the cheek. Hell, my heart nearly stopped. As she closed the door she told me if she was off the next day and I wanted to, we could go to Mindil Beach for a swim; she'd pick me up at nine o'clock she said.

"I walked to the nearest bus stop and sat on the bench, unaware she could see me and also too stupid to realise buses had ceased to operate as it was too late.

"I sat there for some time, head in my hands pondering what had just happened, when I heard a voice behind me, "Hello country bumpkin, gee you're something," she sang and taking me by the hand led me back to her flat.

"From that day on we were an item."

Now even Sam had tears streaming down his face as he continued.

"Within three weeks we had married and purchased a house with two spare blocks in Darwin. Carol worked at her job and lived in the house until I returned from Vietnam. On my return we promised never to be parted again. We kept our promise until her death. I joined the police force and for ten years we lived and worked in Darwin. Though we tried, Carol hadn't been able to conceive a baby at that time, however, we had each other, our passion and love was insatiable, just as I have found again with my beloved Monica.

"After ten years we let the house, purchased a caravan and headed off working all over the top end and the Kimberleys in various jobs. The life of nomads suited us, we were in love and free, we were so happy.

Then while working at a remote cattle station on the Gibb River Road, we discovered, to our delight, that Carol was pregnant.

"Our daughter was born in Broome. When I saw her first appear, I thought my heart was going to burst, it was amazing. Carol decided to go south, being over protective of our infant because of the twenty year wait for her arrival. She thought the heat may affect her, our little pride and joy.

"And so we ended up in Tasmania finding a hundred and twenty acres on the banks of the Derwent River with an old homestead on it. We renovated the old place, I got a job at the local paper mill and so we spent twenty six of the best years ever, raised our daughter, educated her, and stood with hearts bursting as she graduated.

"I had reached sixty and our daughter had by now, with our help, purchased her own home and was busy with her own life. We decided to go on a pilgrimage in the caravan visiting old places we had spent our time in. We also decided to sell the house in Darwin just as we'd previously sold the blocks to pay off the farm.

"I had been home, only a few weeks into retirement when one cold snowy day, I went off to feed our cattle some hay. Carol never complained and hated going to doctors, but she did, this once, actually admit she didn't feel well and had heart burn as she called it. I tried in vain to get her to let me call the doctor and she agreed I could if she still felt unwell in the morning. You know, I think she knew she was going to die.

"As I left the house she gave me her usual peck on the cheek and said something I found strange. ""Take care country bumpkin, life with you has sure been something."""

With tears streaming down his weather beaten face Sam looked old and vulnerable, but he was determined to finish.

"When I came back Jacky ran straight to her chair and started howling. I saw her angelic face and I knew she had died of a massive heart attack.

"I sat with her for hours, unsure what to do. I think without my daughter I would have ended my life. Carol had been my very reason for living, my one and only true family.

"I phoned my daughter and of course she came straight away, in shock, and managed to make all the arrangements. When they took her away I couldn't stay in the house and my loving daughter took me into her house; she had a unit underneath and made that comfortable for me.

"We buried Carol in an old graveyard on our property overlooking the willow lined river that she loved so much. Unable to return to the house, because of all those memories, I locked it up and it is still locked today. But I now feel Carol would be happy to have sunshine and laughter back in the old house, if Monica will still have me. I want us to live the rest of our lives there and be buried with Carol.

"I spent the last two years doing up an old boat to fill in my time," Sam went on, "My helper, an old friend, passed away and it was then I decided to hitch up the caravan and do the trip we had planned, then clean up the house in Darwin and sell it."

Sam sighed and splashed water over his face. He had bared his soul and felt absolutely exhausted, like an old man for the first time in his life. Monica slowly got up and walked over to Sam holding his kindly, old face to her bosom. "You sure are something you beautiful old country bumpkin," she cried.

Victoria and Mary sat quietly, their energy sapped, gazing at Sam in his grief.

Victoria broke the ice. "Sam please forgive me, I will never forgive myself. God what have I done?"

"No Victoria, I really feel better now. I've gotten this terrible sadness off my chest, from my very soul." He then turned to face Monica. " It is you especially who has changed my life. I never dreamt I would find so much happiness again. So you see it is you who I should thank and I do from the bottom of my heart."

Sam stood up in the water, and picking Monica up like a small child he called Jacky and strode to the bank. Looking at the others he said, "Come on cheer up, its over and life is so short. Let's enjoy our trip and each other. I feel much better now for sharing. Let's look forward to a wonderful wedding and a great trip home."

Sam and Monica decided to take Jacky for a walk while Victoria had a lay down in the caravan. It had started to cool down a bit with evening setting in.

Mary was cooking the evening meal and opened up a draw looking for a can opener. She had not looked in that drawer before and came across a photo album. Opening it up the air expelled from her lungs as she looked at Sam and who she knew must be Carol. The same height as Monica, though with a slightly bigger chest, a lot of similarities were obvious.

Feeling guilty she showed Victoria. "My god," she exclaimed. "No wonder Monica is his fatal attraction, they are so similar. Look at the shorts and boots. To Sam she is Carol."

When Sam and Monica returned, he noticed the draw still open and he took out the album and showed Monica. She commented on the excellent choice Sam had in women, noting she and Carol were the same size and hair color. It now seemed a new era had begun, all past lives had been exposed with secrets, old desires, relationships and dreams excised. The disclosure formed an even stronger bond between the four who had been part of it.

Chapter 12

Tired after the heat of the day and the traumatic gut wrenching story of Sam's life, all slept soundly, only wakened by the call of birds and cattle bellowing while drinking from the creek.

They all ate a hearty breakfast before Sam drove back onto the highway. Spirits rose as they looked at the magnificent scenery that now started to appear: huge mountain ranges with flat tops on the ridges. Mary commented one could almost imagine Indians streaming down the hills like in the old westerns.

Filling the land cruiser up at Turkey Creek, they enjoyed a cold drink while sitting on a bench in the shade, watching the caravans and campers pulling in and departing.

Back on the highway Sam reckoned they should try and make it to Wyndham that evening as he wanted to phone his daughter. It was the day he had agreed to phone her each week.

Late in the afternoon they reached the fork in the highway and Sam turned west towards Wyndham. Mary and Victoria dozed in the back while Monica and Sam chatted.

Darkness had crept over the land before they arrived and pulling into the caravan park, Sam paid the fee for two nights and parked under a giant Boab tree. Before the evening meal they enjoyed a swim in the pool. It was romantic under the stars and Sam and Monica embraced each other like life itself, as if afraid the dream might suddenly end.

Sam later phoned his daughter, immediately telling her

about Monica and her friends. He also told her they were heading to Darwin to be married. Felicity at first was shocked but warmed to the idea as she realised that since the death of her mother,he had been like a lost soul.

Calling Monica over he passed the phone to her. Alarmed, she promptly took the phone and a feeling of trepidation came over her, used to the manner in which her own daughter spoke to her. She managed a weak, "Hello."

Felicity introduced herself and in a bubbly voice, congratulated her on making her father so happy. In fact, she said she would take leave and head to Darwin to attend the wedding. Wishing Monica a safe trip she told her she was looking forward to meeting the wonderful lady who made her precious dad so happy. Monica was ecstatic when she passed the phone back to Sam.

After the meal they retired early, it had been a long day and they fell asleep in a short time.

Monica lay against Sam, feeling her love for him had no boundaries. His amazing life story only strengthened her feelings for him. The conversation with his daughter also had a remarkable effect on her. The only one she had not told was her daughter, who had absolutely no contact with her own brother, but this was the only fear she had.

The following day they carried out the usual chores associated with traveling by caravan: washing and cleaning the van. Sam then gave them a tour of Wyndham, the port area and the large statues of aboriginals in the centre of town and they all posed for photos with the giant crocodile on the main street.

Resting and reading in the afternoon, they drove to the Bastion Car Park at the Five Rivers lookout and watched the sun set. It was, as always, an amazing experience.

The four had easily formed an amazing relationship. All appreciated each other and the simple way they showed their care. A strong bond had been formed between them..

Returning to the caravan park and enjoying a refreshing dip in the pool, they enjoyed an evening meal of Barramundi before retiring ready for an early departure.

Leaving Wyndham they arrived in Kununurra at mid-morning, touring the green oasis that is the fertile plains of the Ord Scheme. They had lunch at an establishment that served ice, cold smoothies and they sat beside a beautiful lagoon with colorful Water Monitors.

Driving the short distance to Lake Argyle, they only had time for a quick shower before boarding the boat for an evening barbecue and swim. Cruising the vast area of water, listening to the boat operator explain the construction and capacity of the scheme, they found it more than interesting, and wondered why so many people in Sydney had not even heard of such a huge scheme.

Sam and Monica, with several others, dived into the water. Mary and Victoria declined a swim although Sam assured them that the thousands of freshwater crocodiles were harmless, floating about in the vast expanse of water.

Again, Monica had trouble comprehending how she came to be in the middle of the lake with a man who was to be her husband and with whom she was deeply and totally infatuated.

That evening they gave Mary a rest from cooking and bought a meal of Silver Cobbler at the dining area of the motel. Sam informed them that the fish was farmed from the lake and was, in fact, catfish, however, they enjoyed the meal and conversation with fellow travelers.

Again Sam had not unhooked the caravan so after an early breakfast they set off for Darwin, anxious not to be late. The wedding had been planned for the following weekend and the girls let Sam know they needed a few days to make preparations. Monica's son had made all the arrangements, according to Sam's instructions along with the celebrant's.

It was a glorious day as they reached the highway and headed east towards Katherine, their destination for the night. It was not long before they left West Australia and entered the Northern Territory. Fueling at Timber Creek, the little party drove on aiming to reach Katherine. Apart from their excitment at the coming wedding, they were all keen to help Sam clean up the house he wished to sell.

The scenery changed dramatically keeping all spellbound at the magnificence and starkness of the landscape. It was about four in the afternoon when Sam pulled into the caravan park on the highway, just before the main town of Katherine.

Parking the van he invited them for a swim in the stream nearby. Leaving the park by a rear gate they were surprised to see a small stream flowing with absolutely crystal, clear water. As they entered the warm water they relaxed immediately, finding it to be very therapeutic. Jacky entered into a game of diving into the water yapping madly with several aborigine children all having a magnificent time.

After their evening meal they went to bed, only to talk for several hours, excited about the coming wedding; even Sam was enthused as he constantly gave Monica a peck on the cheek. His absolute enchantment and love of her shining like a beacon and infectious to all in the caravan they shared.

Waking later than usual they had a quick shower and breakfast before again heading north towards Darwin on the final leg of their journey. They were aware they still had quite a trip after the nuptials and that Sam would be attending to business in Darwin.

Sam stopped at Adelaide River and they had lunch. He then guided them on a walk around the cemetery where service personnel were buried, those who had given their lives in defense of their country.

They were impressed on seeing the excellent job the government did to maintain the area, it was beautifully manicured, as it should be, they all agreed.

It was just after midday when Sam pulled into a small caravan park on the way into Darwin. When he had arranged connection of power to his house, he suggested park the caravan in the driveway and use the facilities there while they cleaned it up for sale.

Monica phoned her son Allan though he was still at work. His wife, Margaret, invited them all for lunch the following day. Glowing with happiness at the invitation from her daughter-in-law, Monica hung up the phone.

The camping area Sam had chosen was at the rear of a service station some way off the highway. It appeared at some time it had been intended as a huge tourist park and plans had been put on hold. The area where Sam parked was beautifully covered with magnificent shade trees and colorful flowers everywhere. A swimming pool was set in amongst lush lawns and shaded by towering sweet smelling trees. They all enjoyed a cooling swim in the pool before dressing and using the barbecue next to the pool. The evening was warm and sultry.

They made plans to go into Darwin early. Sam intended picking up the keys from the real estate agent to his house, that had now been empty for several months and arranged for the electricity to be connected. The three women planned to shop for outfits for the wedding. Victoria let it be known that she and Mary were shouting a night for the newlyweds in the best hotel in Darwin on their wedding night, so they could be alone.

Sam tried to intervene. "Just having you two wonderful friends present is enough."

"Out-voted again Sam, your harem has spoken," said Victoria as she held her finger up.

That night, as everyone lay in bed, conversation reigned for some time. It was incredibly hot, even with all the windows wound out and a fan circulating air throughout the caravan.

Victoria drifted off to sleep and waking some time later, rose to go to the toilet and noticed Sam and Monica were not in their bed. Mary, having woken also, decided to accompany Victoria to the toilet.

As the two made their way both had to pass the pool. Moving through the shadows of the overhanging vegetation they realised Sam and Monica had been for a swim. In the moonlight, oblivious to the two people watching them, in silence, they were in the throes of making love. Victoria held Mary's hand as both froze, watching the spectacle unfold before them, unsure what to do. Hidden under the shadow of a huge tree they watched in fascination at the scene being played out before them.

Sam and Monica, glistening with water and perspiration, like two finely tuned musical instruments, both oblivious to the world, pleasured each other in an erotic and lust filled sexual embrace. Monica's small, pear shaped breasts rose in rhythm as she sat on top of Sam and with her head back, cried out in ecstasy as she pleasured herself while Sam lay motionless, cupping her buttocks, allowing her to play out her own agenda until climaxing.

The two hidden women watched, frozen to the spot, captivated by the act playing out before them.

Completely oblivious to everything around her, Monica plunged madly up and down on Sam, shuddering as her body arched in ecstatic orgasm. With her breasts heaving from the exertion, she bent down and gently kissed Sam in an act of pure emotion. She rose above his throbbing cock and crawled forward over him, stopping to let him smell the aroma of her womanhood. Opening up her legs and pushing her buttocks back, she laid her head on the ground, presenting herself to Sam so he may sate his lust on her. Sam rolled over and coming up behind her, drove his cock deep into her, causing her to moan in pure ecstasy.

As the two women continued to watch in awe, in one final thrust, Sam drove deep into her his body, shuddering as he climaxed, the moon highlighting the sweat dripping from him as he gently withdrew from her. Monica turned around and stood up, pulling Sam's head to her firm stomach.

Ashamed at herself, Victoria pulled Mary back along the path as they both hurried back to the caravan, quite sure the two love-makers had not been aware of the prying eyes.

It was not until they lay on their beds that Mary spoke. "I feel ashamed that I stayed and watched that," she said.

"Not much else we could do. It was so spectacular I just froze to the spot."

"God what passions those two have," said Mary. "I never saw sex as anything other than an act men expected women to perform."

"Well, I am glad I had my time in the sun. As a matter of fact, being honest, even at my age, I miss it. I admit to being aroused watching them give so much pleasure to each other."

"Sadly, I have never experienced such passion or satisfaction from sex. Monica was enjoying every minute of it. She was insatiable wasn't she?" said Mary.

"Hell Mary, what was wrong with you? Sex is one of the most satisfying experiences one can have, with the right partner."

"If I tell you a terrible secret Victoria will you promise never to tell anyone?"

"Really Mary, you out of all of us, the most stable. I never thought you would have dark secrets."

"Yes, they all think that, old Mary never complains, but you see Victoria, some of us do live with dark and terrible memories."

Engrossed, Victoria said, "Really, my dear old friend, I promise. I never realised you held such a terrible dark memory in your past. I promise that what you tell me will die with me."

"Okay. Well, my father abandoned us and Mum went to live with the grocer, a mean little bastard with glasses, he reminded me of Gerbil the Nazi. I suppose Mum had no choice really in those days. Well the bastard penetrated me at only eight years of age and my sister who was nine. He sent the boys to live in the barn but allowed us in the house so he could abuse us.

"My sister used to cry when she heard him coming into our room of a night so I played his game to protect her. I learnt to wank him off and give the prick a head job to avoid us both being raped as often. We left as soon as we were old enough to work and found our own accommodation. I'm sure because of that, I was never able to enjoy sex. I was lucky I had a hard working husband who was not passionate and more interested in his work. I had four children but only had sex to please my husband. After watching tonight it made me realise what pleasure two people can give each other."

"My god Mary, how did you live with that all your life? Why didn't you report the bastard, even years after?"

"Like Sam, I feel good I have told someone. To your question, what is the use of dwelling on the past? Life goes on. Why embarrass your husband and family publicizing such a terrible thing?"

"I feel so sad for you Mary. I would have told the authorities, it's the right thing to do you know."

Mary sighed. "Would it have stopped one rape in the past? It was all over and I coped, I made myself forget Victoria and I survived. That is why in many ways I envy Monica, so passionately in love. Did you watch as they pleasured each other, knowing what each other liked? Totally caring for the wants of the other, giving their bodies without reservation to the wants of the other."

"Yes you are right, as always, my wise friend. I was so blessed to have a magnificent relationship and I still miss him every day, every hour. But at least, like Monica, we enjoyed what we had, soaked up the essence of each other as those two did tonight."

Mary turned off her light. "Let's sleep. We have a busy few days coming up."

Victoria turned over pulling up her sheet. "Yes. Thank you for thinking so much of this old, unworthy friend, for allowing me to help cleanse the darkness from your past."

Mary yawned. "Sleep well Victoria, I am sure Monica will."

Chapter 13

Unaware what time it was, they were awakened by the ringing of Sam's mobile phone. "Hello, Sam here, who's this?"

He immediately sat up in bed smiling. "Hello love, where are you? In Darwin? When did you get here?"

Felicity must have let Sam know she arrived the previous night, hired a car and driven straight to her pre-booked motel.

Sam listened intently, as if on instruction, and passed the phone to Monica. "Felicity here," came the happy voice. "I know Dad has a few things to do, so I am on my way to pick you girls up to take you into Darwin to do some shopping and for some girl chatter over a morning coffee," she laughed.

"Sounds great. I'm really looking forward to meeting you. We'll have a quick breakfast and get ready," said Monica smiling in delight.

Putting the phone back on the small table next to the bed, Monica flew out of bed in a great panic. "Come on ladies," she spluttered. "Felicity is on the way to pick us up."

Sam suggested that they all meet at Monica's family home for lunch as previously planned. He would leave the van where it was for another night and then move it to his house in the morning.

An air of excitement immediately came over the occupants of the caravan. Sam, excited at the arrival of his daughter, took off in a hurry to the showers. With Monica and Victoria also being keen to impress, Mary had a job to keep up with her two enthused friends. "God," she exclaimed. "Slow down or one of us will collapse."

Sam had taken Jacky for a short run and the little dog seemed caught up in the moment. He had the uncanny ability, like most dogs, to sense some event simply by the behavior of those around him.

They had just settled down at the table under the branches of an overhanging tree when a car drove up. A tall, strikingly good looking woman in her late twenties jumped out and ran to Sam, throwing her arms around him, happy to be reunited with her beloved father.

"Sorry," she said, as she looked at the three standing around the table taking in the display of unbridled daughter and father love.

Before the others had time to respond Felicity hugged Monica. "You must be the amazing woman who is making my dad so happy," she said and then began to sob.

Wiping her tears as Sam introduced her to the three women, Felicity sat and shared a coffee while breakfast was finished. Mary, and especially Victoria, immediately warmed to Monica's soon to be step-daughter. Victoria looked at Felicity, and thought, *this girl is the daughter I would have wished for, confident, poised, a beautiful smile along with an infectious bubbly personality. The result of two loving parents and a happy and loving upbringing.*

Felicity looked at the three women and innocently asked, "So how did my dad come to be so lucky to have met three such nice ladies?"

All looked a little shocked but Victoria as usual laughingly replied, "Well Felicity, we all jumped naked into his vehicle on Cable Beach."

Victoria went on to tell Felicity the whole story and the other incidents since the four had teamed up. Felicity laughed until tears streamed down her face.

"You three are amazing," she smiled. "You all remind me of my late mother. Dad seems to attract outgoing and carefree women."

"Okay, come on my little Monica, the apple of my dad's eye, let's take you shopping for something nice to get married in to a very special man," said Felicity as she grabbed Monica by the hand.

With everyone talking at once, Sam proudly watched the two most precious women in his life now, hop into the car, with Mary and Victoria giggling as they climbed into the back seat.

A silence descended over the space where so much activity had been happening a few moments ago. Sam felt lonely. It was the first time they would actually be apart for a few hours since they became lovers and he missed her already.

Locking the caravan he opened the door as Jacky bounded into the front passenger seat and they drove off into the city.

Sam went straight to the real estate agent to collect the key. As they had let the house for Sam, over the years, they tried to talk him into a new lease, however, Sam thought it unfair to the prospective tenants to let for such a short time. The senior agent then asked Sam what he was going to do with the home and Sam told the agent that the house was to be put up for sale.

The agent soon told Sam that property was scarce in Darwin now and he would get a good price. Sam whistled when he was given a figure. They agreed to meet at three that afternoon to inspect and list the house on site at the home.

Sam found it hard to believe that a home he paid twelve thousand dollars for was now worth so much. He walked the short distance to arrange for the electricity to be reconnected and paying the fee, a helpful employee promised to have it connected that afternoon.

Immediately, Sam drove out to Rapid Creek and pulled up in the familiar driveway. Old memories flooded back, good memories that the house reminded him of. The original was destroyed in Cyclone Tracy, though luckily, Sam and Carol had been on leave in Bali and missed the terrible catastrophe.

When they returned, Sam arranged for a friend to bring up a caravan from Perth and he and Carol stayed on, having no children to care for, both were able to help with the cleanup.

It had taken some time for services to be reinstated. Their house had been insured and they re-built, making a cyclone proof residence. They missed the old house; it had stood high on cement piers with a laundry and open space underneath.

Sam was happy and surprised to see that the inside of the house, although now a bit dusty, was in excellent condition. The agents had managed the property well. The garden needed a good tidy up but apart from that he found no damage. As he wandered around, a technician pulled up in a van to connect the power. Sam could not believe how quick the service was. The technician explained that he had a job in the next street and when he received the call with the connection order he was able to do the job straight away.

No furniture remained in the house. Sam switched on the hot water and checked that the toilet flushed. He was pleased they could use the facilities when he collected the caravan.

As it was early and he had not booked in for an additional day, Sam decided, on the spur of the moment, to go and move the caravan before meeting the girls for lunch.

Returning to the park he collected the van and in an hour he had it set up in the drive of the house. He had a shower and then looking at the time decided to drive to Monica's son's house in Ludmilla.

Allan and Margaret saw Sam pull up outside. They walked down to meet their new step-father to be. They quickly warmed to Sam, he was exactly what they had hoped for: warm and friendly, with a great personality.

They had two boys named Brett and Roger. Sam would

meet them at the weekend as they were currently on a school trip.

Glancing at Sam, Allan spoke directly to him as they enjoyed a cold stubby on the balcony while Margaret started cooking steaks and seafood in readiness for the arrival of the women.

"Sam, I know my mother is very happy right now. Even I, her own son, can't believe the change in her. I don't like airing dirty family linen but I must tell you a few things.

"My father doted on my sister. She was the first born and for some reason he hated me. Mum had suffered at the hands of the bastard during her entire marriage and the treatment he dished out to her is unforgivable, abhorrent.

"I left home after high school and entered Military College to escape watching her suffer. My sister treated her like a slave and openly, with the assistance of my father, verbally abused her, made her believe she was useless, even bloody well inhuman.

"I begged her to leave many times but I think she lost the confidence to do it and even though I begged her to come and live with me, she felt as if she would be a total failure if she left her marriage."

Sam replied, "I'm aware of the life Monica had. My heart really does cry for her. I promise to look after her, you have my solemn word on that. I love her deeply, she is an amazing woman, far from useless. I find her bright and honest, truly a lovely and kind individual."

Allan shook hands firmly with Sam.

"Welcome to our strange family Sam. It's a pleasure to have you as my step-father, " said Allan as they hugged.

Then Allan said, "Another thing we should discuss is Mum's money."

"Oh heavens?" Sam replied taken aback. "I have money for us both. I would never consider using Monica's money."

"Sorry Sam," chuckled Allan at the misunderstanding. "Don't misunderstand. You see my sister has all of Mum's assets and even though I know they are in Mum's name, she has total control, bullying mum into submission. My father used Mum to hide assets and she just signed whatever he told her to. The whole stinking matter needs ironing out. Believe me Sam I don't want one cent but I know Mum has earned that money and why not? She can use it to make life enjoyable for both of you."

Sam pondered for a time and replied, "Unfortunately, I am not well educated and not up with high finance. I've always just put our spare money, safely I assumed, in a bank account. If Monica needs help then I will do all in my power to do so."

"Sorry to bring up unpleasant matters at such a happy time Sam but it's something I wanted to discuss with you without having mum present," explained Allan as he patted Sam on the back.

Jacky was having a marvelous time with the family Labrador. Like all small dogs, and people, he was cocky, bossing his new friend around and having a ball. Margaret, on seeing that Allan and Sam had concluded their mens' talk, ambled over with two fresh stubbies. "Welcome Sam. What a refreshing change in fortune for Monica, truly wonderful," she said and turned back to her cooking.

At that time, all four women, laughing and chatting, came up the driveway. Introductions were made as they sat down in the shade and tucked into the ample feast of fish, steak and salads prepared by Margaret. Sam noticed Monica and Felicity sat close. He supposed that with both doting on the same man, the bonding between them had been instant. Sam noticed they placed their arms over each others shoulders, giggling, and wondered what his cheeky daughter was revealing.

Sam told them about the move of camp sites and that the caravan was now parked at his old home. Allan volunteered to bring his lawnmower around and spend the afternoon to help with the clean up. Enthused, everyone agreed as they insisted on helping Margaret clean up before a small convoy headed to Sam's house.

Arriving, everyone organised by the matriarch Victoria, hopped into vacuum cleaning, window cleaning, gardening and general tidying up.

Monica was looking radiant in her new shorts and boots. Allan approached her and gave her a warm and welcoming hug. "Mum, I find it hard to believe you are looking so great, so tanned, fit and so bloody happy, good on you."

Monica looked at her son proudly. "I still find it hard to believe too Allan. I am so happy my heart is bursting."

"You deserve it mum. How did you find such a nice man?"

Again, unfortunately for Monica, the conversation was overheard by Victoria, so she again told the story which gained in detail and exaggeration each time.

"Not my mum," Allan yelled. "Serious? I can't believe it. Well done mum. I'm so bloody proud of you."

He picked her up and gave her a big bear hug, swinging her around, laughing madly.

The women chatted, planning the events for Saturday which was only two days away. They decided to have a relaxing day on Friday before the hectic wedding day. Arrangements to have hair done at a salon in the city had been organised and the honeymoon suite booked for the bridal couple.

The celebrant pulled up in her car to get final instructions and for papers to be signed so she could deposit them at the registry. Giving both a quick run through of her simple ceremony, she got to the part of 'if any person has any information as to why these two should not be married' when Victoria spoke up. "Yes! Two other oldies have the hots for him."

The celebrant and all around burst into laughter. Sam looked sheepish and smiled.

As the men began loading rubbish onto the trailer the real estate agent appeared. He got Sam to sign the sales agreement and placed a sign on the fence advertising the home for sale.

After loading up the trailer and the lawnmower, Allan and Margaret headed for their home, looking forward to seeing everyone early on Saturday.

"So where *are* you getting married Dad?" asked Felicity.

"Well its a special place, where I married the other great love in my life. I hope Monica agrees. It's a glorious spot on lawns overlooking Darwin Harbour and out to sea."

A tear ran down Felicity's cheek as Monica ran to her dad.

"I will be proud to marry you in such a special place Sam. what can I say?"

Felicity looked at Victoria and Mary and said, "Okay, now girls why don't you come and stay with me at the motel and let these special love birds have the day before their wedding alone. I have booked a room next to mine for you both."

"What a kind gesture Felicity, but please let us pay our own way?" replied Mary.

"Certainly not. If it had not been for you two, dad would still be lonely and sadly moping about. I owe you all big time. Besides, spending time with such wild, decadent ladies will do me good."

Victoria liked Felicity and said with a wink, "No problems here, it is a great idea. Only hope you can keep up with us Felicity and that we don't make you too tired,"

Laughing, they gathered some clothing from the van, and waving, drove off into the city.

Taking Sam by the hand, Monica suggested a nice shower and then a lie down. The day had been long and she felt tired. Sam agreed and after the shower they retired into the van, happy, content and very much in love.

Chapter 14

Sam and Monica awoke to the barking of Jacky trying to get out of the caravan. His ears cocked, he obviously heard something outside. Glancing at the clock, it showed nine in the morning. Exhausted from all the activity of the previous day, they had slept in. Pulling on some clothes Sam heard a tap on the caravan door. Making sure Monica was covered, he opened the door and stepped out, a young couple stood before him.

"Sorry for waking you up sir, but my fiancee and I have been looking for a house and we saw your sign," the young man said.

Sam looked at the two standing there with their eyes pleading; he realised houses were in short supply and in a booming market even harder for young people to get into. Reaching into the caravan he grabbed the keys to the house and told them to have a good look around. He even invited them to have a coffee after their inspection.

Monica and Sam sat under the shade of the trees on the lawn enjoying breakfast as the young couple checked out the house. Returning after the inspection, Monica invited them to sit down while she went for extra cups. Looking at Sam the young man said, "We love the house though unfortunately, even though we both have jobs, the banks will only lend us a figure that is fifty thousand short."

Sam liked them both and sipping his coffee he looked at

Monica and said, "If my wife, and of course your bank agree, I will leave in the fifty on second mortgage for ten years interest free. Would that help?"

The young couple stood upright, jumping out of their chairs. "Do you really mean that sir? You don't even know us," said the young man.

"Well," Sam replied. "I class myself as being a good judge of character. Anyway, having a mortgage over the property, I have nothing to lose," he went on. "My little and beautiful wife doesn't cost much to keep."

"What do we do now then?" they asked Sam.

Sam smiled. "Pull the for sale sign down as you go, take it back to the agents, ask for Peter Frazer and tell him our deal. I am sure he will arrange everything for you."

Thanking both several times, the youngsters left, taking the sign with them. Monica looked at Sam and said, "That was very kind Sam, not many would have done that."

"Sometimes love, it doesn't hurt one to spread a little sunshine in people's lives. I am aware how hard it is for young people to get a start in life and if I helped them, then that makes me happy. See how much in love they were?"

"Not as much as I am with you Sam. I would die if anything happened to you. My life revolves around you and my heart is in your hands."

Sam suggested a ride into town to explore the city and surrounds, checking out the spot chosen for the wedding. Excitedly, Monica dressed while Sam, as usual, took Jacky for a short walk.

The mobile phone rang as Sam was about to drive off and answering it, he found it to be the agent. After checking the facts he agreed he would sign the young couple immediately and would Sam call during the morning to sign. Sam agreed.

Both spent the morning driving around the parks soaking up the cosmopolitan atmosphere that is Darwin. Sam even suggested going to the Mindil Market that evening for tea. Monica enthusiastically agreed as somewhere she had heard of the place.

Stopping at the real estate office Sam signed the contract and afterwards they strolled along the esplanade to the special place where they were to be married. They stood looking out over Darwin Harbor. Monica realised the significance of the place for Sam and knew he surely must love her for wishing to marry her in this, of all places.

Enjoying a great meal in the city centre it was late afternoon when they returned to the caravan to rest and change for the market.

Monica thought about the last few weeks and the happiness she had experienced. She only had one dark cloud looming on the horizon and that was telling her daughter and the reaction her new found position would create.

Later in the afternoon they drove to Mindil Beach. The car park was crowded but they managed to find a space to park the land cruiser. They left Jacky in the vehicle with the sun about to set, and leaving the windows down slightly Jacky would be alright for an hour or so.

Moving amongst the throng of people Sam and Monica browsed around the stalls, sampling the large range of various foods, soaking up the atmosphere. Sam led Monica down onto the beach to view the sunset, a huge, red ball, slowly sinking over the Arafura Sea.

Sitting on the sand with Sam's arm over her shoulders, Monica looked at the sight. It was romantic, and again, another experience she had never dreamed of. Snuggled against Sam she thought perhaps this was all a dream and she would wake up back at the village. Perhaps I have conjured up this perfect image and adventure from dreaming while watching too many soap operas on television during the many years of loneliness.

Her thoughts were rudely broken by the voice of Mary.

"Found you two old romantics. Please save me from Victoria and your daughter Sam, they are incorrigible lunatics."

Victoria and Felicity had their arms around each other.

"Sorry Sam," Victoria laughed. "You have lost your daughter as I have just adopted her."

Sitting on the beach, the conversation turned to what they had done that day. Felicity and her passengers had toured the town, the old gun emplacements and the museum. Monica told of Sam's house sale and his assistance to the two young buyers.

Mary looked at Felicity and said, "I expect nothing more of your father Felicity. What a find Monica has found, no wonder we are envious of her."

"Yes, there is only one Sam Stewart, but I must admit he was lucky to find Monica. Buggered if I've had any luck sourcing a good man. Perhaps dad has set my benchmark too high," laughed Felicity.

After an hour Monica suggested that perhaps they should all have an early night ready for the day ahead. "It is going to be the best day of my life," she beamed.

Felicity and the two elder friends suggested picking Monica up about mid-morning to have their hair done then meet Sam at Allan's to dress for the wedding. All would leave from there and return after the ceremony for a feast and celebrations.

Returning to the land cruiser to an excited Jacky, they drove back to the caravan, deciding to take the little dog for a short walk to stretch his legs.

On their return they shared the shower, romantically washing each other in the warm, cascading water before drying each other and snuggling into bed, anxious for the sun to rise on their wedding day.

Chapter 15

Sam and Monica had a fitful night of sleep. After talking for hours sleep evaded them. Both felt blessed they had met each other and imagined if it had not been for the mad decision Monica made to do something outlandish they may never have met.

Sitting under a shady tree eating breakfast they watched as a car pulled up and the young house buyers got out carrying a huge bunch of flowers.

"The agent told us about your marriage," the young woman said as she passed the flowers to Monica. "Best wishes to two fabulous people and a heart felt thank you from both of us. We will not let you down."

Delighted, Monica gave them a big hug and thanked them for their kind thoughts. *The day has already started magically* thought Monica, *truly my happiest moment.*

Looking at Sam Monica said, "Thank you Sam for such a wonderful time. Since I met you my life has been one magnificent adventure. Marrying you will truly be the most outstanding thing I have done in my life. I cannot wait until we are back at your home and I can settle into a quiet and happy life with you. Thank you my dear from the bottom of my heart."

"It is I who should thank you. I have a new lease on life, some purpose again, a reason to go on and grasp every wonderful moment. I promise to be a good husband to you

Monica. I find it hard to believe we are so happy, it seems a dream come true."

"Mary once told me to dare to live the dream. Sometimes I wake up in terror thinking it's a dream and I am back in the village. Then I feel you next to me and tears of sheer happiness come to my eyes. Sam promise me we will never be apart while we both live. Please Sam, promise me?" begged Monica as she took Sam's hand.

Sam kissed her gently. "I promise only death will ever part us. I made the promise once before and it was my privilege and happiness to keep it."

Sitting holding hands, as if in a trance, the moment was broken when Felicity and her two companions pulled up in the driveway. Bouncing up the path, Felicity gave her father and Monica a warm hug while Mary and Victoria sat in the chairs.

"Coffee please Monica. Felicity has worn us both out. Now I know where she gets it from. She and her father both always seem to be doing something fantastic," said Victoria.

Chatting away and admiring the beautiful bunch of flowers they had just received, another car pulled into the driveway. It was Allan and his family.

Brett and Roger, Monica's two grandsons, came running up the driveway. "Hi Gran," the elder Roger greeted them. "Dad tells us we will have a new Grand Pop and he has a farm and a big boat. Can we come and stay please, pretty please?"

Embarrassed, Allan butted in. "Steady on you two, let Gran and Pop have a few months to settle in first. Besides we're going to Fiji this year but I promise I will take you to visit for Christmas, if Gran and Pop agree."

Monica hugged both the boys, sad that she had not had the chance of spending more time with them, but looking forward to her new position in life. "I am sure Poppy Sam would love to have you come and visit us anytime."

Sam agreed, telling the boys he would be annoyed if they

did not come and help him on the farm and go fishing on his boat.

Margaret apologised for disturbing them but explained that when the boys arrived home the previous evening, they wanted to come straight over. They had found it hard to believe that Nan Monica was traveling in a caravan, getting married and then going to live on a farm in Tasmania. Neither had been able to sleep either, excited at meeting their new Grand Pop.

Again it was Victoria who broke up the meeting with everyone so excited and talking at once. "Okey, dokey folks, time for us to whisk away the bride for our appointment at the hairdresser. We'll meet back at Allan's about one and then after lunch all head to the esplanade for the ceremony at three."

Allan and his family had some last minute shopping to attend to and said they would see them back at his house when they arrived.

As both cars drove off, Sam, with Jacky sitting on his knee, waved them off. He decided to clean the land cruiser and polish his boots for the wedding. He had decided to be married in a pair of moleskin trousers he kept for special occasions, including a check shirt along with his Rossi boots. He looked at old Jacky and as if talking to a human said, "Well old boy, life sure can change. Looks as if we've been lucky enough to snare another mum to look after us both."

Jacky looked up at Sam, wagging his tail. Sam had always believed, along with Carol, that the little bugger understood every word they said. He had played a big part in their lives since Felicity gave him to them for Christmas many years ago. In fact after the death of Carol he had been a great comfort and companion for Sam.

Washing the vehicle and polishing his boots to a high sheen, Sam looked at Jacky again. "Now for the bad news old boy. Bath for Jacky and Sam, we have to look good for this special event."

Sam bathed Jacky and dried him before showering and changing himself. Checking in the mirror he thought, *not much to work with Sam, but you'll pass.*

Arriving at Allan's to wait for the girls, Sam enjoyed a beer with Allan while Jacky yapped madly about with his new found friend. The women arrived back late and Margaret served up snacks, advising them that she had a mountain of food ready for after the wedding and that she did not wish to have people unable to do the feast justice.

Sam was surprised when Allan changed into his army uniform in honor of his mother's wedding. Sam saw he had the rank of Major and he looked resplendent in full uniform.

Sam praised all the wonderful hair styles, especially Monica's, he never realised she was so pretty. Everybody stood around smiling watching Sam and his bride to be .

Victoria, now firmly in charge, asked Sam if he and Allan would leave in ten minutes and go for a drive to fill in half an hour, then wait at the wedding site a good fifteen minutes prior to the marriage. The bride and her attendants will dress and meet them there for the service.

"Fussing about like an army drill master," Allan jokingly described Victoria to Sam as they left.

Victoria had the proceedings running like a well oiled machine.

Allan drove Sam to the point looking back at Darwin and they walked to the lookout. Again he sincerely thanked Sam for the change he had made in his mother's life, and he went on that he was proud to have Sam as a step father.

Sam told him again that he would do all in his power to make his mother happy and give her a good life.

Allan shook his head and said to Sam, "You can make mum no happier than she has been since you both arrived. I wonder if it is the same mother I last visited in the retirement village? It seems so hard to believe it's actually her."

Allan and Sam arrived ten minutes before the ceremony. The celebrant had a table with two chairs set up for the signing; it had a beautiful white table cloth cover and white flowers in a vase and Sam congratulated her for being so professional.

Allan pointed to the hotel behind them on the other side of the road overlooking Darwin Harbour. "You are booked in there tonight, compliments of Victoria and Mary."

Sam noticed the balconies overlooking the harbour and felt gratitude towards the women.

He then looked in amazement as two large black limousines pulled up to the curb and Felicity and the two older women stepped out, all looking absolutely smashing, hardly recognisable as the two women he had shared so much with.

But it was Monica who took his breath away. *God,* he thought, *she is more than beautiful, she is angelic.* He tried to stop his overwhelming emotions but was unable to and soon tears ran down his cheeks as Monica, flanked by her friends and Felicity, walked up and stood beside him.

The setting was picture perfect looking across Darwin Harbour: boats gently rocking on the aquamarine water, the fragrance of frangipani wafting over the lush lawns, truly romantic as both exchanged wedding vows and gently kissed each other. The tough and resilient Allan even shed a tear, so happy was he for his mother. He stood wiping his eyes as his wife Margaret held his hand, also caught up in the emotionally charged atmosphere. Jacky stood proudly at Sam and Monica's feet, behaving perfectly for the event and looking up at both, wagging his tail.

Victoria noticed amongst several people who had stopped to watch the ceremony, a man about the same age as Sam. He stopped and looked intently at Sam. He was accompanied by an olive-skinned lady, taller than he, with beautiful features.

At the conclusion, amid clapping and congratulations, both sat and signed the formal paper work. Felicity and Allan signed as witnesses for their parents.

Turning around Sam saw the man who had been watching so intently and immediately both recognised each other. Sam walked up with Monica and introduced her, then turning to all present he said, "This is my old friend and army mate, Anthony Wilson, known as AJ, and his wife Sky."

Margaret invited them back to the reception. Felicity and Allan snapped several photos and then the group climbed into the waiting limos to head to Allan's house for the celebrations. Sam found out that Felicity had shouted for the limos and in fact had one booked to take the couple back to the hotel later that evening.

On the way back Monica said to Sam, "What a lovely looking couple your two friends are Sam."

"Yes, they certainly are. They live in Tasmania several months of the year," Sam told her. 'We are lifelong friends. We'll visit them later, when we get home. They're on their way home now."

Margaret and Felicity had managed a super feast. It was a happy gathering as everyone tucked into the mountain of food and drink.

Sam's friends mingled and joined in the celebrations although Sky only drank soft drink. Sam and Monica were deliriously happy with huge smiles, unable to stop hugging each other. Mary and Victoria consumed too much alcohol and caused a sensation by telling the others of the exploits of the happy band since meeting.

Darkness fell over the party as all consumed more food and drink than was usual.

Allan's sons insisted on keeping Jacky for the night; their dog slept on their beds so Jacky could too they begged. Sam agreed and promised to pick him up in the morning. The limo arrived and the guests escorted the newlyweds to the flash looking car to be whisked away, waving vigorously as they drove off.

"What a magic day," Victoria sighed.

AJ and Sky thanked everyone for having them share the wonderful occasion and as they left, gave an envelope to Felicity to give to the newlyweds the following day. Felicity wondered why they had not given it to the happy couple themselves but shrugged her shoulders. She vaguely remembered her father mentioning the couple and another name that she couldn't quite remember.

Sam and Monica arrived outside the hotel. The driver, under instruction, carried the overnight bag for them to reception, only leaving when the happy couple entered the lift escorted by hotel staff to go to their room. Closing the door they fell into each others arms.

"Hello Monica Stewart," Sam sang out. "How is my beautiful wife?"

"Never felt better in my life my most precious Sam Stewart, the best husband a girl could ever wish for," Monica said as she hugged him.

Throwing their clothes to the floor, they climbed into bed, mentally and emotionally exhausted from the day's events. They lay in each others arms soaking up their love for each other and contemplating their life ahead. From the bed, they looked out at the lights of ships in the harbour and while entwined in each others arms, fatigue overcame them as they both drifted off into a sound sleep.

Chapter 16

Monica and Sam enjoyed their breakfast on the balcony. The sea glistened as the sunlight caused the ocean to look like a million diamonds glistening as they danced over the blue waters. It was only seven thirty when they decided to go back to bed for a couple of hours. Dropping their hotel dressing gowns to the floor they lay on the bed talking.

Sam told Monica about Allan's worries over her financial affairs and assured her he had enough money for both of them. He wanted her to understand that he did not need her money. Monica admitted that she was really unaware of her financial position as her daughter handled everything and put two hundred dollars weekly in an account for her to use.

Sam was alarmed when Monica told him she currently did as she had done all her married life and signed any papers her daughter or her husband requested her to. Sam said he did not wish to intrude but perhaps she should ask after her financial affairs and that his daughter was an accountant, and he felt sure, would run over matters for her. Sometimes, he told her, matters involving family can get a little messy.

Monica agreed but begged Sam to let her wait until they were settled in Tasmania. Not until then did she feel that she would gain the strength to approach her daughter on the matter. Sam told her he thought she might like to visit her daughter in Sydney as they passed through. Monica seemed to become upset at the proposition and again pleaded with Sam to let her wait until they had reached Tasmania.

"She was so upset with me as Victoria told her to fuck off on the last visit. I don't reckon she would visit for perhaps another few months and then only to have documents signed."

Sam soon woke up to the fact that Monica had a fear of her daughter, as indeed she had of her late husband. Both had bullied and treated her with an absolute over-riding power and control.

Pulling her to him, Sam told her that if she chose not to, she never need contact her again, he would take care of her. Monica felt safe as she snuggled into Sam. He realised she found even the conversation distasteful and unsettling so he decided never to raise the subject again.

They had dozed back to sleep when Sam's mobile rang. Jumping out of bed he answered, it was Felicity.

"Hi Dad," she said. "Get ready. We will pick you up in half an hour to go for a crocodile cruise on the Adelaide River then onto Jabiru for lunch."

Before Sam could answer she went on. "Jacky is fine, he is playing with Allan's boys, having a ball, see ya."

Sam did not have time to reply as she hung up. Throwing the phone on the bed he told Monica it was Felicity and it appeared they were off on a day trip with her and Monica's two companions.

Monica pulled Sam onto the bed. "Sam sorry for being so weak with my daughter but I always found it better to go along with her and my late husband. I guess I put peace before my dignity."

Sam kissed her gently. "Let her try something on you now," he replied. "It will be a different story I can tell you and if I have to kick arse I bloody well will."

Felicity pulled up outside the hotel exactly on time; she had inherited her parent's ability to keep to a schedule. They enjoyed a relaxing and happy day. Monica and Mary loved the crocodile cruise, they all enjoyed the billabongs and bird life of Kakadu, some of the birds were spectacular.

Felicity was leaving for home on Thursday morning so for the next two days they visited Leitchfield and several of the springs that surrounded Darwin. Wednesday evening came too quickly and they sat around the table having their last meal together. Victoria insisted on shouting everyone, including Allan and his family, to one of Darwin's top restaurants for a slap up celebration. After the meal Victoria stood to make a toast. "To our new family," she called as she raised her glass.

"I find it incredible to think now that we three sat so bored and lonely in a retirement village, look at us now. This is because we met a wonderful man, Sam Stewart, who, even though we all burst into his life naked, changed our lives forever. I now have an extended family, a new daughter Felicity, who has looked after Mary and I beyond belief for a younger person, no doubt a lesson learnt from her amazing father. Thank you and god bless you all," she finished wiping a tear from her eye.

It must have had an effect because Margaret, Allan's wife, rose tapping a spoon to her glass. "On behalf of Allan and our family thank you all for giving Allan's mum a new and wonderful life. I sincerely hope that you all have many happy years together. What a remarkable group of people you are. Thank you from the bottom of our hearts."

Caught up in the moment Sam also rose in response. "We are leaving in the morning but I beg of everyone, never let our meeting here be the last. Our modest home in Tasmania awaits you all and we'll be disappointed if you don't come and stay soon."

Victoria, always the comic, jumped back up. "No worries there Sam. Will next week be alright? I for one can not imagine life without you guys. Felicity being my new daughter also makes it a must that I will be winging my way to Tassy sooner rather than later."

"That goes for us all," Allan broke in. "Do you really think our two sons will not have us in Tasmania within a few months? It's a shame, we've already booked for their upcoming holiday, but I intend taking some leave and heading south, like Victoria, sooner rather than later."

They said sad farewells after the meal was over. Monica hugged her two grandsons, now sad at losing their new exciting Grandmother and their Grand Pop, though both promised to have their parents take them to Tasmania to visit and see Jacky as soon as possible.

Felicity was catching an early flight and looked forward to seeing them in Tasmania within a couple of weeks. Allan and Margaret gave them many hugs and a few tears were shed as they all parted. Sam and his passengers were already packed, ready for an early start on the last leg of their journey.

Unable to sleep properly Mary suggested at four in the morning that they pull out there and then and head south stopping early that day when they might sleep better. They agreed and while Sam hooked up breakfast was prepared and Jacky taken for a short walk by Victoria and Monica.

Daylight crept over the land as they passed through Adelaide River, stopping at Katherine for morning tea. The girls purchased supplies for the evening meal. It was good to be back into the old routine and they were enjoying it. Sam felt a little tired so they decided to pull into Mataranka for the night, leaving the caravan hooked up while they soaked in the warm springs for a couple of hours, talking to other travelers and relaxing.

Enjoying a small evening meal they retired just as darkness descended over the land. Exhausted, no-one spoke and deep sleep soon overcame the four, even Jacky was quiet, having played for three straight days, he did not stir until daybreak.

The following morning after breakfast they returned to the

Stuart Highway and headed south. Victoria noticed both Sam and Monica now seemed anxious to return to Tasmania and start their new life together. Turning onto the Barkley Highway later in the day at Three Ways, it seemed as if Sydney was looming closer and closer to Mary and Victoria, sad at the thought this was in fact too true.

After an eventful day they stopped at The Barkley Roadhouse in a nice quiet caravan park behind the road house. Sam shouted them to a nice meal in the dining area and again they all retired early; the constant traveling starting to take its toll on the two older ladies.

The following day they left the Northern Territory and entered Queensland, deciding to stay at Mt Isa for the night. They booked into a caravan park Sam chose because it accepted dogs.

Chatting to the couple next door, Sam and Monica decided to go to the local Irish Club for the evening as a country and western band was playing. Victoria and Mary explained they were way too tired and if it was alright they would take Jacky for a walk and then retire early. The couple next door had a small dog called Fife and asked Victoria and Mary if they would mind looking after her also; they had an enclosure around their annex which kept Fife penned in.

Monica and Sam had a magnificent time dancing to the slow music, the meal was excellent and their new friends turned out to be great company. They arrived back at midnight, relaxed and tired after a wonderful evening.

Trying to be quiet, entering the caravan, both Sam and Monica found Victoria and Mary waiting for them. "Did you give them your names and address?" whispered Mary.

"Well yes, our names, but they only know we live in Tasmania," Monica replied.

"Thank god," exclaimed Victoria.

"Why? What happened?" asked a perplexed Sam.

"Well when you left we took bloody Fife out of her enclosure and along with Jacky we went for a walk behind the caravan park. We did not get a hundred metres when old bloody Jacky was knotted into Fife with one of the most satisfied looks on his face ever. Took ages before they parted. Just look at the old bastard. Still with a satisfied look on his face," explained Victoria.

Sam and Monica burst into laughter.

"I'll tell them in the morning so they can give her the morning after pill. There's a vet just down the street and I'll pay the cost. You old devil Jacky, " laughed Sam.

Awakening in good time Sam was too late as his neighbors had already left.

"I hope they are going west," said Mary, "or both Victoria and I will be up for pup maintenance."

The four felt glad to leave Mt Isa and head to Cloncurry before swinging south onto the Landsborough Highway. The day was clear and breathless though they were glad the temperature did not seem to be as hot and humid as it was further north. Stopping for several meals and rest stops they arrived in Longreach as the lights of the town began to twinkle in the still evening air.

The following morning Sam visited the Stockman's Hall of Fame and decided to drive only as far as Blackall that day. The next morning the little group was on the road early and after another long day arrived in Dubbo late in the evening. As the women had never visited The Plains Zoo, Sam suggested a day exploring there and then resting before their last drive together into Sydney.

The next day Sam and the three friends enjoyed several hours looking at the animals in the open plan zoo. They felt it was a pity, with the zoo being so close to Sydney yet not one of them had ever visited such a fine display of the world's wildlife.

Over the evening meal all seemed a bit sad that their extraordinary adventure now was over. Before bed, they hugged each other fiercely, shedding more than a few tears. This was to be the last night for Mary and Victoria in the caravan that they had shared so many good times and adventures in.

"The dream is ending," sobbed Mary.

They seemed to linger the following morning, a somber cloud had come over the group, and leaving, they were silent as they headed out for the final leg of their remarkable trip.

Sifting through her bag, making sure she had her key, Victoria pulled out an envelope. "Oh hell," she cried. "Felicity gave this to me to pass on to you. It's from your friends, they gave it to her for you after you left for the hotel, after your wedding."

Passing it to Monica she in turn went to pass it to Sam.

"It's for us," Sam said. "Open it and see what it is."

Monica opened the envelope and gasped. Inside was a cheque for twenty five thousand dollars and a card. Looking at Sam she read the card that Sky had thoughtfully written. "'Dear Sam, thank you for the bravery you showed in going to the defense of Anthony and his wounded friend, I will never forget you. Our best and kindest wishes to you and Monica. So glad you have found such happiness again. Kindest regards always. Sky and AJ.'"

Monica looked at Sam and wondered if he wished to tell them about it. She knew that he would have if he'd wanted to. *Perhaps he would talk about it in his own good time,* she thought.

"You can use this to start our joint account when we reach home. I would refuse it but I know them well and it would deeply offend both."

They arrived back at the retirement village mid-afternoon and Victoria directed Sam to the car park and went into the office to speak to management. Noticing that the duty manager seemed unimpressed at a caravan parked in the car park Victoria cut her like a sword. "As we each have a car space in the park and no cars consider what stands before you as mine and Mary's cars," she snarled.

As she left, the manager scowled and thought, *Welcome home you old bat, back to making our life a bloody misery.*

Monica went to the office after making Sam comfortable in the small villa she owned then informing staff she was leaving and would like to put her place up for sale. The duty manager explained to her that as the village had a waiting list the sale would be immediate. Signing the papers she left smiling, even after being told of the costs kept by management. *They can bloody have what they like,* she thought, *I am out of here.*

Monica left her new address to post the money from the sale and requested that it not be given to any other persons, including family members she warned them.

Both Monica and Sam decided to leave in the morning and the three girls packed Monica's personal things. Victoria promised to sell the furniture and other items she did not want to keep.

Sadly, Monica realised she would miss Tracy Brown and wrote her a long letter and left five hundred dollars of her own money in the envelope. She thanked her for her kindness and friendship and invited her and family to stay with them in Tasmania. 'I have found love and happiness for the first time in my life' she wrote. 'You, apart from Victoria and Mary, are the ones I will miss most. Your loving friend'. She signed it and gave it to Mary to pass on.

No sadder departure occurred than the one that now played out in the car park as Sam and Monica made to leave. Mary and the usually stoic Victoria wept openly and uncontrollably as their two adventurer friends drove off, promising to reunite in Tasmania as soon as practical.

Chapter 17

As they drove across the Sydney Harbour Bridge Sam kept intently to the task of driving. He hated big cities and the congested traffic. Monica guided him onto the Hume Highway and it was only at this time Sam found out she in fact held a driver's license and had a car garaged at her former home. She spoke sadly of her Volvo which she loved to drive, now kept by her daughter since she transferred into the retirement village.

As they left the city Sam noticed that Monica became less agitated and more relaxed. At the village in her bungalow the previous night, she had seemed nervous and full of anxiety. Now she had become more settled as if leaving Sydney, a place she had lived her entire life, had forced the lifting of a dark cloud that had hung over her.

As he looked at her, at how vulnerable she really was, Sam realised that she had placed the balance of her life in his hands. Her face now a picture of contentment as the city disappeared, they entered the open country of New South Wales.

Stopping for lunch at a rest area, Sam phoned the office of the Spirit of Tasmania and was thrilled to be able to bring his booking forward to the following evening. Both now just wanting to return home and begin the start of their new lives.

By mid-afternoon they arrived at Holbrook and booked into the caravan park, preferring to stay close as they had a whole day yet to fill in the next day. Sam told Monica they had to reach the terminal an hour or so before departure as no parking existed on the wharf.

He informed her that once this was not the case and most travelers parked on the wharf early to avoid peak hour traffic and chatted while passing the hours away. Unfortunately everyone had to arrive now in time for direct loading.

They took Jacky for a long walk in the paddocks behind the park. The weather became a little chilly as evening approached. Returning to the caravan Sam put on the fan heater while they both went for a shower. They felt relaxed when they returned and enjoyed a small meal of tuna and salad. After washing up they retired to bed and read for a short time. Monica had found a new mind broadening hobby in reading, she was so glad Sam had introduced her to such an amazing new world.

Darkness crept over the park as lights twinkled. The sounds of heavy trucks slowing as they passed to travel either north or south rose to a crescendo making sleep almost impossible.

Stepping out of bed to turn off the heater, Monica suggested a cup of Milo and Sam watched as she slipped her dressing gown off in the warm air. He realised she knew he was aroused by her perfectly preserved and firm body.

Transfixed, he felt his excitement rising as she made two cups of Milo and turned towards the bed. Looking at her smooth, inviting vagina, unable to control himself, he swept the sheet back exposing his throbbing cock. With a wicked smile on her face Monica placed the two cups on the bedside table and mounted Sam, swept up in the wild animal lust both produced in each other. Sam tried to control himself as he rose into her, climaxing fast, disappointed he was unable to oppress his lust enough to keep going.

With Monica still sitting on him they kissed passionately. She held him tightly as if she would never let go. To his surprise, he felt himself expanding in her again as both entwined in a session of unadulterated wild and uncontrolled passion, ending after what seemed an eternity with both crying out in ecstasy, absolutely sated and gasping for breath in a frightening climax.

Lying on the bed panting, this was the first time since meeting that they had been truly alone. Monica rose from the bed and Sam watched her use a face washer to slowly sponge herself down, then gently holding Sam's deflated manhood, wiping him clean in warm water. Slipping back into bed she snuggled back against Sam, already drifting off into exhausted sleep. A slow smile came over her face as she thought, *at last a man who desires me, more than that he is crazy for me, as I am for him.* Their erotic lust for each other was like a raging fire.

The following morning Monica cooked Sam his favorite breakfast of bacon and eggs, it was their last breakfast in the caravan where they had enjoyed so many good times together. Unable to dismiss the fervor of the previous night Sam reminded her of the wild passion she aroused in him, almost uncontrollable and admitting he was never satisfied, always feeling like more. She had an effect on him which sometimes made him feel ashamed. Kissing Sam, Monica admitted she felt the same, like an uncontrolled fire driving her crazy and she confessed she loved his desire for her and the wild passion both extracted from each other.

It was nine o'clock before they pulled onto the highway, entering Victoria by mid-morning, however, Sam did not stop until Seymour for lunch. Still tired from the exertion of the previous evening, they dozed for a couple of hours, filling in time so as to arrive and load directly onto the Spirit.

Monica had never been on a ship before and was very excited. Sam found the whole thing a bit daunting, hoping this would be his last time as it had become a real task fighting traffic and getting to the ship in the small window of time allowed.

He told Monica of the times Carol had gone on ahead to the room while he loaded the vehicle. All meals were included then in the cost of the ticket, but the old times were well and truly gone, he sighed.

Monica was excited, as was Jacky, who knew he was heading home as they drove over the West Gate Bridge. Diverting off the freeway they soon passed through security who checked under the bonnet. Sam said to her he was unable to comprehend what they hoped to find when tons of explosives might have been in the caravan and under the vehicle. Monica discovered it irked Sam that his free and peaceful country was now becoming a paranoid security zone because some immigrants hated us and our way of life.

After a short wait staff beckoned them on into the belly of the ship. Making sure Jacky had food and water, Sam made up a bed for the little dog and locked the vehicle. Both carried a small overnight bag. Sam decided they should eat first and then go to their cabin later. The pair enjoyed a leisurely dinner as the ship shuddered slightly, moving across the bay for the overnight journey to Tasmania. Sam pointed out the lights of Melbourne as they ghosted into the darkness.

The night air was chilly and they soon made their way indoors, enjoying a glass of wine at the bar on their way to the cabin, which, they discovered, had four bunks. They felt a little stunned as they looked at each other.

Sam hated the top bunk and laughed as he told Monica how Carol always grabbed the bottom bunk and he would pull the mattress onto the floor and sleep there. Sam was incredibly tired, the stress of the trip and getting on to the ferry had taken its toll. As he slipped into the single bed, Monica stood before him, a picture of absolute pleasure. She climbed in with Sam and snuggled into her position telling him that no way would she now sleep without him close to her. Smiling as he pulled her to him, he drifted off to sleep.

Both were awakened by the ship's public announcement system advising they would be docking in thirty minutes at Devonport. They enjoyed a quick shower together before dressing.

Sam was so happy to be going home; Monica was excited about her new life with the man she worshiped. She looked at him as he dressed and her heart was nearly bursting with pride. *He is the very essence of my existence now,* she thought.

Making their way towards the deck that the vehicle was parked on, Jacky was beside himself with excitement, yapping madly as they opened the vehicle and sat inside waiting for the huge doors to open for unloading. It was still dark as they drove off the ferry. Monica gave a shout as they touched Tasmanian soil, her new life was really beginning. Clearing customs Sam hit the road. Monica was unable to see any countryside in the darkness. A fog hung low over the road and ice glistened. Sam explained it was a frost, one of the last for the winter, he hoped.

Stopping after twenty minutes to give Jacky a run while Monica made a cup of coffee, for the first time they pulled on heavy coats. After the heat of the north the chill of Tasmania was biting. The area had toilets that they used and Jacky cocked his leg on most of the nearby trees as they had hot coffee, watching his movements as other travelers pulled in to make breakfast before traveling on.

Sam pointed out all the towns as they passed by on the trip, many now bypassed by the new highway. It was well and truly daylight as they pulled into Perth on the Midlands Highway for fuel. Monica was amazed at the lack of population and she remarked that it was more like the north of Australia.

Like a child, Monica repeatedly asked questions of Sam about the house. He told her it was comfortable, old, not flash like she was used to. She told Sam the caravan would do or even a tent as long as they were together.

"I am so in love," she kept telling him, looking into his face as if pleading. "As long as I am with you things will be fine."

They passed Campbell Town, Oatlands and other small country towns to soon turn off at Bridgewater, and passing through New Norfolk, followed the river until Sam pulled into a Poplar tree lined drive. The sign said 'Willow Bank Farm' and Monica knew she was home.

Following the driveway towards the river they turned into a circular drive. Monica gasped in sheer delight. Once again Sam had underestimated and what stood before her was a beautiful Sandstone homestead, verandah front and sides, dormer windows looking out over rolling pastures and the willow lined river ambling along below.

Felicity was waiting outside for them, smoke rising from the chimney. She ran to greet them, showering hugs and kisses over both. Pent up emotion and shock caused Monica to break into uncontrollable sobbing.

Alarmed Sam asked, "What's wrong? I know it isn't much."

"Oh Sam," she replied with tears streaming down her face. "I am crying with happiness. It is all a fairytale, it is the most beautiful sight I have ever seen."

Sam held her while she spilled out her emotion feeling a little overwhelmed himself. At last they were home.

Sam insisted on carrying his new bride over the threshold before gently setting her down at the table. Monica glanced about, all the furniture was antique, beautifully restored.

Seeing her curiosity, Felicity grabbed her hand. "Let's go," she said, "I will show you your new home."

They went upstairs to the main bedroom, a beautiful bed with canopy sat in the middle of the room with a view over the paddocks and river below. A modern ensuite sat adjacent with a beautiful dressing table with large mirror opposite. Monica was spellbound; in her wildest dreams she would never have imagined Sam living in such opulence. She asked Felicity who had decorated the home. "My mother. Dad encouraged her but it was left to Mum entirely. I hope you like it and that you have as much happiness and love here as she did," said Felicity.

"Felicity it is perfect, I will not be changing one thing. What great tastes your mum had, no wonder Sam was so happy," answered Monica still sobbing.

"When Mum died dad was shattered and I really worried about him, he had no zest left for life. If it had not been for his bloody old boat I don't know what would have happened to him. By the way, this is the first time he has been back in the house, since leaving after Mum died. It is marvelous, he is so in love again and so happy, thanks to you little Monica."

They stood for a time clinging to each other, both loving the same man in different ways, a strong bond was forming between the two women.

Monica realised she would never replace Carol but would do all in her power to make both her amazing new family members happy. Monica was unable to take in all of the beautiful home as Felicity swept her through the house, even showing her the overgrown vegetable garden and empty chook pens. All three chatted over a meal that Felicity had ready, though because of a client meeting, Felicity had to leave soon after. Sam and Monica were left in the peaceful surrounds of the neglected gardens of the homestead.

It was Sam who spoke first. "I know this may seem strange, perhaps, but I feel I should show you Carol's grave first. I'm sure she would be happy for us both. I never intended to have another relationship but it seems life has many twists and turns. I still don't know what would have happened to me if you had not come into my life."

"Of course Sam, I would be proud to come with you to Carol's grave. I can tell by your home that it always shone with love and happiness."

Hand in hand they walked over the lush fields where red and white Hereford cattle with calves grazed contentedly. Spring was in the air, wild flowers splashed color over the knee high clover and grasses.

Monica noticed it straight away, on a rise overlooking the meandering river, fenced in wrought iron, neatly painted white. There were several grave sites present.. As they approached they saw Jacky sitting beside a new marble headstone. They had not realised he had been missing since they arrived.

Standing before the site, Monica felt privileged as if she had just met Carol and was now going to share her husband and life in this perfect piece of paradise. The area inside the fence was immaculate. Monica wondered how it was in such perfect condition, doubting that Felicity had the time to tend so fastidiously to the area.

Sam looked at Monica and said, "I also know this is crazy but I have always planned ahead. I want to be buried next to Carol with you on my other side. I feel so incredibly lucky to have met two magnificent human beings who bring me so much happiness. As we lay in life perhaps you can indulge an old romantic and allow me to lay in death between two of life's roses."

"It would be my greatest privilege to do so Sam. I feel content at the thought of being buried in such a peaceful place."

"Well, that's over, let's not be mournful. Let's enjoy the rest of our lives together. I am glad you like our little bit of heaven. I will never raise the subject again but I had to ask you. You have made me very happy and I love you more than life itself."

Turning, they called Jacky and walked slowly back to the house. Monica agreed with Sam as she pondered her new life. *Indeed,* she thought, *I have entered Nirvana.*

She had discovered she had a high libido yet always thought she was abnormal, suppressing her desires, ashamed at her cravings for physical pleasure. Her first husband, she realised now, had been unable to satisfy her and shunned her, belittling her to hide his own inadequacies.

Her daughter was allowed to sleep with any boy and prance around the house in skimpy revealing underwear, another shame her husband forced her to endure. They had both spent weekends on the yacht with companions, indulging in wild parties, trying to impress and not even trying to hide the fact from her. She threw herself into raising Allan, her reason for living. Her husband and daughter ignored them both. She felt it such a huge contrast between her past relationships and the normality of her present relationships: loving, caring with desire for each other.

Both unloaded the personal items from the caravan that Monica had packed in Sydney then Sam backed the van into a shed and unhooked it for the last time, parking the land cruiser next to it.

He then showed Monica the old car he had under cover. It was an early model Mercedes and in excellent condition. Using jumper leads they started it, much to Sam's delight and he suggested going into New Norfolk for supplies at the supermarket. The battery needed charging and he said the run would do it good.

Pushing the trolley while Monica filled it to brimming with groceries, Sam suggested only buying enough meat for the weekend as he would send a vealer off to be slaughtered. This alarmed Monica but she realised now she must face the fact of where meat really came from.

By the time they returned and unpacked the groceries both were tired, it had been a long day. Monica phoned Victoria and Mary, filling them in on the details of their arrival and explaining enthusiastically about her new home.

To Monica's surprise, they told her they would be arriving to stay with Felicity in two weeks time. Victoria said they missed her and Sam terribly, unable to stand life at the village without her, especially after their great adventure. Felicity had kindly offered them Sam's old unit for as long as they wished. "Tell Sam to prepare the boat," Victoria instructed. "The crew are on the way."

As darkness enveloped the landscape, more than ready for sleep, they withdrew to the master bedroom, relaxing in the spa under heat lamps that hung overhead. Monica looked at the huge inviting bed. Sam got out of the water and passed her a towel. Drying her back, both slipped into the soft bed and sinking into the comfort of Sam's arms, Monica was asleep in minutes.

Chapter 18

Monica woke to the sound of music and the aroma of bacon and eggs wafting up the stairs from below. She looked around the room, unable to comprehend the last few weeks of her life and the dramatic turn it had taken. Never had she felt so relaxed and happy.

Climbing out of the soft luxurious bed, she paused and sat on the edge of the magnificent four poster, gazing out at the scenery below her: green grass waving in the morning sunshine and dozens of sleek cows grazing as calves cavorted about with mothers occasionally raising their heads to check on their offspring.

Pulling on a dressing gown, she stepped into her slippers and started down the stairs to be met by Jacky wagging his tail furiously as if to say, where have you been, it is well past time to start work?

Entering the kitchen she was amazed at the old fashioned Houn pine benches, slate floor and utensils hanging above on wrought iron framework. Monica fell in love with the place. It was obvious that a lot of love and care had gone into the whole house.

Sam looked up from his cooking and smiled. "I was going to surprise you with breakfast in bed," he said, turning down the music.

"Thanks but I don't want to miss one second. At the moment I have so much to see and explore and learn about in my new life."

"No rush, you have the rest of your life. I thought we would have a tour of the property first then start cleaning up the gardens and plant some vegetables. Nothing beats fresh home grown vegetables."

"That's great Sam, but please be patient with me, my only experience is shopping in Coles or Woolworths for meat and vegetables and I am totally ignorant."

"Did you garden?" Sam asked in amazement.

Sheepishly Monica answered, "No, worse luck. I was not allowed to garden. We had a gardener come in and do that for us. It seemed my husband thought such work undignified, only for the lower classes. But now Sam you must teach me everything, I want to grow my own vegetables and beautiful flowers."

They sat chatting and enjoying Sam's cooking. After cleaning up Sam suggested Monica wear her jeans and boots as it was still a bit chilly for shorts just yet. He warned that as it was early spring there, the winds could be suddenly and bitingly cold.

Monica was surprised when Sam led her to the barn and pulled the covers off two quad bikes. She had only ever seen bikes like them up north on the trip. Sam backed the smaller of the two bikes out and explained the basics of operating it. He patiently stood by as she rode several times around the driveway, very nervously at first.

Jacky insisted on sitting on the back, delighted to be home and back at his old duties. Monica soon learnt the fundamentals of riding and setting off behind Sam, on her first inspection of the property, she soon warmed to the freedom of the bikes as they cruised over the paddocks. The ride was invigorating and she fell in love with the feeling of powering along with the wind flowing past them, along with the smell of wild flowers and new pasture.

Several calves, being inquisitive, started to chase them,

kicking their heels into the air causing Jack to become excited and start barking. Caught up in the thrill she began laughing, it all seemed surreal, an experience she absolutely loved.

As they headed down the lane that ran through the centre of the property, lined with towering Poplar trees, Monica drew up next to Sam.

"I feel free, thoroughly invigorated, young again. Can we go on for another drive?" she shouted.

Sam smiled, waving his arm forward, indicating for her to follow him. Stopping at a gate, Sam left it open as they made their way along the river onto the next property. He had permission from the owners to use the access to go along the river to fish and hunt. The track was smooth as Monica flew past, hair blowing back in the wind with eyes sparkling, having the time of her life. Sam, becoming a little alarmed as she had no experience, indicated to slow up a little. When the bush thickened he decided to turn for home. Closing the gate as he entered back onto his own property, they soon pulled up at the shed. Monica jumped off the bike and grabbing Sam she thanked him for the best experience she had ever had. "Can we do that often?" she inquired.

Sam promised her every day if she wanted as he pushed her bike back into the shed.

Both enjoyed a morning coffee as they sat on the verandah. The low growl of a car made them look towards the driveway. To Monica's alarm, an early model Holden ute with a massive bull bar on the front roared in through the farm gate, aerials whip lashing backwards and forwards.

Several dogs jumped out of the back as the driver jumped out of the sticker festooned vehicle and rushed straight into Sam's arms. A perplexed Monica stood up, noting the driver was perhaps in her late twenties, tall, blonde, wearing jeans, a large belt, short-sleeved shirt and blundstone boots.

"How the bloody hell are you?" the woman asked as she

looked admiringly at Sam. Turning to Monica she said, "This must be the little woman who won my Sam's heart. Monica?" she said rushing and grabbing Monica in a bear hug expelling all the air from her lungs before plonking her back on the ground, dazed and confused.

Sam laughed. "Sorry," he said to Monica. "This is Sandra Young. Sandra looks after the farm and gravesite for me."

"Shit yeah," she replied. "Sam is my best mate. I suppose you wont want me to look after the cows now Sam, I understand if our deal is off."

"Absolutely not. I am sure Monica will agree with me that our deal still stands. Sandra looks after the cattle and we go halves in the profit," he informed Monica.

Monica gaining composure replied, "Absolutely Sandra, we would think of nothing else, you have done a marvelous job and if Sam is happy well so am I."

"Geez thanks, would miss not coming here and the extra bucks are handy. Saving for me own bit of land someday."

Looking at Sam she added, "A few calves need knackering Sam, what day suits you?"

"We'll be home everyday except Wednesday, we have some friends coming. I need to check out the Matilda and fuel and provision her for a trip to Port Davey."

"Fine, see ya Saturday," Sandra replied. "Sam, would you mind if I come with you on this trip, please, please? The boss owes me three weeks holiday and wants me to take it. Hate to be a pain in the arse but I'll help you on the boat?"

Sam laughed. "You are more than welcome Sandra, it will help me pay you back for the help you have been to us."

"No wuckin furries,' she yelled, waving goodbye as she slammed the door on the ute, gunning the engine as a pack of dogs scrambled into the back, and took off out the driveway in a shower of gravel.

"Wow," Monica laughed. "That was some girl Sam and she

sure loves you."

"Sorry," said Sam with a grin. "I should have warned you. Sandra works next door, a rough diamond one might describe her as, but inside all that bluff beats a heart of gold."

"I can tell that Sam. I like her. She sure is something though," chuckled Monica.

"Well you're right there," Sam laughed. "But I'll never forget the help she gave me and offered never to have to be asked, so I give her half of what the cattle make."

"Ï hate to ask Sam but what does knackers mean?" She looked at Sam seriously.

Sam smiled. "Well you might not wish to know once I tell you but it means parting the bull calves from their testicles."

Monica shuddered. "You sure are right Sam, wish I hadn't asked that one."

They enjoyed the rest of the day cleaning up the flower garden. The cattle stood at the side fence waiting for weeds and grass to be thrown over. By evening both Sam and Monica ached from the exertion of the task. They basked and relaxed in the spa, laughing about the days events.

"Life sure is interesting with you, you old country bumpkin,"Monica laughed.

Neither felt like much to eat and retired early. Happily contented and hopelessly in love, Monica snuggled into Sam's embrace and sighed with contentment. For the first time in her life she had found happiness.

The next morning sunlight danced over the bed as both stirred, still stiff from the previous day's effort in the garden. Muscles unused to physical work ached and Sam groaned as he went to move. "I reckon we went a little overboard yesterday," he said.

"I actually enjoyed it Sam. It reinforces that I don't ever want to leave here again. I feel so content here with you."

Sam hugged her closely. "I know how you feel. I'm going

to sell the Matilda after this trip. I call her Sam's folly, but it did save my sanity and gave me an outlet after Carol's death. We also owe Victoria and Mary a very large favor, after all, they *are* responsible for us meeting."

"Yes that's true, I am being a bit possessive, but I am so happy here. I just love everything about this place, it really does shine with love and happiness."

"To be honest I feel that way myself. Just the two of us in our own little world. It will happen eventually but I have made promises for now. Also I class Victoria, Mary and Sandra as very special friends, you know, even family."

"Of course you are right Sam. I feel as if I am being selfish. They are my only friends and without those two girls I feel I would not have survived in the retirement village. I always felt I was a bit too young to be in such a place but Celia insisted."

"I just can't understand your daughter. How ever one could treat a family member that way, let alone your own mother, sure beats me."

"My dear Sam," Monica replied "You must understand what her father was like and the upbringing Celia had. In spite of everything I still love her, she is my daughter, I gave birth to her."

Sam squeezed her hand and replied, "I am sorry. It's true, one must never judge until they have been in that person's shoes. I just find it so wrong that she treats such a wonderful lady so badly and you're her own mother."

"Yes, true. I only have one more wish and that is that we can all be one big happy family and have a relationship like the one you have with Felicity. I feel so sad that my daughter can't be like her. What a wonderful thing it is to see the love you two have for each other."

"Well, one day perhaps. Please don't let it consume you dear, let us be happy together. Anyway, as we are too sore and stiff to work, perhaps I will take you for a nice drive to see my old flat under Felicity's house. We'll join her for lunch and stock up the Matilda ready for the trip. Twelve days will soon fly by before the girls arrive."

"Excellent idea Sam. I have you and nothing else matters. I'm looking forward to seeing Hobart too," she said as she slid out of bed.

Both burst into laughter as Sam had to help Monica dress, her body so stiff she was unable to bend. "I always thought men helped pull ladies pants off, not help put them on?' laughed Sam.

"You can take mine off anytime Sam but right now just pull the bloody things up. I think we will attack the gardening a little slower next time."

"I'm going to let the cows into the veggie garden this morning, they can eat all the rubbish and I'll get Sandra to help me put the rotary hoe on the tractor and I'll work it up with that," said Sam.

They ate breakfast and Sam went to let the cows into the old vegetable garden. Always interested in some new feed the mob came running and started eating furiously at the milk thistles and numerous weeds.

Sandra had the cattle in two mobs of about thirty. This particular mob had calved earlier and the bull was again in with the cows. Monica stood watching as the bull reared onto a cow and served her.

"Good lord Sam," she said, "that was quick, how come she is the only cow with a husband?"

Sam spluttered laughing, "We only have one bull with the lot," he replied. "That is the way it is with breeding cattle."

Monica blushed. "Sorry Sam, I have a lot to learn. Just don't get any ideas though, this old cow is not sharing you with anyone."

"No chance of that," he laughed. "My old cow is more than I can handle anyway."

As they made their way to the garage Sandra came belting up the road in her usual style, coming to a halt in a cloud of dust, dogs yelping and running everywhere. Even Jacky barked furiously, excited at the arrival.

Grabbing a box out of the back of the utility she shouted, "Go ahead folks, only dropping a few chooks back in your chook yard Sam. Thought you might like some fresh eggs."

"Thanks Sandra," Monica yelled in the mayhem. "I was going to ask Sam about chooks."

"No bloody rooster though," Sandra shot back. "Bastard dropped dead, too many hens I reckon, looks like he was happy when he croaked it."

They stood and watched as Sandra opened the box and ten bedraggled chooks dropped into the pen. Tossing the empty box back in the ute, she again made the usual departure and one dog, a little slow and missing the takeoff, landed where the ute had been and then took off down the driveway in hot pursuit of the driver.

"See ya Saturday," she yelled, waving madly in the air as ute and dogs disappeared.

Unable to control herself Monica burst into fits of laughter. "Sam, please tell me whether you have any more Sandra's in your life, she is a mini cyclone, unbelievable."

"No they only made one Sandra, broke the mould after that, and yep, she sure is special," laughed Sam.

He backed the car out and Monica sat in the comfortable seat, still bemused by the scene she had just witnessed.

Chapter 19

The morning was clear though chilly as they drove down the highway through the town of New Norfolk towards Hobart. One thing Monica noticed was the lack of traffic. The Brooker Highway was light with traffic as peak hour had passed and she commented to Sam about the difference between the gridlock of traffic in Sydney to the traffic in Hobart. Sam cut around the Domain and onto the Tasman Bridge.

"Sam," Monica exclaimed. "What a beautiful sight. I had heard Hobart was beautiful, it truly is. What a wonderful part of the world you live in."

"Australia is a magnificent country," Sam replied. "I love it all, but yes, Tassy is special. Only hope too many don't find out and ruin it."

Turning left towards Lindisfarne, Sam turned into a bay and pointing out to Monica a flotilla of boats swaying at anchor. She immediately saw the name, Matilda, on a massive boat dwarfing many of the yachts crowded in the bay.

Parking on a jetty that jutted into the bay, Sam undid a small dinghy tied there and assisted the still stiff and sore Monica into the little vessel. He rowed the short distance out and as they got nearer to the boat, Monica, in a concerned voice looked at Sam and asked, "How is one supposed to board such a vessel Sam? It looks bloody huge, a bit like its owner," she batted her eyelashes at Sam smiling.

"I'll just grab you by the bum," Sam laughed, "and hoist you up the side where the rope ladder hangs over the other side."

"Is life ever dull with you Sam?" she asked.

"I always thought I was a bit dull really. I try to keep myself amused and happy. Idle people are usually unhappy people," he replied.

"Have to agree with you there Sam. Until I met you that sure was my life.".

Pulling alongside the freshly painted boat, Sam helped Monica up the rope ladder. She found it difficult to squeeze between the railings that ran around the ship and finally standing on the deck, she had her first look at the Matilda. Sam came up over the rails and tied off at the punt alongside the boat. Taking Monica by the hand he led her to the wheelhouse and unlocking the door she was surprised at how neat it all was; several screens sat above the wheel with a huge chair positioned near a console for the operator.

Sam suggested she go below and check out his handy work. He explained how he had removed the freezers below and made bedrooms, as well as extending the dining and kitchen areas. He also explained, as he started the engine, how he and a friend, spent eighteen months living and working on the old boat. She had been tied up after the government purchased the license from the owner as the fishery collapsed due to over fishing. She was used to long line sharks off the continental shelf. She was fitted, he explained further, with a Gardner 8LW, continuous rating, two hundred and eighty horse power diesel engine.

Sam went on to explain that all the winches on the deck had been removed and the old girl has a top speed of ten knots only. Sam chatted away proudly continuing to tell Monica all about the boat, she did not understand a thing that was detailed to her, but she listened intently aware this old ship was indeed Sam's savior after the heartbreak of Carol's death.

Monica felt the thud of the huge motor as she went below,

followed by Sam. What a surprise she received. The dining area was huge and even included a bar, forward was a compact kitchen, aft she found four bedrooms all neatly furnished, two with their own showers. Sam told her he had also fitted a new two thousand litre fuel tank for extended cruising. He sheepishly admitted he'd had delusions of grandeur while refitting the old girl. He and his old departed friend had even discussed cruising north to the Pacific.

"Old mens' dreams," he laughed, "perhaps to keep us going strong, well, we were both lonely and had lost wives. When Peter, my mate died, I didn't feel sorry for him, he wanted to go with his wife, in fact, he died happy, hoping somehow they would meet up. Old mens' delusions," he soberly went on.

He tried all the lights and instruments above the console devices and showed Monica how they were used to guide them to any destination in the world and showed charts of all the local area.

Sam seemed to enjoy showing her the array of sophisticated gear at his disposal. "We will take her into the wharf then go and get supplies, apart from perishables, to stock the kitchen, and get some grog. If I am showing the girls the sights we had better have some wine too," he smiled.

"I'll go and check what is on board while you take us to the jetty," said Monica.

"Great, there's a fair bit on board now, but never can tell on an extended trip what we will need so better stock right up for a while, possibly up to a week."

Monica heard the rattle of the anchor as she opened up the ship store. She gave a low whistle. There were more supplies there than she thought were needed but Sam must have a good idea.

The old ship shuddered as Sam engaged the gear making the huge propeller churn a trail of white foam spewing out the rear. The ship started to slowly move in a huge arc towards the jetty.

Monica looked at the screens above as Sam slowly moved the ship in close to the jetty. Sam showed her the position of the vessel on one screen with the jetty approaching.

As they approached the huge pylons Sam reversed the huge propeller as he gently placed the ship alongside. Leaving the wheelhouse he then threw ropes over the steel anchors on the jetty. Monica was happy to see Sam open up a gate on the railings and push a gangplank on to the jetty.

"We'll go and get some supplies at Eastlands," said Sam. "The company I phoned will be here at midday to fill the fuel tanks too."

As Sam headed down the gangplank Monica said, "What about the engine Sam, it's still going?"

"We wont be away long and I want to charge the batteries up a bit; they last for weeks but I haven't given her a run for at least four months."

Leaving the jetty Sam drove them to the shopping centre. Monica enjoyed shopping there and Sam promised to bring her back for a browse another day, not wanting to leave the Matilda unattended for too long.

After purchasing two shopping trolleys full of tinned food and long life milk, both headed to the vehicle and unloaded before pulling into the bottle shop where Sam purchased three dozen bottles of various drinks including 'Bundy and Rum' cans for Sandra and he grinned at Monica.

Unloading and packing the supplies took longer than expected. The fuel truck arrived and refueled the vessel while they trudged backwards and forwards to the car carrying bags of supplies. After finishing the task, Sam paid the fuel supplier and they sat in the dining room of the Matilda enjoying a coffee with cheese and biscuits.

"The only thing we have to bring with us when we leave is some meat and vegetables. We'll catch fresh fish hopefully on the trip," said Sam.

"Where are we going Sam?"

"To see some of the most magnificent and wild scenery on the planet."

"Really? After what I have seen and experienced since meeting you I can only say I am looking forward to the trip, it will surely be something,"

"I am sure you will not be disappointed."

Sam then suggested that Monica wait on the jetty while he return the ship to anchor, getting down was perhaps harder than boarding using the rope ladder. Monica gratefully accepted and stood watching as Sam let go of the ropes and pulling the gangplank in, reversed the old queen back to her mooring point.

Monica was amused that Sam found it a bit of a task getting back into the dingy. He smiled back at her aware he was still stiff from yesterday also.

Rowing back to the shore Sam looked at Monica and a feeling of tenderness came over him as he watched her waiting for him. She was indeed a pretty sight, perfectly formed and still beautiful for her age, and a beautiful human to boot.

Tying up the dingy Sam climbed up the ladder and taking Monica by the hand, kissed her, his passion for her so limitless.

Driving back over the Tasman Bridge Sam headed to Sandy Bay and his daughter's house overlooking the Derwent River. Unlocking the door to the unit below the house he showed Monica where he had lived since Carol had passed away, unable to stay in the home they had enjoyed for so many happy years.

"Now I am living again and thanks to you life is complete again," he told Monica. "You are my reason for living again."

"Sam love, you are the centre of my universe, my life started the day I met you." Hand in hand they returned to the vehicle, both keen to return to the sanctity of their home.

Felicity worked late so Sam told her they would catch up with her at the weekend. On the way home he had an urge for some fried chicken.

"I indulge myself in the rubbish occasionally," he laughed.

"Strange," said Monica, "so do I and every now and again the colonel calls me too."

Returning home they both inspected and fed the chooks Sandra had dropped off. Monica was thrilled as one nest contained two fresh eggs that she collected and gently placed on the kitchen table.

"Breakfast Sam," she said placing the eggs ever so carefully in a carton Sam had found for her.

Even Jacky was glad to be home, although Monica noticed he seemed to be quite at home on the Matilda, no doubt from having spent so much time with Sam repairing the old ship.

The next few days were bliss for Monica, inspecting the cattle on the four wheelers, gardening and planting seeds, feeding the chooks and gathering the eggs; for once in her life she was deliriously happy.

Both were abruptly awakened early on Saturday morning by Sandra's arrival and the bike starting as she roared up the driveway followed by her dogs to yard the cattle. Sam yawned and looked at the clock, it was only seven.

By the time they both dressed and had a cup of coffee Sandra had the milling beasts yarded and was kneeling down bedside the drafting race extracting testis from a bewildered calf. Monica looked in utter awe as Sandra expertly removed both testis and splashed disinfectant over the flattened scrotum. Sam passed her the NLIS tag and she expertly pierced the flap of the ear to permanently attach it before turning the calf loose, wondering what the hell just happened to it.

Monica watched as they sorted and marked two other bull

calves and tagged five heifer calves. *Much rather be a heifer in the cattle world*, thought Monica as she watched intently. After the cattle spilled out of the yards and started to sort themselves out, all three returned to the homestead for breakfast, followed by Jacky and Sandra's pack of excited kelpies.

Monica prepared breakfast while Sam and Sandra talked cattle, blood lines and prices. She found it quite interesting to listen to Sandra who seemed very knowledgeable on the subject of cattle.

Sam had mentioned to her that Sandra was an orphan, raised by foster parents. He and Carol first met her when she started working for the family next door ten years earlier. Both he and Carol immediately liked her and she regarded Sam as her father; they became very close over the years. Sandra had been shattered at the death of Carol, absolutely heartbroken.

Now as Monica watched the two, she realised both had a special relationship. Sam really cared for the young woman and the feeling was obviously mutual. As they ate breakfast the phone rang and picking it up, she recognised the voice of Sky, the beautiful olive-skinned woman who had attended their wedding.

"Hi Monica," she said. "Glad to see you are both home safely. Sorry to disturb you out of the blue but AJ would like to see Sam. Will you be home this afternoon?."

"Thanks Sky, yes we made it home safely, "Monica replied. "I'll put Sam on. I'm sure he would love to see you and AJ, we both would."

Sam took the phone. "Of course Sky, come and stay the night, please. Love to catch up with you both and my god, *thank you* for the generous wedding gift."

After a short conversation Sam replaced the phone. "Sky and AJ are in Hobart to pick up some gear. They've accepted our invitation and will be staying for a night. Hope you don't mind love, we go back a long, long way."

"Sam, they are a lovely couple and it will be wonderful to have your friends stay," Monica replied, now aware that with Sam, action would never be far away, with some event always about to happen.

After breakfast Sandra helped Sam put the rotary hoe on the tractor and worked up the garden to a fine, soft bed ready for vegetables. Eager, she volunteered to take a vealer to the slaughter house on Sam's stock trailer that afternoon also. Monica realised how keen Sandra was to help Sam, so willing to assist her older friend. *What an odd pair,* she mused, watching the two working away together. One quiet and reserved, the other completely opposite.

Monica prepared a light lunch while Sam and Sandra loaded a steer onto Sam's trailer. Over lunch, unexpectedly, Sandra asked Monica, "Have you met Sam's friend AJ and his wife Sky? You know he had two wives at once? Worked well, both got on like good friends."

"No, Monica hasn't been told the story, though perhaps I should tell her myself before they arrive."

Sam told Monica the story of how AJ met Sky in the woolsheds of New South Wales and that they became parted, through no fault of either, and lost contact. He told her of the birth of Sky's daughter, how AJ met Prudence, and then went off to war. As if reliving a past life, Sam went on to tell her about a fellow soldier being wounded and AJ carrying the friend to safety; how he was there in the thick of it and ran forward to give covering fire to his comrades. Sam told her about how AJ came to meet both women, how they came together in AJ's life, and how they decided to share him, both loving him enough to share his life.

Prudence was a remarkable woman, he went on, explaining every detail, how they built a cattle empire and then with the death of Prudence, her wish that Sky and AJ marry at the grave site. They had four children, two from each of his loves. Two still live in Sydney, one in Tasmania and one in the Kimberleys near Fitzroy Crossing. Sam told Monica that the eldest, Mary, was a lawyer in Sydney, the others still involved in the cattle business that Prudence created.

At the conclusion he looked at Monica. " It is a remarkable story about three remarkable people. Sky is of American Indian, Spanish, Scottish and Aboriginal blood, a truly spiritual and kind person."

Monica was looking at Sam, her face an ashen color. "Is the daughter in Sydney called Mary Brown-Wilson? Surely not, it would be too much of a coincidence."

"Yes, that is her name. How do you know that?" Sam asked astonished.

"I met her and her grandmother, Mary Jones it was, and Prudence at the graduation. You see Sam, she graduated with my daughter from university for god's sake.

"I was sitting alone and Prudence came up to me and introduced herself. I wondered at the time why her daughter had such a beautiful, light-brown skin and dark hair, as Prudence was light in colour. I just figured she had a dark-skinned husband as the grandmother was light-skinned as well."

"Well, in fact Mary was neither her real grandmother nor Prudence her mother. Sky is young Mary's mother but both always introduced themselves as the mother of all four children."

"What an amazing story Sam, one of absolute love and commitment. They must have be two very remarkable women."

Sam filled Monica in about Mary Jones who had taken claim to the grandmother's role in the story. Also, he told her that Sky believed *he* had saved AJ in doing what he did, but went on to say that it really made little difference, both had experienced a fair bit of luck at the time.

Sandra piped up. "Sorry Sam, didn't know the full story. Carol told me once about the trio after you had been to Prudence's funeral, I thought it was a magic story. If I ever found a man that liked me, I couldn't share him. They must have been special people."

"Yes, they certainly were. I found out about it when both sent some revealing photos to AJ to cheer him up and just happened to look over his shoulder and saw them both posing for him in crotchless panties. Sure did cheer him up."

"Your life never ceases to amaze me Sam, you are so casual about everything, yet what you've done is amazing, even more so the people you know. Right here now, Sandra I think you're a pretty amazing person."

Sandra laughed. "Well, Sam sure is special. So happy he has met you Monica, you are one special lady too. Better get this beast to slaughter Sam. I'll bring the cruiser and trailer back tomorrow if you don't mind, want to call in to the footy and watch some well built boys play and imagine one is mine."

"No problem at all. You'll find someone special one day, look what I landed at my age."

"Tell Sandra how I jumped in your car naked Sam with two other ladies."

Blushing, Sam told Sandra the full story.

"Bloody hell Monica. I knew you was special, what a great story," Sandra giggled. "Promise not to tell no-one Sam though I might use it as blackmail," Sandra replied, laughing uncontrollably.

"Go on, get going," laughed Sam. "I'll blackmail your bottom one day with the electric cattle prodder."

Monica and Sam waved her a happy goodbye as she drove off; her dogs in Sam's vehicle with their heads hanging out every window and the steer in the back on its last trip.

Turning, Monica said to Sam, "Lets get busy and make sure your friends have a good night. What do you suggest for dinner this evening?"

"How about the fish we picked up on the dock this week? If we thaw it now it'll be ready."

"Sounds great. I'll put some soft drink in for Sky and some beer for the two boys and I shall crack a bottle of wine."

Chatting, they entered the house, anxious to look after their coming visitors.

Chapter 20

Monica and Sam busied themselves in the kitchen. Monica was keen to impress Sam's old friends and marinating the fish and placing them in the fridge ready to cook later, she made a mixed salad to go with the fish. Both enjoyed making a caramel slice for sweets; they did not usually eat sweets but this was a special occasion.

Sam was in a playful mood and constantly toyed with Monica, she loved the attention he gave her. It was Sam who suggested they go and have a spa before the guests arrived. Monica agreed knowing full well Sam had other thoughts in mind and she instantly became aroused, flushed with expectation of a sexual tryst.

Sam ran the spa while she undressed. Turning, Sam looked at her and tearing off his clothes, picked her up as she feigned alarm, and threw her onto the bed, pinning her arms back and opened her legs wide exposing her swelling pink vagina.

Kissing her, Sam rubbed his cock up and down between her swollen sex until she was begging him to enter her. Unable to control himself any longer he slid into her. Looking at the glazed look in her eyes and hearing her muffled cries of pleasure, he slammed uncontrollably into her until climaxing, disappointed he was unable to hold back the explosion of passion that streamed into her wet vagina.

Sitting in the spa, fondly looking at each other, it was Monica who broke the silence. "You big, cruel person you Sam. You nearly drove me mad teasing me like that."

"You drive me crazy all the time you little sex pot. We'll finish the business we started when we get to bed tonight."

"You torment. Now I will be aroused all night waiting for us to get to bed. God I'm shameless, hogging for sex with you all the time," blushed Monica.

"Feelings mutual. In fact, we had better get out of here and dress or if I sit looking at you oozing sex much longer our guests will have to wait while we bonk some more.

"Can you wear the nice little number you had on the first night we had a meal at the resort? It shows your perfect legs and bum."

"So that turned you on did it, you dirty old man. If I had known I would have waited and let you make the first move."

"Not really. When I passed the towels into the three of you, I have to admit I looked straight between your beautiful legs and I was sold then, couldn't sleep that night thinking about you."

"So all my scheming to get you in the sack was a waste of time. You are a cruel, old man Sam Stewart."

"No way," Sam replied. "Frankly I didn't know what to do. Inexperienced in that approach to things really. My two loves both did that for me thank goodness or I would never made a move. I never dreamed you would be interested in me. Same with Carol, don't really understand what you both saw in me."

Monica laughed as she headed down stairs. "Well Sam, hidden talents maybe? I went from a weenie to salami and more sex than I had in forty years of marriage in just a few weeks."

"You are an awful sexpot Monica Stewart and I will make sure, health holding, you get a good, bloody site more. Also it's great exercise, supposed to be good for the heart."

Monica looked radiant, unable to stop smiling, now turning the tables and teasing Sam, wiggling her bottom at him and batting her eyes as they opened a bottle of wine.

Sitting on the porch, soaking up the scenery on this beautiful spring evening, both relished each others company as they sipped wine. Monica felt the calming effect of the golden liquid as it warmed her spirits. Three wines later, in a playful mood, Monica straddled Sam and was kissing him with passion when the mood was broken by a car pulling up in the drive. Springing up off Sam, she began to straighten her hair feeling extremely embarrassed. AJ entered and seeing the situation, immediately defused it with, "The spoils of true love. We both sure are lucky Sam to have two such beautiful women."

Sky grinned at Sam. "It is lovely to see you both happy, love is a wonderful thing. It is great you have given your heart to each other."

Monica greeted and hugged them both. "I am so happy sometimes I think my heart will burst. Take a seat, Sam will get you both a drink."

The friends sat watching as the sun sunk slowly in the west, the last shards of light disappearing as twilight descended over the land; the last rays of sunshine danced over the meandering Derwent River. Monica would remember the evening many years later, the four seemed to get along so well together, something she had never experienced. She noticed the passion her two guests also had for each other as Sky hardly took her eyes off AJ, following his every move and seeming to soak up his presence.

After the meal both men sat in the large chairs by the fire, while Sky and Monica cleaned up. They both chatted and Monica found Sky to be one of the most spiritual and honest people she had ever met. After they had finished, both sat on the lush carpet between the legs of their husbands talking well into the night. The feeling of domestic bliss felt by Monica was like a dream, her past life in the mists of time forgotten and not wanting to be remembered.

At midnight, they all retired to bed, agreeing to have a sleep-in the following morning. Monica was tired, the wine had taken its toll completely. Forgetting Sam's promise, she was surprised but happy when undressed, he pulled her to him and mounted her in wild thrusting, pent up with desire. Monica became alarmed that the guests, although downstairs, might hear the wild lovemaking Sam was giving her. Too tired and with the effects of too many glasses of wine, she felt pinned to the bed as he rode her in one of his lustful acts of pure animal desire.

Monica was too tired to clean herself up as usual after Sam had ejaculated in her. She rolled over and dropped off to sleep; her mouth felt dry and she knew a headache awaited her in the morning.

Both awakened to the sound of Sandra returning the trailer with Sam's vehicle. Monica was too weary to get out of bed, and as she predicted, had a bad headache caused by too much wine. She also smelt the aroma of sex from the night's activities. Sam suggested a nice spa and he would make her a coffee. Reluctantly she agreed. Sam filled the spa and carried her into the ensuite, gently placing her in the foaming water.

"I've been a bad girl Sam. Never drank in my life, just can't hold it but still love the feeling of a few wines, but never again, two is my limit from now on," said Monica, looking very ill.

"Well it does slow you down a bit. First time you never showed enthusiasm for the old sex trick," laughed Sam.

"It was still okay Sam, but I enjoy it better sober, for sure."

Sam returned with a cup of coffee plus some Panadeine Forte to ease the pain. Drying herself, Monica lay back on the bed, sipping the coffee.

As Sam left the room he noticed her sleeping soundly. Sandra had already left when he went looking for her. She would have realised they were still been in bed.

Returning to the kitchen, he started making breakfast, noticing it was eight o'clock. After he ate, he placed the remaining food in the warmer and took Jacky for a stroll.

Sam returned at nine o'clock and found Monica and the two guests eating. Surprisingly, Monica seemed to have recovered quite a bit in a couple of hours.

They waved goodbye as AJ and Sky drove away, needing to return home early as the pump part they had picked up was urgently required back at the farm. Sky gave Monica a card with their phone number for their Tasmanian farm and numbers for Sydney and the Kimberleys, making her promise to keep in touch and visit when possible.

As they drove down the driveway, Monica pulled Sam to her. "Take me back to bed please sexy. I feel like crap and need a couple more hours sleep."

Sam decided they both could do with a couple of hours extra sleep and as he cleaned his teeth Monica noticed his wallet on the bedside table and slid Sky's card inside. Settling in to become entwined in each others arms, both drifted off to sleep, a prerogative of older people; so Sam had often commented. Both were jarringly awakened by the shrill ringing of the phone by the bed. Rubbing her eyes, Monica answered. "Hello, Monica speaking."

"Hi Monica," a cheery voice came back, it was Felicity. "Sorry I've been tied up at work, as usual. I am on the way up for a couple of hours. Are you ok? You sound a bit tired."

As Monica looked at the clock, shocked to find it was nearly three in the afternoon, she said, "Fine now. To be honest I over indulged last night, not used to it, never again."

"Just like Mum," she laughed. "Must be small people unable to handle the grape. After every headache she swore off it."

Monica, feeling better, laughed. "Well, take my word for it, two drinks are all I am having, from this day forwards, it's not worth the pain."

"I'm bringing some chicken for you both, save cooking at such short notice. Have you any salad?" Felicity asked.

"Sounds great. Yes, I have plenty of lettuce and tomatoes. We'll see you soon.".

Both felt refreshed as they dressed and decided to take a short walk. Jacky had been waiting by the bed all day patiently watching for movement.

Monica picked some fresh flowers and suggested walking to the grave site and replacing the flowers. Sam seemed pleased she suggested the idea.

When they returned, Felicity was just driving along the driveway. The evening was relaxing. *Domestic bliss,* Monica thought, *something I only ever dreamed of.*

Felicity left at nine that night for the return journey, anxious to have an early night ready for the coming week. Even Monica was glad to sink into the warmth of her bed, still feeling slightly unwell from her over indulgence.

The following week seemed to fly by as both enjoyed the tranquility of the farm: gardening, walking and enjoying the wonderful company both gave each other.

Many times they agreed that neither felt the urge to travel or leave the peace of the life they now led. After the coming boat trip, Sam suggested selling the Matilda. He would take Monica's grandsons on one last trip however, before the sale.

On the Saturday, they found themselves, along with Felicity, waiting at the Hobart Airport for Victoria and Mary. As they came into the arrival area, Monica and Sam ran towards the three, hugging and laughing in glee at the reunion, even though it had only been three weeks.

"Seems like an eternity," Mary shouted above the crowd. "Did we ever miss you lot? Life at the bloody village will never be the same. It seems like six months since we last saw you."

Collecting the luggage, Felicity helped to load the cases into Sam's car, promising to come up the next day and pick them up after the four had the evening together. Sam suggested they stay full-time with he and Monica, but Victoria refused point blank. "You are practically still on your honeymoon," she said. "We have imposed too much on you both already. We will explore Hobart ourselves and spend time with you on the boat."

"If the weather looks good, we will head off the following weekend," said Sam.

Felicity drove back to work as the four once again chatted madly, laughing about the great times they had since finding Sam, keen to inspect Monica's new home.

Sam drove and listened, unable to get a word in. He gleaned from the conversation that Celia was still unaware that her mother had even left the village. Mary had received only one visitor, her grandson, a police officer, having visited her twice. It seemed other members of her family were far too busy to visit.

Monica's villa had been sold and the managers had moved the new occupant in three days after she left. Victoria had to dispose of Monica's furniture fast and sold the lot to a secondhand dealer. She apologised for not getting much for it but Monica laughed and said she really did not care. Sam had beautiful furniture in his house and money meant little in her new life.

It became evident that both women had become terribly unsettled since the trip and their return to the village; their lives seemed unbearably boring after such a wonderful adventure. Tracy Brown sent Monica her love and a lovely letter thanking her for the money. Mary said that Tracy had cried when they gave her Monica's letter and the cash. Tracy had vowed one day to save up enough to visit Monica and her new love Sam. She had all the news about how they met and details of the wedding; she was thrilled and happy for both.

As Sam drove across the Tasman Bridge, both passengers commented on the beauty of Hobart. Monica pointed to the right where Sam's boat was anchored; Victoria seemed excited about the upcoming trip. However, complete silence descended within the car as they drove up the tree-lined driveway to the homestead. The two women gasped as they stepped out to behold the picture perfect home Monica now shared with Sam.

Mary wept as she hugged Monica. "I am so unbelievably happy for you. What a find our Sam was?"

Always the comic, Victoria piped up. "Tell you what Sam, if Monica ever leaves you, I know two women who will happily share your life."

Monica laughed. "Absolutely no show of that. Come on in and we'll show you to your rooms, and my little bit of heaven."

Excitedly they inspected the house while Sam unloaded luggage into the spare rooms; both had double beds. Sam could hear the giggling and exclamations as they looked over the master bedroom upstairs, sounding like young schoolgirls; he was happy for them. He was terribly fond of the two older ladies.

Over lunch, they caught up on all the news. Jacky was more than happy to see his two friends back in the fold again, with both ladies happy to have him sitting on their knees, lapping up the attention.

Victoria pulled out some wine she had brought with her for the occasion, and suggested drinking a couple of bottles to celebrate. Monica told them about her problems with over drinking and said she believed it had only been so since meeting the two absolutely decadent women.

"I will only have one glass," she laughed. "Off the stuff for life."

"I just cannot believe you are the same Monica I knew all that time back at the village," Victoria quipped.

As they sat around the table, Sam kept piling it with food and wine. Monica had one glass and then drank orange juice, not wanting to suffer like she had previously.

Both the older guests became slightly inebriated, they were so happy to be reunited with their fellow adventurers.

Monica suggested taking them on a tour around the farm the next morning.

Sam smiled, the wine had taken effect on him also. He quietly sat back and basked in the happiness felt as the friends talked and laughed and recalled good times.

He turned in for the night at nine o'clock and was asleep when Monica finally ushered her two friends off to bed. They found it hard to end the magnificent time they were having, reminiscing over the last adventure and the consequences of having met Sam.

The following morning, to Sam's surprise, Victoria and Mary rose early, anxious to check out the farm before Felicity arrived at lunchtime to take them to her house in Sandy Bay.

After breakfast, Monica suggested taking the two quad bikes with the trailers hooked up for the women to sit in as they explored the farm. Mary and Victoria were thoroughly taken with the property after only a short time. They rode over lush pastures watching Herefords grazing with their calves contentedly and they stopped occasionally to watch the river meandering past.

They pulled up on the rise next to the old family cemetery that held the grave of her predecessor. Standing silently, looking at the beautiful headstone that marked Carol's grave, Mary said, "Sam, I can see why you both chose this property and why you were so happy here."

"Yes, we had many happy years here. I'm sure Carol would be happy to see Monica living here and bringing the same happiness back into my life. Both are remarkable women, I feel unworthy of the love of both."

"Told you once Sam, you under estimate yourself, you are the best of the best," said Victoria softly.

Monica suggested going back to the house to have a barbecue before Felicity arrived. She watched the arrival of Sandra with the freshly packed beef. "Must warn you about Sam's best mate Sandra. She seems a bit overboard but she has a heart of gold and loves Sam dearly. She's coming on the Matilda with us this weekend.

Sandra stayed for the barbecue lunch of steak and salads, getting along marvelously with her fellow crew members. Felicity turned up and Sam wondered how he had attracted such a large gathering of the opposite sex, all talking at once.

After lunch Felicity left with Victoria and Mary who were both anxious to check out Hobart. Sandra also headed back to work taking an esky of meat Sam insisted she have.

Plans to meet early on Saturday at the Matilda were finalised unless weather conditions made the departure for Port Davey unwise.

Once again, peace and quiet descended on Sam and Monica. For the next few days they relaxed, completing several tasks they had previously started, both looking forward to the looming departure on the Matilda and for Sam to fulfill his promise to Victoria.

Chapter 21

On the planned Saturday morning, after checking the predicted weather forecast over the next few days, Sam decided to depart on the boat trip south. Felicity promised to drop off her two guests at about eight o'clock and Sandra decided to leave her ute at Sam's and travel with he and Monica to the boat.

Sandra's employers had promised to look after her dogs for a few days while she accompanied Sam and Monica. Sam had decided to leave early to prepare the boat for the arrival of his guests who were excited about the upcoming trip, especially Victoria who kept phoning Sam to check on departure times and asking what to take.

It was still dark on Saturday morning when Monica shot out of bed, wondering what all the noise was downstairs. Jacky was barking madly as noises floated up from the kitchen. Shaken awake, Sam rolled over, rubbing his eyes as Monica whispered, "Sam. Sam someone is downstairs, can you hear them?"

Sam looked at the clock and smiled. "Sandra. I bet she's getting breakfast ready, no doubt trying to hurry us up."

"God Sam, I thought we were about to be killed in our bed," Monica laughed.

Dressing, they carried their bags downstairs to be met by Sandra and Jacky, both filled with enthusiasm at the coming trip.

"Here, have Sam's favorite," grinned Sandra. The smell of

bacon and eggs wafted around the kitchen.

Sandra and Monica chatted incessantly while Sam enjoyed his breakfast. Even Jacky, sensing an adventure, kept scampering to the car waiting for departure.

It was nearly seven thirty when they arrived at the jetty. Sam immediately rowed out to the Matilda while Monica and Sandra unloaded the cases and extra food they had brought along for the trip. Sandra parked and locked the vehicle while Monica and Jack waited for Sam to dock the Matilda.

Meanwhile, Felicity pulled up with Victoria and Mary, both caught up in the excitement, unable to sleep the previous night.

Victoria gave a low whistle as she watched Sam bring the Matilda alongside. She seemed huge compared to the yacht Victoria had spent so many happy years cruising on. Sandra assisted in tying up the Matilda as Sam lowered the gangplank. Jacky was the first on board and he was soon followed eagerly by everyone else. The work area of the boat was huge: all the drums and equipment had been removed, all that remained was a fourteen foot dingy on a swinging winch, ready to be lowered if needed. Sam had fitted a winch for hauling in cray pots and a small fish cleaning table that neatly folded up when not in use.

Unable to contain themselves, the three older women friends explored the bowels of the ship. Victoria was more than surprised with the fittings and renovations that Sam had carried out.

Felicity and Sandra helped Sam transfer all the personal items to the rooms, and packed the perishables in the freezer unit that Sam had started with the engine.

Felicity waved goodbye as the Matilda and smiling crew pulled out and Sam guided her down the Derwent River and under the Tasman Bridge. They all stood in the wheelhouse enjoying the coffee as they cruised down past the Casino, marveling at the picture perfect vision of Hobart as they glided by.

Sam explained he was going to take them down the the D'Entrecasteaux Channel and on the way, he hoped to stop and catch a feed of fresh fish, hopefully flathead.

The morning was clear although still a little chilly, yet not a cloud appeared in the sky as Sam opened up the controls to glide along at ten knots.

The passengers went up onto the decks and apart from a small swell, conditions were perfect. Of his friends who stood on the deck, Sam realised Victoria was enjoying it the most, he could tell she loved the sea.

Slipping in between Tinderbox and Dennes Point, on Bruny Island, Sam watched as Sandra pointed to various landmarks. He thought to himself, *I'm glad she came along, always eager to help and make people happy, a great asset to the trip.*

At midday, as they passed Satellite Island, a stiff breeze sprung up forcing everyone into the wheelhouse. Sam decided to pull into Great Tailor's Bay and stop there for lunch.

As Monica prepared the food, Sam dropped the vessel out of gear while Sandra tried for some fish and yelled to the others to come as they must have been drifting over flathead. Sam baited several hand held lines while Sandra, Victoria and Mary pulled in enough fish for the evening meal.

While Sandra cleaned fish, Sam dropped the anchor to stop the vessel moving, not being necessary now after having caught sufficient fish.

Monica had prepared an excellent meal and all were ravishingly hungry, the sea air and early start making for good appetites. Mary commented on how efficient and fast Sandra filleted the fish.

"Plenty of practice," she laughed. "I always seemed to get that job when we went out on the old girl with Peter and Sam."

Two hours passed before they decided to move on. Sam

wanted to make it a leisurely and enjoyable trip. He and Victoria - who wanted to have a go at operating the Matilda - went to the wheelhouse, while the other three cleaned up. Sam showed Victoria how the old vessel functioned and was surprised at how quickly she picked it up; she seemed to take to the controls effortlessly, a natural because of past experience, fully able to comprehend all the nautical terms used in the operating of a vessel that size.

"You have to watch out for bullies," Sam said, "the only problem with inshore cruising with such a large vessel."

"Got me there Sam," Victoria smiled. "What is a bully?"

"A submerged rock. Smack you and take your guts out."

Sam directed Victoria to go around the southern end of Bruny Island where he showed his passengers seals on the rocks, going as close as he dared. All but Sandra went on deck to have a close look at the magnificent animals. It was not long before all returned rather hurriedly.

"Bloody hell," Mary said, "do they always smell so bad?"

"Yep," laughed Sandra, "that's why I stayed inside, bad enough in here."

Sam decided to pull into Recherché Bay and anchor in the river mouth for the night. Victoria had now taken over the controls, absolutely soaking up the adrenaline that the new position gave her.

"Sam, I cannot get over all the sophisticated equipment you have fitted. Where were you planning to go? Cruise around the world?" Victoria asked.

"No. Old mens' dreams, but thought I may have gone north to Queensland and perhaps the Pacific; old mens' dreams though."

"Tell you what Sam, if you ever do go, old Victoria is in like Flynn. Your boat would be ideal for extended cruising, it is so stable and comfortable. What is the fuel usage like?"

"Very economical really, for the engine size."

He again explained to Victoria, as he had to Monica, all the specifications of the engine and the ship, as Victoria expertly threw the motor out of gear, dropping the anchor in the calm waters off the area Sam had intended staying overnight.

Making sure the anchor was not dragging, Sam went below where Mary had the fish frying. Monica was making fresh salad and Sandra was passing drinks to everyone, including popping a can of 'Bundy and Rum' for herself.

While eating and drinking for the next few hours, all agreed it had been a great day and that it was good to be back together on another great adventure.

Much to the chiding from her friends, Monica only had two wines, informing everyone of her low tolerance to the grape and of the results each time she over indulged, which left her feeling like total crap.

The gentle thud of the engine and slight sway of the ship had a drowsy effect on the little party and at ten o'clock, all decided to head for bed.

Dawn broke with the sun's rays streaking from the west over the land. Refreshed, all hurriedly ate breakfast, anxious to continue the journey to Port Davey. Sam had whetted their appetites with stories of wild scenery and of the family who once lived there mining tin.

Pulling the anchor up again, the old queen of the sea, head held high as the huge propeller left a trail of foam, made her way out to sea and south down the coast. They now noticed the wild country and coastline, devoid of human habitation, as the awesome scenery passed slowly by.

"The sea is beautiful and wild here Sam, it's dark blue and menacing, not like the aqua blue waters of the tropics. I bet it can get rough here," said Victoria.

"Sure can. We'll watch the weather closely. We have a nine hour trip back from Davey under full steam."

"Can we shelter in Port Davey if the weather does cut up

rough?" asked Monica .

"Sure," Sam replied, "the fishermen go in to sit out rough weather; as a matter of fact in real rough weather you can't get out."

"Completely different from the north of Australia: it seems harsher, wilder, untamed," said Mary.

"Yeah, something special about this part of the world. There's nothing between here and the Antarctic but wild ocean."

As the Matilda sliced through a two metre swell, the old ship rolled slightly, slicing across the rolling waves. Mary felt seasick and said, "I reckon Monica knew what she was doing, not indulging in too much wine last night." She moaned and went below while Sandra found her a bucket.

Rounding south east cape, Sam kept hugging the coastline, giving his passengers a good look at the rugged scenery that passed by. Lunchtime saw them passing De Witt Island and Sam told them of the girl who once camped on the island years before, making headlines.

"She must have been lonely," said Victoria.

"Had a few fishermen call from time to time," Sam informed her.

South West Cape passed by and Sam told them that the island on the right was Mutton Bird Island. The entrance is only half an hour away, a now enthused Sam reported.

Mary made it back into the wheelhouse aware that the entrance to their final destination was looming.

Entering the Port Davey area, the roll eased as Sam pointed out landmarks the fishermen had showed him. "On the left is the Sharks Jaw. The Carolyn's on the right."

Passing Break Sea Island it was late afternoon when Sam decided to anchor in Whaler's Cove for their first evening in Port Davey.

Sandra suggested dropping two cray pots before stopping

for the night. Sam readily agreed as he liked freshly cooked crayfish and had obtained two licenses, one for himself and one for Monica, allowing both to catch five each per day.

Baiting and dropping the pots, they anchored the ship; their anchor point was now flat calm, the evening pleasant and thedecision was made to have a barbecue on deck. Placing chairs about and setting up the barbecue, they sat around enjoying a few drinks in one of the most wildest and isolated parts of the planet, while Sam cooked large steaks from the vealer he had sent for slaughter.

Sitting and thoroughly enjoying the magnificent surrounding wilderness, the sensation of isolation was broken by a fishing boat that had also decided to spend the evening at Whaler's Cove.

The two men on board rowed over and all enjoyed a few drinks and general discussion. It seemed the boat was a cray boat and would pull their pots up in the morning, and then return to Hobart. Both had known the old Matilda and Sam gave them a tour to show his handiwork; both were surprised at the transformation, congratulating Sam on a fine job of reinvigorating the old vessel. The fishermen offered three crays for the evening meal and happily accepted an invitation to stay for the meal. Sandra cooked the huge crustaceans and while the fishermen preferred the steaks, the others cleaned up the crayfish, relishing the now expensive treat.

Sitting on the deck, rugged up against the evening chill, the talk continued for several hours. Both the new guests kept everyone enthralled with stories of the area, about rough seas and even tougher men who made a living from the area.

Bidding a fond adieu, their two new friends departed, wishing Sam and his passengers a safe and interesting trip, adding that if they wanted to visit Melaleuca, it was possible to get the Matilda in, and even tie up to the old jetty there built by the King family.

Sam thanked his new found friends and wished them a good haul and safe trip back to Hobart, promising to catch up at a later date.

The following morning, Sam pulled up the cray pots; they held seven crays, only three being of size, but enough, he thought, for a good meal. After a good breakfast, Sam cruised up to Bond Bay and anchoring, he lowered the dingy. After lunch they enjoyed a trip up the Davey River to Davey Gorge.

On the way up, they all agreed that again, Sam had indeed filled his promise to show them something spectacular, enthralled at the scenery and isolation.

"It's so wild and isolated," Mary said," it makes one wonder how long it will remain so. Mankind seems to be destroying the planet at a fast rate."

"Unless they find mineral wealth here, or need it," Sam replied, "it may have a reprieve for a few years yet."

Returning to the ship in the late afternoon, the excitement and adventure since leaving Hobart began to catch up with everyone and Victoria's suggestion for a quick afternoon nap spread with enthusiasm. The ship's rooms were comfortable and the steady thump of the engine had a calming effect.

Later that evening, one by one, they came straggling at intervals into the dining area and no-one felt like cooking a meal. Instead, they all made snacks to suit themselves, before retiring back to their rooms for the night.

At daylight, Sam and Sandra woke the others with the clanking of the anchor being pulled and the ship slowly starting to get underway. Sam had decided the previous evening to leave early to enter Bathurst Harbour and tie up at the jetty at Melaleuca.

Sam told the story of the family who once lived there and how the wife had passed away. The husband had walked to Cox Bight and alerted a fisherman who had returned with him to collect the body.

Before long, passengers with coffee cups in hand came up to the bridge, anxious to experience the trip into Bathurst Harbour. Sam, being unused to the area, watched the instruments intently as he guided the Matilda through the entrance past several islands into the harbour, and turning south, they eventually tied up at Melaleuca.

This was the first time they had walked on land since leaving Hobart and they enjoyed an afternoon walk, including Jacky who was pleased to be on terra firma once again. The afternoon was dead calm, not a breath of wind, as they relished in the exercise of exploring the area, including the old mine works.

"The people you told us about must have been exceptional to live in such isolation in this wilderness," commented Victoria.

"Sure were. They were quite a rare and remarkable family. Some of the children still live in Hobart I believe."

"If I had not actually visited this area Sam, I honestly believe I couldn't have imagined such stark beauty without experiencing it first hand," said Mary.

Back on the boat, Sam decided to return to Whaler's Cove for the night. He and Sandra would set some cray pots to pull the next morning before they set off on the return trip.

The water was like glass and the afternoon reflections of the surrounding country on the mirror-still surface was magical, broken only by the wake left by the Matilda.

Anchoring back in Whaler's Cove, Sam and Sandra set the two pots in the spot where they had found such good luck previously and sat in the dinghy catching a few fresh fish for the evening meal; not a breath of wind stirred.

The three friends sat on the deck, enjoying a quiet drink, reflecting again on the absolute change in their lives since that rash decision to go to Broome on one last adventure. Even Monica forgot her decision to cut back on alcohol and became caught up in the atmosphere as they watched Sam and Sandra pulling in fish. The sun set on the picture perfect vista before them.

Looking intently at Monica, Victoria said, "Monica, Mary and I have something to discuss with you, away from Sam. Now would perhaps be a good time."

Monica looked surprised. "Go ahead but I have nothing to hide from Sam."

"Absolutely not," replied Victoria, "but we just wanted your opinion first. You see, we both already have talked this over with Felicity, it was in fact she who made the offer."

"Come on you two old bloody schemers, just what is going on?" an inquisitive Monica asked.

"Well since our trip, neither Mary nor I can settle at the retirement village, our lives have been changed. We have been so bloody miserable, just sitting in that place of misery, playing cards like rejected animals waiting to die. I can't understand our society shunning the elderly as if we are less than human, categorising us as useless and unfit to make our own decisions; we may be old but our spirit still remains. Well, if you don't object, we'd like to rent Sam's old unit from Felicity and come to Tassy to live," Victoria said tentatively. "We promise not to intrude on you and Sam, just visit occasionally. Being around you two now is like heaven itself, your love for each other and Sam's infectious grip on life makes us feel young again."

Monica looked stunned and exclaimed, "Hell that's great. Sam will love that, he really likes you two. In fact, he blames you for meeting me. I know I might seem possessive of Sam, because he is my one true love, but I love you two also. Remember our pact, sisters in arms forever?"

Mary stood up beaming. "Let's have a toast. To our move to Tasmania and old friendships."

Quickly sitting down again, Mary went quiet, and holding

Monica by the hand said, "I have a confession to make and so does Victoria."

"Come on, what is it now? You two and your plans," chided Monica.

"Well, not plans really this time. Remember when we stayed in Darwin at the little park before going to Sam's house?" asked Mary.

"Yes, very fondly. What a lovely little oasis that was."

"Well, Victoria and I went to go for a wee and walked unintentionally on you and Sam making love."

"Oh hell. We did get a bit carried away," Monica said embarrassingly.

"A bit is an understatement. You bonked each others brains out. We stood paralysed, couldn't move as you pleasured each other, transfixed to the spot, it was unreal."

"I think I do go overboard sometimes and I seem to turn on the animal in Sam, but it is the first time in my life I feel in control of my sexuality," blushed Monica.

"You overboard? Hell we are jealous, go for it you lucky bugger. We are the ones apologising for being voyeuristic and watching you in awe," said Victoria.

"Good grief no I am not ashamed, in fact, I cannot believe that shy man out in the boat is such a wonderful lover and it is all thanks to you two."

Monica then relayed that Sam had told her of looking at her the first day in the car with no clothes on and all roared laughing at that and all the other stories each remembered, exaggerating the details with every drink.

Sam and Sandra returned to three happy fellow adventurers to be told the news. Sam was ecstatic and said it was a very welcome decision.

He lashed down the dinghy ready to depart early, back to Hobart. They would pull the pots up from the deck, once underway in the morning.

Sandra filleted yet more fish and then showered, joining the others and scoffed a few 'Bundy and Cokes', enjoying the company and atmosphere her older friends generated.

Retiring to bed, Monica told Sam of the confession that her two friends had made to her about seeing their lovemaking in Darwin. Sam pulled Monica to him laughing. "Well sexy, I think it's about time we parted the puss and christened the Matilda."

Monica grinned. "The old puss is more than ready to be parted. The thought of us making such a spectacle excites me a bit."

They sank into each others arms, drifting into contented sleep, their lust quenched; sleep and the act accentuated by too many glasses of wine.

Chapter 22

Sam woke early the following morning. A strong wind had come up during the night. Turning on the radio, he was alarmed to hear a low was coming in from the west. The warning had been sent out at midnight for all boats to head for shelter. Waking the others, he told them the latest weather report and it was decided to sit it out in Port Davey as they had plenty of food and water.

Sam decided to head to Bond Bay; he and Sandra had just pulled the pots while Victoria cruised slowly past the buoys. They had just pulled the second pot when Mary and Monica came hurrying down the deck towards him, he could tell both were alarmed.

Sandra emptied the pots, measuring five legal sized crays and then stored the pots below as Sam listened to Monica.

"Sam someone is sending out a may day. It seems as though they have lost engine power or something. Victoria is talking to them now."

Sam hurried to the wheelhouse where Victoria handed him the radio. "They're in big trouble," she said.

Sam listened to the tinny radio voice. "This is Wayne Bond and deckhand Joe Harris on the fishing vessel Lorraine east of Maatsuyker Island. We have lost our engine and are adrift. The seas are picking up and we require help. Over."

"This is Sam Stewart on the Matilda in Port Davey. We are underway and will come to your assistance. Hopefully we can still exit the entrance. Over."

"Thank god Sam, I know the old Matilda. Can you tow us back to Port Davey? Hopefully things will not get too bad. Over."

Sam looked at the worried faces surrounding him. "I know it is a big ask but we have to help with this, I feel we have no other course."

"Not even a question Sam. We are all human and others need our help," said Mary.

Sam opened up the old motor to full-cruising speed as they turned towards the open sea.

Turning to Victoria he said, "You'll have to take control when we get near the Lorraine. I'll put on the safety harness and we'll rig two lifebuoys to some rope that we can use to throw to the vessel. Sandra and I will tie a heavy rope to secure her to us for the trip back here. Sandra will standby if I need help. Mary and Monica will look after Jacky and please stay in the wheelhouse no matter what happens. I'll get life jackets right now for everyone to put on."

Sandra already had two ropes, furiously tying on lifebuoys and anchoring them to the Matilda; she was running now as the waves started to make the deck slippery, crashing over it as they entered the open sea.

Already the clouds descended and the sea looked foreboding as the swell rose to four metres. All clung to the handrail in the wheelhouse as the old queen punched into the fury of a westerly screaming in from the great southern ocean.

Sam looked at his frightened crew. "Sorry for bringing you into this," he shouted.

"Nothing to do with you Sam. If we all go down so be it though it's young Sandra I feel sorry for," Monica shouted back.

Sandra yelled loudly above the roar of the wind. "Privilege to be with such fine people. Don't worry about me."

Victoria clung on to a chair as Sam strapped her in,

shouting, "It is my entire fault, I insisted'.

"That's nonsense, all for one and one for all. If we have to go to Davey Jones's locker, I am proud to go with such wonderful and brave people."

This seemed to resolve the steel in everyone and each bravely looked ahead for sight of the stricken Lorraine. The sea's fury heightened as the radio crackled, "Wayne here Sam, we're drifting towards rocks on Maatsuyker, the sea is rising, god help us I have never seen anything like this, the waves are now up to eight metres."

"I can see the island Wayne, we're still perhaps ten minutes away. Agree about the sea, never seen nothing like this before, although I am not that experienced," Sam replied.

"Thank god Sam, we are close to being driven onto the rocks. Will not last long if that happens. Tell my family I love them if you can't make it in time."

Those on the Matilda could feel the terror in the voice, making their own position seem less dangerous. They felt a sense of helplessness as the Matilda powered through the massive sea with water at times completely covering the wheelhouse and deck. The old vessel, acting as though aware of her responsibilities, rose again into a gigantic wave to plane down the other side.

It was Sandra who yelled out. "I can see them Sam. Geez they're close to those big rocks. Can we make it?"

"I don't think so," yelled Sam. "She is about to be driven onto them."

On the Lorraine, Joe, a hardened veteran who lived in Triabunna, loved his footy and his drinking. He also loved a fight. Single, tough and resilient, he along with his experienced skipper knew the inevitable was about to happen.

"Been a pleasure skipper," Joe said as they pulled on life jackets, both knowing they would not last too long once the wooden vessel smashed onto the looming rocks. Their bodies would be pulverized against the rock face of the island.

As both stood in the wheelhouse waiting for the grinding sound of rocks smashing the vessel, Wayne Bond saw the Matilda. She was doing a huge arc ready to make the dangerous approach to try and pick them up.

"Shit," he yelled. "Surely they aren't foolhardy enough to try and pluck us off here."

A huge backwash gave the Lorraine a reprieve but both knew the next monster coming would deposit them onto the rocks.

Sam looked at his bewildered crew. "No-one comes on deck," he yelled. "No matter what, understand? If I manage to get the lifebuoy to them, pull out Victoria, to a safe distance and throw her out of gear until they are onboard or the propeller will get them if we try to bring them on under power. I'll take her in as close as possible and then throw the buoy to them; both are old hands and will jump into the sea. With god's help we may just pull this off. If all seems impossible, no matter what happens to me, head back out to sea when you can, the navigational device will take you back to Hobart. Keep her head into the waves at all costs," Sam yelled.

Crying in fear for Sam, Monica yelled, "Surely you can't go out in that."

Sam bent down and kissed her with passion. "A man must do what a man must do; we have to try and save these poor souls."

Sam pulled the Matilda in as close as he dared, putting her head directly into the huge sea as a wave drove her dangerously back towards the Lorraine, already on her side and fighting her last battle with the sea.

He opened the door and hunched against the salt spray as the backwash held them from smashing onto the rocks with the Lorraine. He worried about the giant propeller churning slowly. *It must be close to hitting the rocks,* he thought.

Grabbing the lifebuoy, he threw it with all his might as the two fishermen, wide-eyed and with adrenalin pumping realised this was it, and threw themselves into the foaming backwash, both popping up miraculously. Joe grabbed the rope and stroked over to his skipper who latched onto the rope as well.

Unable to see what was going on, Victoria decided to open up the throttle as the next wave came towering in. She looked back in satisfaction as Sam waved her forward. The old Matilda shuddered as she gained full throttle and rose into a massive wave.

Sam turned to see the two men still holding the rope. He noticed the lifebuoy between them with neither man using it to place over himself. Obviously not wanting to disadvantage the other, they stubbornly linked arms and held on like death itself and then the the strain tightened, pulling them away from certain death.

Sam watched and cursed as a giant wall of water smashed him into the railing. Immediately he knew he was in trouble. The impact from the railing and the freezing tide of water broke several ribs; he struggled to keep conscious with the mayhem before like a haze. He felt warm blood ooze down his trouser leg as he slipped into unconsciousness.

Seeing what had happened, Sandra, without hesitation, catapulted down the deck. She knew that in order to get Sam safely inside, she must first get the two frozen men on the line to safety. She grabbed the rope holding the two fishermen and wound it around the cray puller; she hit it into gear, aware that Victoria would throw the Matilda out of gear when the rescued men came close to the deck. In her haste she got her little finger caught in between the rope and winch drum; the pain that shot up her arm was shearing. Yanking her hand free with all her might she saw raw bone. As if acting in a dream, she looked at Sam and stuck to her task, hoping her old friend was going to make it.

Victoria looked back and thought they had gone out to open sea a fair distance but perhaps not quite far enough. She knew the two men on the end of the life rope would be exhausted by now and growing weaker. Throwing the Matilda out of gear she closed her eyes and prayed.

Joe was the first up over the side as a giant wave hit once again. He immediately grabbed his skipper and with one enormous effort, hauled him over the side, both laying against the safety railing on the deck that was covered in freezing and foaming water.

Monica, wild-eyed, thought Sam was dead and in panic opened the door before Mary or Victoria could stop her. A wave hit, washing her down the deck like a rag doll, her small body smashing against the dinghy frame.

Joe, quickly summing up the situation, ran like a man possessed, throwing himself over her as the next wave hit. This one was not so bad as Victoria now had the old Matilda under full throttle again and she effortlessly rose up over the immense wave. Joe picked Monica up as the boat careened down the other side and bent as he hurried to the wheelhouse where Mary had the door open.

Looking behind he saw his skipper and a girl dragging the elderly man who had saved them, along the deck, bent against the freezing wind and salt water.

As they dropped inside the wheelhouse the old Matilda rose defiantly into the next wave of water smashing over it.

Wayne Bond looked at the old lady in control and in utter disbelief could not believe they had just been saved by old pensioners and one young girl.

Summing up the situation he spoke to Victoria. "I'll take over if you like and you can help below with the injured."

Victoria, still wild-eyed and surviving on fear alone, gladly agreed, fighting to stay upright as she made her way below.

What greeted her was alarming. Sandra was wrapping up a finger, red blood oozing everywhere. Joe had stripped flesh from both hands in the supreme effort to save his skipper. Monica lay oblivious to all and Sam was coming to, groaning slightly in pain.

Quickly, Victoria regained control as she felt the old Matilda fighting the furious sea; the roar was deafening and high winds now blew foam in off the thrashing water. Hurriedly, she began to remove the wet clothes from Sam, with Mary's help, cutting them off with scissors.

Trying to move below deck was difficult with the constant pounding and heaving of the boat.

Drying both Monica and Sam carefully, they found dry blankets and covered them for warmth. Monica was coming around and smiled when she saw Sam breathing next to her. Closing her eyes, she quickly drifted into a deep sleep.

Joe changed and sat in a chair bolted to the floor, both hands heavily bandaged, sipping the welcome spirits that Sandra had found.

Going up to the wheelhouse, she passed clothes and whisky to Wayne and he gulped down some of the liquid. Drying himself, he changed, grateful to be out of the freezing clothes he wore.

"I thought we'd had it," he smiled at his savior. "Who the hell are the brave people with you?"

Sandra told him all about Sam.

Wayne asked how the injured were and Sandra was able to report that they were resting quietly, both unaware of the full extent of their injuries.

By now the incident was making headlines all over Australia, the media was in a frenzy; for once, a good news story.

Wayne was swamped with questions from search and rescue who had been unable to send any help because of the wild sea; he told them the story of his rescuers and word broke like a tidal wave, jamming the airways.

Wayne informed Sandra he was heading to Hobart, a distance of seven hours full-steaming away. Police had opened up Constitution Dock and ambulances were on standby to take the injured to hospital.

By this time, Sam and Monica were both awake, looking at each other smiling through the pain, both grateful to have survived the ordeal, even though it was not over. Sam had great faith in the old Matilda, being used to the great Southern Ocean, she was built strong and relished the heavy going.

By mid-afternoon they passed the Iron Pot and then they knew the ordeal would soon be over. Wayne had been told that the dock in Hobart had become a media frenzy with hundreds having turned up, including Sam's daughter Felicity, who he had talked to on the ship's radio, along with his tearful wife and family.

The police launch, along with dozens of vessels, heralded their arrival in the Derwent River, escorting the proud old vessel to Constitution Dock.

Both Sam and Monica had little recollection as they were carried off the Matilda to waiting ambulances. A tearful Felicity hugged her father and Monica as flashlights and TV cameras jostled among a cheering throng, as the survivors relayed the amazing story of their escape from certain death.

Doctors immediately gave the couple pain killing injections and the wounded were ushered into a string of ambulances for the short trip to hospital and treatment.

Victoria and Mary stood proudly before the cameras, telling the amazing story of the rescue, while concerned officials tried to usher them into waiting ambulances for check-ups at the hospital.

All of Australia became caught up in the amazing story of survival as television crews raced to get exclusive coverage from anyone who would cooperate. At the hospital, police refused entry to any media as they raced to get to air what they had collected to feed a waiting nation on the latest news.

Chapter 23

Celia Spielberg sat in her office, exhaling and watching the trail of cigarette smoke rise lazily. She looked out of her door at the receptionist's breasts, nearly fully exposed. *Gossiping on the phone to god knows who*, she thought.

Glancing at her watch it was three in the afternoon. *Time to go*, she thought and scooping up the papers on her desk, a raft of papers she had spent the entire day preparing for her mother to sign, she headed out.

Leaving the office, she glanced at her husband, Ronald Lacey - she much preferred her own name, that of her late father - she caught him glancing at Susan, the secretary. Susan had been given the job even though she was hopeless, by her late father in order for him to screw her when he pleased. Since he had died in Susan's arms, the business had gone backwards at a fast rate. Known for taking on high risk litigation, she had been unable to succeed like her father and now was in debt, needing to access more of her mother's money and assets. Her late father had used her compliant mother to hide assets he did not wish to put at risk.

Over the last few weeks, Celia had become restless. Her marriage to Ronald was only one of convenience; both had separate bedrooms and lives. It had been at her late father's insistence that she had married him; he was purely an asset to the business, ruthless in court and feared by many adversaries. Celia also realised, to cement her position, Susan had been humping him, She often smirked at Celia when she became frustrated at her lack of ability.

The life they both pursued was high-maintenance and required vast amounts of money; something the firm now lacked. Several high profile cases had backfired and clients now refused to pay, causing more cost. Taking them to courts already jammed, the waiting periods becoming frustrating.

This weekend, she planned to visit her mother, who she had not seen for several weeks because of an altercation with the vinegar-titted old bitch she had befriended in the retirement village. Now desperate, she planned to attack head on, and knowing her power to control her mother, would go straight for the throat. *Times are now desperate*, she thought.

Celia realised that without access to her mothers small fortune, her world of high socialising would collapse. Their property portfolio was not performing well, having paid high prices for inner city studios, which had now lost value along with other failures. She knew something had to be done.

Cursing the traffic, she thought of Brendan the gardener, her lover for the past twelve years. Although she had only started the relationship for sex, she cared for him. She also knew he was besotted with her, putting up with her temper and arrogance; his good nature, much like her own mother's, infuriated her sometimes.

Pulling up in the entrance to her house, she smiled, knowing that Brendan Moore with his lovely smile and blond hair would be working away in the garden as happy as a pig in mud. *How come simple people with simple lives always seemed happy?*, she pondered.

Unable to find Brendan, she went to the potting shed where she heard the sound of his singing wafting from the lower part of the garden. Turning, he saw her shadow over the door, and grabbing her, he kissed her passionately. She relaxed, and he lifted her onto the table, parting her legs. She felt him enter her roughly. *God I need that,* she thought, becoming instantly aroused. Kissing, they both became lost in passion for a short time. Celia forgot her dilemma and the problems she had to somehow overcome.

They climaxed and pulling down her skirt as she slipped from the table, she said, "For heaven's sake, wait till the bedroom next time, I think I have got splinters in my arse."

Lighting a cigarette, she chatted to him for a short time, grateful not to be talking legal jargon and money, as all her circle seemed to constantly.

Brendan was simple in conversation. He loved flowers and gardening, he also kept a few animals which he always talked about, rather proudly. Several times, when her husband was interstate, they spent weekends on her late father's yacht. Her mind snapped back to reality as she realised it was still in her mother's name.

Brendan seemed disappointed, like a scolded puppy as she paid him his day's wages, informing him that because it was getting late, he would be unable to come up to the house that day.

Entering the house she opened the flood of bills, some overdue, and putting on the jug for coffee, she turned on the afternoon news.

Stirring the coffee, cigarette in mouth, she suddenly dropped the cup which smashed over the tile floor. Standing with mouth open, she watched her mother being unloaded from a boat in Hobart and she listened with absolute horror as the story unfolded about Mr. and Mrs. Sam Stewart, and a motley crew, including that horrid Victoria, having been involved in a drama of survival and the rescue of two fishermen. For some minutes she sat glued to the screen, shaking in disbelief as the story was told in detail before her. Gaining her composure, she immediately phoned the retirement village.

"Please tell me what my mother is doing on an old rust

bucket with some illiterate fisherman in Hobart please?"

"Mrs. Spielberg sold her villa some time ago and I believe she does live in Tasmania with her new husband, " replied the manager,

Slamming down the phone, Celia, desperate, immediately phoned her husband to find he had left the office. Searching through her phone book, she located his mobile number and immediately dialed.

A puffing Susan answered the phone. "Hello Celia, can I help you?" she purred.

"Certainly," Celia snapped. "Put my fucking husband on the phone and fast you bitch or I will personally come over and fucking kill you."

"What's wrong?" a startled Ronald answered. "How dare you threaten Susan."

"Listen you bloody dipstick," Celia fumed. "I don't give a rat's arse about you, and your little dick humping that slut, but something has happened that needs your undivided attention now or we may all end up in the fucking can."

Ronald sat up in bed, a cold sweat came over him. He realised many things they had done were not exactly kosher and never had he heard his wife speak like that before, she purely ignored him as he did her. Pulling on some clothes, he left, slamming the door, without even answering a demanding Susan.

On the way home, he thought about their situation. He knew that the firm was in financial trouble. Their behavior, thought by many in the profession to be beyond reason, and to some, an embarrassment to the already bad name his profession had.

Leaving the car in the driveway, he ran into the kitchen. Celia was pointing to the TV screen almost speechless.

"My mother, the only person who can save our arses, is married to some bloody old codger in Tasmania for fuck sake," she fumed. Ronald looked in horror as the story was repeated, a lump swelling in his throat, fully aware that without the constant access to the money Celia's mother had in her name, they would not survive the bad period the firm was facing.

"OK," he said, "we somehow have to get her back to Sydney, under our control. I told you to get power of attorney and have her classified unfit to control her finances."

"How the fuck did I ever in my widest dreams, imagine she would be living in bloody Tasmania, the arse of the world, humping some deadbeat old boaty," Celia yelled.

"Well, I suggest you get off your arse, hire an air ambulance, and get her back to Sydney into a private hospital under the care and protection of a security guard, *like tonight*. If anyone checks on what we have been doing to her finances, we are rat shit." Ronald hissed, red faced, feeling his heart racing. For once, he was not in control and very aware of the consequences should an investigation uncover everything.

Both grabbed phones: Ronald booking a room in an exclusive private hospital while Celia hired a twin-prop air ambulance and staff for immediate take-off to Hobart. Packing quickly, she threw last instructions to a rattled Ronald.

"Listen you useless shit, I thought you had some guts. I'll be back hopefully before daylight tomorrow. Hire security guards to watch her room on my return and make sure they understand that no-one, apart from hospital staff, is allowed to enter her room, or fucking else."

Ronald wiped the sweat from his brow as he watched Celia jump in his car.

"Also," she yelled, "spend some quality time cleaning your dick and preparing court documents to lodge so we can get Monica classed as unfit. We'll have to try and get the bloody marriage annulled," she screamed, spinning out the driveway.

Three hours later, she strode into the Royal Hobart

Hospital, an ambulance hired and waiting in the unloading dock, while three attendants she had brought with her, ran alongside with a trolley. At reception, a night nurse stood upright and said, "How may I help you?"

"We are here to pick up Monica Stewart, whatever her name is now, my mother. We are transferring her to Sydney for specialist treatment," ordered Celia.

The nurse appeared alarmed.

"No one told me of this. Perhaps I can call the duty doctor."

"Please do so," snapped an irate Celia. "Make it quick or I will take great pleasure in suing the arse of you and this bloody hospital."

Upset and confused, the nurse stammered. "Sorry it just seemed inappropriate madam, she is in room 114."

Celia, with the flustered nurse running in front, stormed into the room. Monica was sound asleep, heavily sedated, not waking as the attendants lifted her onto the trolley. Loading her into the waiting ambulance, they sped off into the night for the waiting plane and trip back to Sydney.

The nurse returned to her desk, immediately phoning the young doctor on duty and filling him in on what had just occurred.

"Busy," he replied, "must have been a slip up, no-one told me, but that would not be unusual. Don't worry, all seems in order if the ambulance was waiting."

The plane landed in Sydney at five in the morning. Immediately, they transferred Monica to a private hospital; the attending doctor giving her more sedatives under instructions from Celia.

A security firm, previously used by Celia's company, had two of its best men waiting. Celia gave instructions to them and the hospital staff that her mother was in danger and she would personally break them both with lawsuits if any person came within a bull's roar of her.

Celia then left the hospital as day was breaking. Ronald was still busy trying to sort out the best method of attacking the enormous problem they faced.

"What a balls up. Now what is our best plan of attack?" she complained to Ronald.

"We are on shaky ground. Do we know any psychiatrist that will openly lie for money?" he croaked.

"Listen Ronald, anyone can be bought, my father proved that. This one we have to win. Mum knows nobody here and we can manipulate her. All we have to do is push an early hearing and keep any other bastards away from her."

"Still it is the biggest gamble we have ever undertaken," he squeaked.

"Listen Ronald, get some bloody backbone. Call all our partners into the office early, we'll get our heads together and prepare the best case we ever had. If we fail, we're totally fucked," said Celia, looked positively ill. *My life is out of control,* she thought as she raced to the bathroom, retching violently .

Chapter 24

Sam woke with his mind trying to recollect the last twenty four hours; his head ached and he felt sick. Laying there, he felt bandages wrapped tightly around him and his thigh. He recollected the doctor telling him, and a worried Felicity, flanked by Victoria and Mary, that he was indeed lucky only to have sustained a deep gash, two broken ribs and some severe bruising. Monica's injuries comprised of a broken arm and one fractured rib, with several minor lacerations. Both would recover nicely with time, Sam had been informed.

Understanding the stress both had been through and then not being able to see each other, the hospital had arranged for Sam to be placed in room 114 that morning with Monica. A bed was being readied for his removal from intensive care. Initially staff suspected Sam had sustained worse injuries.

Exhausted, Felicity, Mary and Victoria, had left for home about midnight, promising to return early that morning after a night's rest. They were incredibly relieved that things were not as bad as at first believed.

It was Felicity who came rushing into the room first; Victoria and Mary following closely.

"Monica is gone, Dad," Felicity sobbed. "Her daughter signed her out during the night and has taken her to Sydney."

Tears welled in Sam's eyes as he gave a heartbreaking sob.

"Why? Just why would she take my angel away from me Felicity? We were so happy."

Victoria stood steadfast.

"As god is my witness Sam, we will get her back. God knows what our poor Monica signed under the control of that bitch. I just don't understand what power she holds over her."

"Sam, she might have signed control of her life and assets over to Celia; she always seemed under her spell," said Mary.

Felicity sobbing, replied, "What can we do Victoria? We have to get her back again, look at my Dad, he is devastated."

"Sam," Victoria whispered, "can you get the Matilda to Sydney?"

Sam pushed determinedly up to a half-sitting position on his pillows.

"By god Victoria, I can be there in two plus days."

Felicity was alarmed.

"Dad is too ill Victoria, look at him."

"Felicity," Sam said grabbing his daughter by the arm. "Your old dad is dead without Monica anyway, just do as I ask please."

"Well okay. I don't think you can go through two losses dad, what do we do Victoria?"

Victoria looked at the people in the room, her eyes like steel. "Celia is bloody smart and we are legally dumb; attack and surprise is our motto. First, let us get her in our clutches not us in hers. Sam will take the boat to Sydney, and anchor in Rush Cutter's Bay, then we will search without tipping Celia off and somehow plan to kidnap Monica from the place they have her held."

It was as if a light had gone on in the room. All looked determined and prepared for whatever might happen; Monica would be saved. Felicity, deep in thought, said, "Perhaps we should see a lawyer and find out the legal situation?"

Mary spoke up, "Bad idea, that would tip Celia off and it may take months even years to get Monica back. Victoria is right, we will grab our little friend and take her somewhere safe."

Sam was trying to dress with the help of Felicity. "We can go north. Do you know somewhere safe Victoria?" Sam asked.

'No bloody fear Sam, we can hide out in the Pacific for years, that is my playground," Victoria answered.

At that time Sandra came in. She had been kept in hospital overnight and then discharged herself. Felicity explained the situation and Sandra, with a scowl on her face, said, "I am in on the deal Sam. I am coming on the boat too and don't even think of saying no, Sam Stewart, I'm bloody well in."

Everyone, including Sam thought it a brilliant idea, a doctor entered as Sam was leaving. "It is against my wishes that you leave Mr. Stewart, but I can not stop you. Just sign yourself out on the way." he said

"Thanks Doc," Sam replied, "but a man's got to do what a man's got to do."

Felicity drove Sam and Sandra to the dock. The old Matilda stood proud, it was early and no-body was around as Sandra cast off, with Sam sitting in the chair backing the old girl out into the Derwent River

"To the airport," Victoria ordered. "We will wait on standby for the first flight out."

On the way, Felicity phoned work, her boss being quite aware of her father's ordeal, gladly gave her a few days off. No-one dared divulge what was really happening.

Sam opened the old diesel up and the Matilda plowed along at a constant ten knots. Sam knew he had sufficient fuel to get to Sydney; he would refuel there and checking he had his wallet, settled down for a long journey as Sandra made breakfast.

By late afternoon Sam was steaming up the East Coast. The weather had settled and they were making good time. They were relieved to have received reports of good weather forecast for Bass Straight over the next twenty four hours. Sandra took over as Sam went to lay down for awhile. He still felt discomfort and took two painkillers that the hospital had dispensed and insisted he take with him.

At that time, Felicity and the two determined friends of Monica, landed in Sydney. Collecting the baggage they caught a cab to the retirement village.

Immediately, Mary called her favorite grandson Tom, a policeman who was about the same age as Felicity or slightly older, and requested his presence. Alarmed at the voice of his beloved grandmother, Tom went straight to the village. He knocked on Mary's door and as soon as he entered he knew something was wrong, his grandmother appeared distraught.

Felicity told Tom the full story, trying to remember every detail. After thinking for some time he finally said, "I really think this is a legal matter girls. Your plan to grab Monica may compound the situation. I wonder if Celia has legal rights to manage her mother and affairs. That is a serious step any judge would have been cautious about."

Mary answered in tears. "Well Tom, Celia is smart. If you will not help, then please don't tell anyone about it, and just go and leave us in peace," she sobbed.

"Steady Gran," Tom replied. "Let's make a plan then, to hell with it, I need some excitement in my life."

Felicity laughed nervously. "I feel like Bonny and Clyde," she said.

"I'll take Felicity and get some hospital gear from a party shop. We'll need a van also to take all of us," said Tom.

"So what is the plan?" asked Felicity.

"Same as Celia's, you are Doctor Felicity and we need a nurse to accompany you and push the wheelchair as well."

At that moment a knock sounded on the door, causing everyone to jump. Looking out the curtain, Mary relaxed. "Here is our nurse," she said. "Tracy Brown."

Opening the door, Victoria explained to Tracy the task ahead, which she jumped at.

"Heard you came back," she said. "Glad to hear you are going to leave this shit hole too, it would be my honor to help Monica."

Victoria grabbed Tracy. "You are leaving too, Tracy," she said.

"How can I do that?" Tracy sighed.

"Because Victoria is paying off your house in the morning. I have no one and what is left over will more than do me for the rest of my life," she said. " You helped us and was kind to us all during our incarceration here. Only one stipulation you: must leave here and then bring your family to visit us occasionally."

"Where will you be?" Tracy asked.

"This nightmare will end someday," Mary replied, "and we can all live in peace. I'll let you know."

Felicity and Tom left, promising to collect the items required the following day. Victoria made Tracy promise to pick them up in the morning to collect some money for the trip ahead, and to pay off her home as Victoria had promised. Tom assured that he would discreetly find out what hospital Monica was being held in.

Tracy rushed home, informing her husband of Victoria's generosity. He was gob smacked; he knew the close relationship his wife had with the three women but never in his wildest dreams did it occur this would happen. The effect was immediate. Now Tracy would stay at home and raise the kids and their lives would change forever.

Tracy never told anyone about the plan and of her one last favor to her friends. Lying in bed that night, she rehearsed for her best performance ever.

The following day Tracy and her husband became the proud owners of a debt free home. It was a great weight that had been lifted from their shoulders. Driving to the village, Tracy resigned and when she returned home, she wrote a long letter to the department, dealing with the aged and telling them of the appalling food fed to residents.

Victoria and Mary placed their villas on the market and arranged for Mary's family to come and take any furniture they wanted the following day; the rest they left to charity.

Mary's family seemed happy that she was going to live in Hobart, aware she was having a good time with Victoria and Monica. It was easy to see the misery that residents suffered in the supposed high-class village.

The following evening, Felicity received a call from her father. She and Tom drove to Rush Cutter's Bay and picked Sam up while Sandra stayed behind with the boat to refuel.

Like a well oiled machine, that evening after dark, Tom dropped Felicity and Tracy off at the front of the hospital. Felicity looked professional in a dark suit with stethoscope around her neck and wearing a nameplate with 'Dr Rita Dowling' emblazoned on it. Tracy had on a sisters' uniform and confidently pushed the wheelchair in front of her as they strode into the hospital.

Tom watched nervously, along with Sam. The only sound in the van was the heavy breathing of the occupants.

Felicity and Tracy strode to reception asking where Celia Spielberg's mother was. Without a glance, the receptionist gave them the room number, too engrossed in a phone conversation to give them more than a cursory glance.

Smiling to each other in confidence, they approached the security guard at the room door. "We are here to take the patient for an x-ray," Felicity spoke firmly and confidently.

The guard looked at the pair and said, "No problems doctor, I just have to get you to sign this form."

"*Really.*" Felicity scowled. "And who the hell now tells medical staff what to do?"

Tracy looked worried. *For hell's sake*, she thought, *don't go too far please Felicity*. The guard smiled slightly taken aback by the comment. "Sorry doctor. The daughter has given us strict instructions," he replied.

Grabbing the board, Felicity scribbled on the form thrusting it back at the embarrassed security guard. "Well the least you can do," she snarled, "is help us with the patient."

Entering the room, they were shocked at the ashen-faced Monica lying in a bed quietly crying. Confidently, Felicity winked at her as her facial expression changed.

"Doctor Dowling and Sister Jones to take you for x-ray Mrs. Stewart. We have the Matilda room ready for you."

Monica did not speak as the compliant security guard helped load her into the wheelchair. As they left the room with the security guard pushing Monica in the chair, Felicity said, "Thank you for your help, we can manage now."

"Sorry doctor, my instructions are not to let her out of my sight."

"Well I can tell you, you pervert, no-one is watching while my patient strips bare. I will call the police, this is madness," Felicity fumed back.

"Oh geez, sorry doctor, of course. I didn't understand," the shocked guard replied. "I'll wait here for you to return."

Tracy, fighting off laughter, strode as fast as she dared, pushing the wheelchair down the passage and through the front doors; the receptionist did not even look up.

As the night air hit Monica she started to cry again. Tom saw them come out and drove right up. Mary slid the door open as Monica looked up and saw Sam sitting there. With new found strength she hopped into the van into the arms of her love. As they held each other, tears streamed down their faces causing everyone to be overcome with emotion. Tracy pushed the wheelchair into some rose bushes and she and Felicity jumped in as Tom drove off into the night.

Expertly, Tom sped through town, taking side streets. He had planned the trip to avoid as much traffic as possible and arriving at the Matilda, Sandra told Sam that she was refueled and ready to go.

Sam, worried that Sandra really was sacrificing way too much to help out, insisted she stay behind and return to her job. All on board gave Felicity, Tom and Sandra fond farewells as the determined group of oldies cast off for a journey into the unknown.

Standing with arms around each other, confused and tearful, the three left standing on the pier watched as the old Matilda proudly steamed out of sight with the people they loved most, united once again as they disappeared into the darkness.

Standing on the jetty it was Tom, who spoke first. "In the morning I'm going to confess," he said. "Then I'm going to find out what the hell is going on, surely this madness must end."

Sandra sobbed, "Me and Felicity will come with you. I can't go on wondering what will happen to those old people, what ever will they do?"

"What will become of them? Something is terribly wrong with the law if this sort of thing can happen," sniffed Felicity.

Tom replied, "I am determined, now that I've done as they wished, to find out just what the legal position is. If I lose my job then so be it. Both of you can come back to my place tonight and tomorrow we will face the music."

The three, united in grief and worry about the four older members of their families, drove off from the jetty, determined that the following day they would do their utmost to clear matters up.

Back at the private hospital, the security guard looked nervously at his watch, it had now been over two hours. Picking up the clip board, he looked at the signature the doctor had scribbled. A look of total defeat came over his face as he groaned. On the pad was written 'Get fucked Celia'.

Phoning his employer he explained what had happened and knowing that he would be immediately sacked, he decided not to wait around for the arrival of the boss and Celia. Picking up his bag containing his thermos, he left his hat and firm ID card, walked to his car and drove off into the night grinning now. *Bloody convincing pair,* he thought.

Celia sat drinking, still thinking of the court application three days ahead, sure they had enough to convince the judge to pass a ruling in her favor. *The old bastard hasn't even turned up to try and rescue Mum,* she thought, *this will be a walkover.*

The doorbell rang and being on her own she requested who was there. It was the manager of the firm she had hired to protect her mother. He stood nervously as he passed her the signature explaining what had happened.

"I will see you in court you useless bastards and don't expect payment. Now piss off. Just the look of you makes me fucken sick," she fumed, shaking with rage.

She sank to the floor, totally defeated, knowing her case was now weakened if her mother turned up to court acting normal and worse, with council to represent her. She did not even consider phoning her husband. *The prick can go down with me,* she fumed.

Chapter 25

Tom had not slept a wink and at two in the morning he got up to make a hot drink, worried about his grandmother and her cohorts, by now well out of Sydney Harbour and heading north. *Confused, brave old people* he thought. Loyalty and an undying friendship had driven them to help each other regardless of the cost. Even though he would face the consequences of his decision to assist in the kidnapping of Monica on that day, he lay awake and actually felt proud of his small contribution. Sipping his drink, he was happy to see Felicity enter the small kitchen.

"So I am not the only one who can't sleep," she said.

Tom yawned. "That's for sure. I just can't relax, I am so worried about those brave oldies. I'm really proud of my grandmother and her loyalty to her friends. You know Felicity, my career may end today, but I would not change a minute nor one thing I have done that I shouldn't have."

Felicity smiled. "Same here Tom. You remind me of my Dad; a rare person in today's greedy, self-interested society. All you would have to say is 'A man's gotta do what a man's gotta do' and you would be him."

"How is Sandra sleeping?" asked Tom.

"Poor girl is exhausted. She's a pretty special person you know. Came all that way with my father out of the love and respect she has for him. What is more, he had a job to stop her from going on with them; Dad always said if he was fighting a war, Sandra would be his number one pick as a comrade in arms; defiant, loyal and a fighter. You know she was an orphan? She regards Dad and Mum as her family and I am proud to call her a sister."

"Thanks, from the bottom of my heart Tom. What you did was above family loyalty. My other worry is Jacky, Dad's faithful little dog; he is still at home and my neighbor is feeding him but he still misses Dad terribly; they really are inseparable."

"Sure has been an awful business. This Celia must be some bitch." said Tom.

"You know Tom, I wonder what motivates her: power, greed or what? I hope to meet her one day and find out."

Both sat until daylight talking, finding comfort in each others company. Many times during the long morning hours Felicity looked at Tom and thought, *I wonder why some lucky girl hasn't latched onto him.* For the first time, she also had time to reflect on the happenings of the last three days; events had happened that fast that she had only just begun to think of what had transpired.

"Tom, if Celia, for instance, hasn't had her mother certified or whatever as unfit to control her own affairs, this may have been a complete waste of time."

"I had just begun to think along those lines myself but the oldies seemed so upset and determined, even fearful, of Celia and her power. I got caught up emotionally in the whole thing and went along for the ride."

"Do you know where we can find out?"

"Of course. If she was court appointed there would be records. Good god Felicity if there isn't we have to let them know."

"What time does the records section open?" asked Felicity who now felt hopeful.

"In one hour," Said Tome as he looked at the clock.

"We had better wake Sandra, she would never forgive us if we

191

left her out of this."

When the records office opened the three burst into the reception area anxious to access information that may or may not be good news.

Felicity filled out the necessary forms and paid the fee. A short time later the clerk came back carrying several pieces of paper.

"I have good news and bad," he informed them. "No order of any type exists at this time, however, a hearing is scheduled in three days time to apply for power of attorney over the affairs of Monica Stewart and to have her declared unfit to manage her own affairs. The applicant is her daughter Celia Spielberg."

"Do you mean to tell me that Celia had no power to remove her mother from Hobart and take her to Sydney?" blurted out Sandra.

"Absolutely not. Unless her mother gave permission it would be tantamount to kidnapping," the clerk replied.

The mood of the three changed immediately as they looked at each other stunned.

"One last question," Tom looked at the clerk. "Do you suggest Monica attend the hearing with a legal team and defend this application due on Friday?"

"Certainly," said the clerk, "although courts are reluctant to issue such orders it would depend on the case in support of the application."

Thanking the helpful man they left the building and congratulated each other, laughing with relief. Felicity looked at the other two and said, "Better not celebrate yet. We have to get them back and I doubt if the radio is on to call them; they may be suspicious of any calls. Don't forget, we are dealing with four paranoid old people prepared to defend their friends to the last."

Tom grinned. "Might cost us a bit but my mate runs the

helicopter rescue service. I can get them to lower me onto the deck to deliver the good news. Hopefully, old Victoria will have headed straight out to sea to evade detection, smart old bugger, but it may narrow the search area down."

By the time the trio arrived at the helix pad the pilot had the chopper fuelled and the blades rotating as Tom ran to jump in the machine. It powered off with both girls waving.

The pilot calculated, using Tom's information, that in the time they had been underway, the Matilda would only be eighty nautical miles out to sea and with a little luck they would locate the vessel by its black paintwork and name emblazoned on the hull.

Victoria was sipping coffee chatting to Mary. Both felt tired now with the adrenalin gone and realising the immense task ahead. Sam had taken the first three hour shift while the rest slept. He and Monica now slept soundly, having been so exhausted that neither had been able to sleep much for three days and the effect had taken its toll. Both still swathed in bandages, they were deliriously happy to be reunited.

As Mary checked on them a tear came to her eye. They lay with hands locked, a look of contentment on both faces as the faithful Matilda fled to safety.

Victoria felt old and worn out but her determination and loyalty to her friends made the task one she had no regret undertaking. Her thoughts turned to what may have been just a few days earlier; celebrating their move to Hobart to spend the last of their days amongst friends.

Arriving in the wheelhouse, Sam broke her train of thought. Mary had gone to lay down, exhausted, *but as always*, Victoria thought, *a loyal, trustworthy and faithful friend.*

Victoria and Sam chatted for some time, their conversation broken by a helicopter coming in fast from their rear. Both knew they had been caught and a lump formed in Sam's throat.

They watched in absolute surrender as the aircraft circled

over the bow, hovering above the deck. By now Monica, extremely distressed and with Mary holding her hand, came up from below. They watched as a man lowered to the deck from the helicopter and then unclipping his safety harness, waved the machine off and ran ducking for cover to the wheelhouse grinning from ear to ear.

"It's Tom," Mary cried out. "What has he done to us?"

Tom burst into the wheelhouse, grabbed the wheel and spun the old vessel back towards Sydney. "Celia had no order of any type," he yelled in delight. "She actually kidnapped Monica, however, she has an application before the courts for Friday to have Monica declared unfit to manage her own affairs and we are going to beat that hands down."

They all stood there, absolutely stunned, emotion and the strain of the last week finally catching up with them. Crying and clinging to each other, they sobbed in relief that the ordeal was almost over. "Go below," Tom ordered them. "I'll wake you up as we enter through the heads. Sandra and Felicity are waiting for us."

Tom switched on the radio and relayed the good news to Felicity and Sandra who were elated to hear from him.

Since the disappearance from Hobart of the rescue heroes, it had again turned into media frenzy. As to what had happened to the players in the drama and the Matilda, it seemed as though they all had disappeared off the face of the planet. When Tom had been relaying his success in finding the Matilda at least two reporters with listening devices had picked up the conversation.

Sandra and Felicity stood on the jetty in Rush Cutter's Bay, knowing the Matilda would be several hours. They felt unable to do anything else but just wait there for the return of the people they loved most in the world.

Sitting on the jetty it was just past midday when both looked in surprise as several car loads of reporters and television crews pulled up, all trying to beat each other to the unfolding story as they began to piece things together. Looking at each other in surprise it was Felicity who spoke first."Listen Sandra, I feel it's better if we just tell the truth. Lies turn into more lies and it may help our case on Friday if the truth is out now."

As the throng of media surrounded them Felicity held up her hands. "Okay, set up whatever and I will tell the full story," she said. "The truth and the whole truth, warts and all."

Surrounded by the mob of journalists Felicity explained every detail since the rescue, exactly as it happened. An absolute hush came over the milling crowd as they listened to the amazing story of love and loyalty. Felicity told every fact so well, including the upcoming court case on Friday, that no question came after.

Just as the reporters had arrived, all left in a flurry to make their reports. Felicity knew that when the Matilda eventually arrived the place would be wall to wall with the media.

Celia sat in the kitchen smoking and drinking coffee although not watching the TV as it droned on with some soapy show. Her husband still had confidence in the success of the upcoming court application and laughed at her depression. 'Just shows she *is* bloody mad," he told her.

Her attention soon became focused on the screen as the program was interrupted to bring a news flash. They described the story as a true Romeo and Juliet saga. The reporter told of the kidnapping of Monica by her daughter Celia Spielberg and her subsequent snatching under the nose of security. The most amazing part was that Monica's husband, a decorated Vietnam war veteran, had sailed from Hobart in the well-known Matilda, under great pain to rescue his beloved.

If the rescue had created a media interest, the latest unfolding story hit the airwaves like a tidal wave and the press went into overdrive on every angle of the story.

Sam Stewart's mate and fellow veteran, Anthony Wilson, travelled straight from Tasmania to help his friend in any way possible and at the airport gave an interview.

"What sort of man is Sam Stewart?" asked the reporter.

"One of nature's gentlemen, the best of the best," AJ replied.

"Is it true that his new wife, and the love of his life, is unable to control her own affairs?" came the frantic question from the throng of reporters.

"Monica Stewart is one of the nicest and most amazing women I have ever had the privilege to meet," he replied. "I attended their wedding in Darwin and visited them at their home. I find the whole thing abhorrent."

"Are you going to give evidence on her behalf in the upcoming hearing?" shouted a voice from the throng.

"It is my greatest wish to do so. I have already spoken to my daughter and she is going to represent my friends in this tragedy of justice and abuse of the legal system," AJ replied.

Another question came though AJ was unable to hear properly and turning to the crowd, he said, "As this whole matter will be before the courts on Friday I will leave it at that. But suffice to say, all their friends look forward to ending this madness so that two decent people can get on with their lives."

Celia held her head between her hands knowing the game was over and knew she would have to do what she should have done a long time ago; face the consequences of a life out of control.

Chapter 26

Tom let the exhausted oldies rest until he picked up the entrance to Sydney Harbour. Going below he woke his charges up and was happy to see all seemed relieved and a little sheepish about the chain of events; angry at themselves for allowing Celia to panic them into such drastic measures.

As they made their way through the heads a police launch came powering out to meet them. Overhead several helicopters appeared with TV crews filming the approaching vessel. Tom saw an armada in the distance of various vessels streaming out towards them. As the police launch pulled aside the Matilda, it was indicated that a member was going to board. Slowing, Tom watched as an inspector leapt onto the rail of the Matilda and Sam helped him on board.

Stepping into the wheelhouse he introduced himself to the wide-eyed occupants. "I have to inform you that we have decided to take you to a secret location for your own safety. At least two thousand people are waiting for you on shore. We have already taken your family members Felicity and Sandra to safety. Behind us is at least two hundred vessels of all types coming to escort you in," the Inspector informed them. "We intend transferring you to the police launch and escorting you to a safe location at Rush Cutter's Bay. We have a huge traffic problem with hundreds that are jamming the roads. Tom and one of our officers will take the Matilda in and anchor her, the rest will come with me now please."

"Why? What have we done now?" cried Mary.

"Nothing," the officer replied. "You've become celebrities after the rescue and now public support for you is absolutely mind blowing. We have companies donating everything including caravans. Law firms offering free service, the list goes on. This is unheard of in my career. Even celebritys' agents are waiting to sign you up. It's unbelievable," the officer said.

Both boats tied up and transfers were made. The Matilda steamed on while the police launch with the passengers on board slipped away as another police boat came alongside and started to escort the old queen. The police launch glided into a quiet bay on the north shore and Sam was surprised to see Felicity, Sandra, AJ and Sky waiting beside two vans with tinted windows.

Stepping ashore, confused and somewhat alarmed, they were hurriedly ushered into both vehicles which then sped off.

It was only then that AJ spoke to Sam. "We're taking you to our house. We have a spare gardener's cottage so you can all camp there until the court case is over. I have a doctor waiting to give you all a check up. Bloody amazing Sam, you are truly an amazing person," he said shaking his head and smiling.

"Well," drawled Sam, "a man's gotta do what a man's gotta do."

"Sam, you came all that way across Bass Strait in severe pain to rescue me. What can I say? You *are* one amazing person," said Monica.

The gates to Kimberley Cottage were opened as the vans sped up and a security guard closed them once both vehicles has passed through. As they stepped out from the vehicles Sam recognised AJ's daughter Mary.

"Hi Sam," she greeted him. "I am only too glad to offer my services; as a matter of fact I have contacted Celia's firm and informed them I will be acting on Monica's behalf and requested full disclosure of the case they intend to present."

Both Sam and Monica were overwhelmed, grateful to their old friends for springing to their defense so quickly.

"I don't practice full time now Sam," said Mary, "but still act in a consultancy capacity. But you have generated so much publicity that two of the top silks in our company have offered their services also."

"What chance do you think we have?" asked Monica.

"I am absolutely positive they will withdraw the application," Mary smiled. "I have also requested they pay costs and pass over all your financial details, kept by them, before we will accept such a move."

"I cannot thank you enough Mary. Just tell me what I owe and I will fix you up. I am not very conversant with the law, just a simple person really, so we are extremely grateful for your help," said Sam.

"Sam," Mary smiled, "it really is my pleasure to help my Dad's old friend. As for money it is also our firm's pleasure to do it for no fee. You would insult us if you refuse to let us represent you at no charge."

Felicity came up and hugged both Monica and her Dad. "I have arranged for Joe and Wayne to sail the Matilda home after the case. Both men by the way, are not happy with you and Sandra for coming up on your own and said they would have jumped at the chance to escort you. Joe kept muttering threats about anyone who might offend you both."

Sandra came up and gave both a tearful hug. "Bloody glad to see you all safe, crazy old buggers," she sniffled.

"By the way," Mary informed them, "I have accepted a freely offered ride home in a corporate jet for you when you leave for home."

Victoria, who for once had just been listening, piped in. "Tell you what Sam, next time three naked women hail you, I can see you fleeing. What an astonishing chain of events that meeting triggered."

Everybody laughed and looked at each other, relived, happy and exhausted. Their hosts placed them in the main house and cottage. Wonderful aromas of food cooking wafted throughout and celebratory drinks were passed around as medical staff changed bandages and checked the tired adventurers.

Headlines in the evening paper read 'Pensioner Passion'. 'One of the most remarkable stories reported in my career' the journalist had written, 'is the story of this rescue. Monica Stewart's virtual abduction and the amazing journey undertaken by her husband Sam and friend Sandra, both in pain from injuries, who crossed Bass Strait to rescue her. How two old women helped showing incredible loyalty and friendship', the report read. In detail they described the ruse played by Felicity and Tracy, reporting a true story, in itself, of bravado and cunning. The report continued. 'Thousands intend to attend the court case in support of the couple with the coming application being described as an absolute abuse of the justice system.'

All watched as the news was saturated with the story, showing images of the old Matilda steaming through the heads and reporting how the police had spirited the heroes away to a safe house. Traffic jams filmed by the helicopter crews aired on all TV channels; even politicians entered the fray commenting that the application was an absolute abuse of an already clogged legal system.

It was Sky who eventually suggested everyone retire to bed early and gets a good night's rest. Everyone was prohibited from getting up early the next morning to ensure they would have a relaxing time. Sky said, with relief, that she hoped the next day would be the end of an unfortunate and harrowing experience for everybody.

Mary was going to the office early, hopeful their opponents would see the inevitable and withdraw the application.

Chapter 27

Celia sat alone in her vast home watching events unfold before her on the television. All day she had felt seriously ill, retching intermittently.

For the first time in her life she felt completely alone. Her many friends had completely deserted her, the society she moved in forever gone; not one of her high society acquaintances had called or even phoned. She knew she was now a leper, forever shunned.

Deciding to sit on the verandah for fresh air to try and think up some sensible solution, she was more than surprised to see Brendan, her lover, walking up the driveway. Celia went out to meet him.

"Come to gloat at an idiot, have you?" asked Celia.

"No. I have always loved you but you wouldn't know that Celia. Whatever you've done I am here to offer any support I can."

"Brendan really, are you serious? No one has ever professed their love for me. I thought you only wanted a good ride like everyone else used to."

"Do you always have to put on the big front? Your father isn't here anymore so you don't have to impress anyone. Behind all your bullshit is a nice person trying to get out. I always knew you'd hit a brick wall one day and that I'd be there to pick you up."

"Really?" Celia replied hurt. "So my gardener loves me and will save me from myself?"

Brendan stood defiantly before her. "If you had ever taken

the time to listen to me Celia... I studied at night school years ago and yours is the only garden I have worked in for ten years, just so I could see you. I manage a large hardware store and have done for five years, worked my way up. I take an afternoon off every week to come over here. If you needed me I gave up my weekends."

"You silly shit, why would you do that for god's sakes? Brendan I've treated you like muck," sobbed Celia.

"Love is a terrible master Celia but just like your mother's husband, men do strange things for those they love," Brendan replied taking her by the hand.

"I'll no doubt have any money or even a house left, my mother owns this place and my husband will claim everything else. I am too tired and sick of the whole thing to fight anymore," she sobbed.

"I have a nice, comfortable home on two hectares in the Blue Mountains ready for you, and if you like, we can sell and move anywhere to start afresh."

"Are you serious? You would do that for me?"

Brendan smiled pulling her to her feet. "Yes, but you must face your responsibilities and withdraw the application against your mother. I always liked her, she is a very nice lady. Oh, and also, no more smoking after this is all over."

As they turned to go into the house, Ronald and two of the partners from the firm Celia's father had started, the one she now ran, came up the drive. Ronald spoke before Celia had a chance to say anything. "We have come to make you an offer and it is one you cannot refuse Celia. The other partners and I have withdrawn the application and made a press statement stating it was a terrible mistake and that you only had what you believed were your mother's best interests.

However, now that you realise your folly, I am leaving you as of tonight and will offer you the following, which I suggest you accept and sign the papers we have prepared."

"So you are offering me, Ronald, the main shareholder and partner in my late father's firm?" snapped Celia.

One of the other partners broke in. "Celia, you have no company. Having you present there, after the events of the last few days, may scare clients enough to abandon us like a sinking ship. Think Celia, we will, as agreed, pay costs on the application to the other party and pay you the sum of two hundred thousand dollars for the interest you have in the firm. You will make a statement that due to health problems, you have resigned and have no further interest in the firm. Please Celia, otherwise we will all go under. God knows it will be hard work to claw back some respect as it is."

"Listen, it was my money that kept us afloat over the last few months, the firm is worth more than that. If it were not for my father none of you would be in the position you are today."

"That may be the case Celia, but accept this offer now, sign the papers and pass all your mother's financial affairs over or we will not stand with you on this whole stinking affair," the partner said.

"Really. If I go, you go with me. It was at your insistence Ronald that I withdrew over two hundred thousand from Mum's personal account," fumed Celia.

"Oh really Celia? Did I ever visit your mother once shoving papers in front of her to sign and not informing her what she was signing?" Ronald snapped back.

Brendan stepped forward. "Just sign the papers. Let this thing end now, why prolong the inevitable? Please Celia, they have obviously ganged up on you, just sign now."

Celia looked at Brendan, his eyes were watering, no doubt feeling sorry for her and she knew he was right.

"Well, I suppose Brendan is right," she replied with a sigh. "I have all Mums' papers in a folder inside. Please get them for me Brendan? They are on the kitchen table in her house which Ronald used rent free for the past two years."

"Can we please go inside and sign these documents? We have a bank cheque ready for you after the signing," said Ronald.

"Like fucking hell," Celia snapped. "Twenty two hard years and I get two hundred thousand dollars. Pass the bloody papers and I will sign right here. And as far as I am concerned Ronald, I want a divorce as soon as possible so I may fuck my lover Brendan as a free woman."

"So now the truth comes out. Yes Celia, my greatest wish is to see the last of you."

"Shocked are you Ronald? It was okay for you to dip your feeble excuse for a dick into Susan and any other woman desperate enough to want a tickle with a weenie," replied Celia as she read the documents.

Brendan reappeared carrying a portfolio of papers and passed them to Ronald.

"So we are having it off with the gardener; how low can one go?" smirked Ronald.

"Really Ronald, he is more a man than you will ever be, and as for gardener, he only came here to visit me. Brendan is manager of the biggest hardware chain in Australia, dickhead."

One partner with Ronald smiled, unable to control himself and said, "Okay, let's finish this unfortunate business. I am sure we all wish to get on with our lives. Celia I am sorry things turned out the way they have but you are not stupid, surely you must see this is the only course open to us."

Celia sighed. "Yes. Unfortunately I have to face reality, as will Ronald. Our high society lifestyle was unsustainable. Good evening gentlemen. Oh, just one last thing Ronald. Please inform big-titted Susan to vacate my mother's townhouse, the one you and she share. No doubt she will find another rental at fifty bucks per week."

Turning, Celia and Brendan walked hand in hand defiantly,

into the house.

"Brendan if I ever needed you it is tonight, please stay with me. I'll pack my clothes in the morning if you haven't come to your senses and changed your mind and tomorrow I will move in with you. It is all a huge relief somehow. I was sick of the whole charade anyway. You know Brendan, I think I always tried to emulate my late father; he was a dead shit too really but I just got carried away with the power and lifestyle, it was like a drug."

"I just ask one other favor Celia. Get on your hands and knees and beg your poor mother's forgiveness please. I'll be a good husband to you but I must beg you to right a terrible wrong."

Celia looked at Brendan and tears welled up and began to run down her face. "Is that a proposal Brendan? After the divorce comes through, do you really mean that? I am eight years older than you and I think I am pregnant. In all the turmoil I forgot the pill several times and I am sure I am carrying your baby."

Brendan clapped his hands. "Of course I want to marry you when the divorce is finalised and for you to have my, sorry, our baby. This is the best thing that's ever happened in my life."

"I will make it up with Mum, somehow, I promise. I am just glad it is all over. Are you sure you want a pregnant, broke, forty four year old for a wife; who smokes, is nasty, bad tempered and a bitch to boot?"

"Do you really think I have hung around for twelve years of my life waiting to let you go now? Deep down I'm sure all you have done was to impress your late father. I can tell you now, you were never ruthless enough, even though you tried and tried bloody hard, you still had too much of the niceness in you, same as your mother has. I often think that's why you treated her so badly, you tried to distance yourself from her in order to impress your father."

Celia looked at Brendan. "And to think I had you all those years for the asking, a kind, gentle person who loved me like you do. Unfortunately you are right, why didn't you pull me up earlier."

Brendan laughed. "Would you have listened? Of course not. I often spoke to your Mum about you; I think she knew I loved you, or suspected. Poor Monica actually feared you, years of intimidation and stand over tactics by your late father broke her spirit, she was a lovely person, my heart really did bleed for her."

Celia again broke into tears. "What an absolute bitch I have been Brendan. I classed Mum as weak but I think all she did was try and please us all. My brother saw the pain she suffered and took off. I am sure he begged Mum to leave and live with him, but she steadfastly stood by her marriage vows. God forgive me for what I have done."

"Tomorrow after we pack, let us personally visit your Mum and I know she will forgive you, she is a kind and forgiving person. You have the rest of your life to make it up to her."

For the first time in her life Celia went to bed in the arms of someone she knew truly loved her, despite all her faults. *Yes*, she thought, *I will make it up to my mother and the amazing and brave man who won her heart.*

Chapter 28

Sam and Monica slept soundly. Since her rescue Sam noticed that Monica seemed to be in a state of ongoing shock, the ordeal of the boat incident, her injuries and subsequent transfer to Sydney being all too much for her. Apart from constantly thanking Sam and clinging to him, the whole episode seemed to be taking her to a place near breaking point. Even the intrepid Victoria feared for her mental stability. Both she and Mary worried for their little friend who had seemed so happy for once in her life. They prayed she would endure and the nightmare would end.

Sam and Monica had been given a room in the main house by their friends and Felicity, Sandra, Victoria and Mary had retired to the guest cottage the previous evening. Sam and Monica were awakened from their deep sleep by gentle tapping on the door. Glancing at the clock, Sam was surprised to see it was nine thirty.

"Sam it's me, AJ. We have some great news. Mary wants to see you both as soon as you dress," AJ whispered.

"On the way." said Sam. "And I can never thank you enough AJ for what you've done for us."

"We go back a long way mate. It's my greatest pleasure to do whatever possible to help."

Pulling on some clothes, Sam and Monica followed AJ to the kitchen. The housekeeper had a breakfast of bacon and eggs cooking; Sam's favorite. Mary, AJ's daughter, sat before a heap of paperwork reading the contents.

As Sam and Monica walked in she smiled and looked up. "I have good news and perhaps to you Monica some surprising news. The application has been withdrawn and the other party has agreed to pay all costs. I have also in my possession, as part of the deal, all your business papers here before me, they have just been delivered from our office as part of the deal we insisted on. It would appear your late husband used you to safely hold assets in your name, unaware, of course, that he was going to die. It appears all assets were held by you."

"I had no idea," said Monica. "I just signed papers he insisted I sign. I can't ever remember reading or being told anything to do with Nigel's affairs. If I asked him he became irritable and said it was normal household business and to leave it to him."

"My dear Monica," Mary said, "I think the fact that your late husband was an absolute arsehole is common knowledge in the legal fraternity in Sydney. What you tell me is of no surprise, however, I always think it a pity Celia tried to follow his path. When I first met her at university she was a nice girl, to be frank Monica, I think your late husband manipulated and groomed her to follow in his footsteps."

Monica began to sob. "Celia and I got on so well when she was younger but Nigel poisoned her against me. Both turned against me and Allen. I tried but whatever I did suited neither. I always felt a failure somehow."

"Well it seems he never planned to die so early, well of course, we don't do we? It appears from your financial portfolio that you own several million dollars in property and shares," said Mary, "including the townhouse your late husband's lover resides in at fifty dollars per week rent."

Monica looked amazed. "Celia always put money in my personal account but in my wildest dreams I never imagined all this."

"Rumour is already circulating that Celia has been pushed

out of the firm your late husband grew from scratch.It also appears she has spent over two hundred thousand of your money in the last twelve months. I am sure you signed papers unaware of what you were authorising."

"Celia only had to ask me and I would have given her everything. I am her mother and still love her."

"I would suggest you go and see Celia Monica, by now she would be a very lonely person. Also we must at some stage, and the sooner the better, give a media interview. In doing so it may end the huge interest in you both. If you like I will arrange one this afternoon with a well know media personality."

Sam spoke up for the first time. "Make it this afternoon, it has to be done. I want everyone to know we are doing it for no fee. Also, I want on our behalf, to donate all the money and goods kind people have given us to three of our favorite charities."

Mary smiled. "I knew you would say that Sam and have even informed the presenter of both facts; he will inform the public of what you wish prior to the interview starting."

Sam asked Monica, "Where is your house? If Celia is still there we will go and see her this morning *before* the interview. This whole episode needs a proper ending."

Monica looked at Sam. "You are right Sam. We can actually walk, our house is in the next street. I can actually see the roof from the front lawn."

"What do you want me to do with your financial portfolio Monica? Will you allow Celia to stay in your house?"

"If she wants to. I feel now that perhaps she needs some help. Can you hold it for me until I decide what to do?"

Mary rose from the table. "Of course Monica. Sam may I have a quick word please on a different matter."

Mary frowned and looked at Sam. "I have just spoken to my brother David who also lives here with his wife and family, though at this time they are all in Darwin. With the mining boom we are short of good managers for our cattle properties and I intend to offer a job to Sandra if you agree. In mentioning it to her she told me she helps you with your cattle so I would not go over your head. However as you are aware she would have several months off in the wet season and if you agree could attend to your cattle during that time."

"Of course I agree, I only have a few cows and give her half for helping. I can tell you Mary, no more loyal and harder working person exists than our Sandra."

"Thanks Sam, we really are in a bind at this time for next season. I can assure you we will pay well and look after her for you."

"Your care and loyalty to your staff is legendary Mary, as was your parents. This is the big chance Sandra has been waiting for."

Finishing breakfast Sam and Monica decided to go and visit Celia and face whatever had to be faced. Monica seemed to steel herself for the meeting; a meeting, she decided, that should have occurred weeks before. *Perhaps,* she thought, *this whole unfortunate episode may have been avoided.*

The others joined the departing couple at the table to be told the good news. They all volunteered to go with them to visit Celia but Sam and Monica declined the kind offers.

Felicity told them that Tom was going to take them out to lunch. Tom had reported that some mad Tasmanian with two heavily bandaged hands had taken over the Matilda. In fact, he was threatening to toss any person overboard who tried to climb on board. Felicity promised to phone Joe and Wayne, who had been joined by Wayne's wife, to let them know their services would no longer be required and that they could now sail the Matilda back to Hobart.

Victoria and Mary intended to leave for Hobart that afternoon. Both desperately needed some rest and looked forward to seeing everyone back at Sam and Monica's the following weekend, anxious for life to return to normal.

Sandra was ecstatic at her new found position in life and promised to return home with Victoria and give her resignation and pack for the drive after Christmas to the Kimberleys, dogs and all.

Sam and Monica promised to attend the TV studio to tape the interview which was already being advertised to be shown that night.

Walking hand in hand, both had more than a feeling of trepidation as they approached Monica's old home; one which had given her so much misery. As they came along the street, Monica was surprised to see the entrance gate was wide open. Entering they both walked up the driveway. Monica was the first to recognise Brendan, their gardener for many years, loading his car with cases and other items. A happy reunion followed as Monica had always liked Brendan; his love of plants and animals gave them many happy moments chatting over the years.

It was no surprise to Monica, as Brendan informed them, that Celia was still asleep; she had not slept for days. He then went on to tell Monica and Sam the whole story. It was no surprise to learn of his professed love of her daughter; she always suspected such and had already mentioned it to Sam. More surprising was Celia's pregnancy and the fact she was leaving to move in with Brendan. He told Monica he always knew she would hit the wall, trying to please and follow her late father; it could never last, he knew it would destroy her. He begged Monica to forgive her as he believed she had changed and really wanted to be given a chance.

Sam was impressed by the loyal Brendan and actually started to feel pangs of guilt at the picture he had built up of Celia. Sam knew that for Monica to ever be truly free and enjoy her life with him, she and Celia must become a family again. He knew Monica would forgive and forget but Celia worried him.

Deep in conversation the three failed to notice Celia walking towards them. Monica turned as if a sixth sense beckoned her and as Sam and Brendan stood watching, she ran sobbing to her daughter. Celia, racked with guilt and shame, was overcome and dropped to her knees, loud sobs of anguish gushing from her as both fell into each others arms. Sam and Brendan stood transfixed by the raw emotion played out before them.

"Please forgive me mum, please forgive me. What have I done, god forgive me?" Celia kept repeating.

Sam and Brendan knew both had no part to play in the reunion of mother and daughter. Brendan invited Sam in for coffee in order for the women to have the privacy needed at a time like this.

"Mum," Celia said. "Can you ever find it in your heart to forgive me. I was out of control and my whole life had become a lie."

Monica soothed her daughter as they held on to each other.

"It is my greatest wish that Sam, Brendan and the two of us lead a family life from here on. You have nothing to forgive, it was your father who guided you and I know you tried to please him."

"That is no excuse for what I have done Mum. I will try for the rest of my life to make it up to you. I have two hundred thousand to repay you for money I wrongly took from your account."

Monica laughed. "Who cares about money, it will never buy happiness. It was yours anyway, I only had it because your father used me to protect assets. He never left you anything so it is yours as much as mine. Anyhow, Sam looks after me and we have more than two simple, old people in love could ever use."

"Can you really forgive me mum? You are too kind, after what I did to you for all those years."

"We can never change yesterday, besides it belongs to the past. I have a wonderful man and a wonderful life. I want you and Brendan to come to Tasmania, Brendan always wanted a small farm. All I wish is to watch my new grandchild grow and for us to become a happy family."

"It sounds like a fairytale mum. Poor old Brendan, he's good-looking, he should have found a nice girl years ago. Why did he ever bother with me?"

"Love, Celia, is a wonderful thing; he always loved you, I knew that."

Hand in hand the two reconciled entered the kitchen. Sam and Brendan smiled happily to see the two women they dearly loved finally together, smiling together.

"Celia, Sam tells me there is a three hundred acre farm opposite his for sale in Tasmania. Please tell me you will agree to sell my house and buy it. I'll get enough for my property to make the move debt free. It is my life's dream to have a farm and I know you'd love to as well," he smiled.

"I agree if Mum does not mind her bitch of a daughter living so close. God, never in my wildest dreams did I ever imagine being pregnant living on a farm in Tasmania."

Monica piped up now, a changed woman. "No, we will sell everything I have in my name, I will pay for the farm as a wedding gift to you both, the balance I will invest for my three grandchildren."

"What about poor old Sam?" asked Celia.

"Well maybe I will keep some but Sam will leave Felicity his farm and assets, which is the right thing to do. Hopefully, everyone will be happy."

Sam joined in the conversation. "Perhaps money and power are not the great drugs of happiness after all; family and helping each other is worth a lot more than money."

"Well I am not quite sure of that Sam but money never gave me happiness that's for sure, so I hope the future holds some happiness and I can tell you I will try, especially for Brendan and Mum. I have to prove to both now that I have changed."

Felicity and Sandra came walking up the driveway, anxious about how Sam and Monica had been received. Sam met them both and explained what had happened, suggesting perhaps now may not be the right time to meet Celia, but that they would meet later in Tasmania.

Sandra and the two older women were on their way to the airport and home. Tom and Felicity would pick up Sam and Monica back at Sky and AJ's place to take them to the studio for the interview.

Monica suggested that Celia might like to stay in the house but she wanted to make the break now. Her new life would start today and she wished to completely block out her old life.

Celia gave Monica the keys and she and Sam waved the couple off, planning to meet in Tasmania on their return. Both planned to fly down to inspect the farm and stay with Sam and Monica.

After they left, Monica turned to Sam. " One last wish Sam. I want to stay in my old bedroom tonight. Do you mind?"

"No problem to me but we leave in the morning for home. I miss Jack, it's the first time we've been apart and I miss the little bugger."

Both inspected the huge home and Monica was surprised that her Volvo still sat in the garage. "I miss my car Sam," she said, "it is the only thing I would like to take home. Sorry to always be a pain but would you mind? It is only three years old and I loved driving it, it saved my sanity."

"We'll drive it home,' Sam replied, "it looks a nice car."

They returned to their friend's house to let them know they would be staying in Monica's old house for the night and then leaving in the morning, both anxious to return home. Thanking their friends profusely for the magnificent hospitality and help, Sky and AJ told the two friends that they also were heading back to Tasmania in the morning and would catch up as soon as possible after things returned to normal.

Felicity and Tom returned to take them for the scheduled interview. Monica was nervous but Sam, as usual, just regarded it as something they had to do. Telling Felicity of the plan to drive Monica's car back, Tom broke in quickly. "I'm going to take a two week break and go to Tasmania with Felicity and we would love to drive the car down for you."

Sam accepted, not really wanting to drive back anyway. He had agreed to please Monica but the thought of the drive worried him as he still suffered pain from his injuries.

True to his word, the interviewer opened with the fact that no payment had been offered or requested for the interview. He went on to say that all the monies and goods given to Sam and Monica had been given to charity, then he reported they both wanted to return to a normal life and hoped everyone would respect their wishes. He thanked the public, on their behalf, for all the support and interest that had been given.

The questions started with the rescue and then the incident of Celia taking her mother to Sydney. Sam answered that Celia had only tried to act in her mother's best interest and although misguided, both mother and daughter had met since the incident and wished to get on with their lives. An unfortunate and sad affair best forgotten Sam concluded.

Monica was asked what she thought of Sam coming valiantly to her rescue. She smiled and said that she expected no more or less from Sam; he was her hero and the love of her life. At the conclusion, the interviewer thanked both for being so honest and for being such easy and cooperative people to interview and wished them well.

Relieved, Sam and Monica had Felicity drop them off at Monica's house for their last night in Sydney. Tom drove

Monica's car away ready for the trip home the following day. They all hoped to meet in Tasmania in a few days.

Showing Sam to her old bedroom, Monica looked at him smiling. "I just don't know how we are going to do this lover," she said, "but even though we are covered in bandages, stitched up and stiff as hell, for once this old bed is going to see some action. Three decades of sexual frustration in it is ending, hook or by crook, tonight."

Sam smiled as he dropped his clothing and pulled the sheets back. "Action stations, but it *is* going to be a self-help project," he laughed as Monica turned off the light.

Chapter 29

Sam woke with a start. It took a few minutes to realise just where he was, so much had happened over the last few days, it had all seemed surreal. He felt at ease when he saw Monica sleeping next to him. Since meeting and making peace with her daughter, a complete change had transpired in her; he reflected it was as if she had purged the demons from her soul.

Monica looked at Sam as she woke up realising where they were and she said, "I dreamt of a knight in shining armor making love to me in this very bed and here he is now, in bed with me and we certainly did make love, injuries and all."

"I hope you know Monica my love, that you have prolonged my recovery by months because of the excesses of last night and this morning."

"It was worth it. I feel now as if I have totally lifted the clouds of darkness from my soul. I am free of the bad thoughts of this place and the fear of my daughter; she is like us all, vulnerable and human. I intend to leave this house and never look back; this morning I have overcome my demons," Monica said looking confident and revitalised.

After breakfast Monica and Sam locked the house and returned to Mary's residence. They found her in the office attending to company business that she and her sister and two brothers ran. Thanking her once again, Monica collected her financial documents and arranged for the car to pick them up and transfer them to the airport. Both were eager to get home and settle into marital bliss and see Jacky who would be eagerly waiting to see his beloved master.

They waved a fond farewell to Mary as the taxi disappeared down the street. Sam's phone rang, it was Allen in absolute panic. He had just read all the papers after returning home from their overseas holiday.

Monica spoke to him for some time telling him about the entire drama since the rescue. He was relieved to hear everything was in order and promised to come down for Christmas in a few weeks time.

Sam phoned Sandra and asked for a favor, not wanting to alert the press of their impending homecoming. She promised to pick up Jacky and meet them at the airport. Sam and Monica had taken up the offer of a private jet home in order to escape the media who were checking on their movements through commercial airlines.

Arriving at Hobart Airport it was a great relief to them to finally be home. Security had allowed Sandra to park near the freight terminal and no sooner had the private jet come to a halt than Sam and Monica were out on the tarmac, much to the delight of Jacky who was going absolutely crazy with delight.

Sandra arrived in Sam's car as it had more room and comfort than the ute she drove. Monica sat in front with Sandra while Jacky and Sam sat in the back seat, excited and happy to see each other again.

Monica reflected that in all her life the sight of her new home again was the best view she would ever wish to see for the remainder of her life.

Sandra helped unload the luggage and making sure both were okay, went straight back to work, after telling Sam the neighbors she worked for seemed pleased she had found a better position but admitted they would miss her.

Sitting on the porch, relaxing with a cup of coffee, Monica looked at Sam. "You know Sam, I hope we never have to leave here again. I just want to live here in peace with you till the day I die."

Sam chuckled. "Feel that way now myself but who knows, one day we just may go for another adventure."

"Well I intend to rest today. First thing tomorrow I'll get on the phone and arrange the cleaning of the house ready for sale and I'll place all the properties on the market, sell the shares and put the yacht on the market too."

"Are you sure? Do you want to think about things for a while?"

"Hell no Sam, I just want peace and quiet. Whatever I pay for Celia's farm I will equal and give to Allen and Felicity as well; they are all family and deserve the same. We'll keep some of what's left and the balance can be set up as trusts for the grandchildren."

"Felicity is not your offspring, she shouldn't be included."

"Who came into that hospital and helped me Sam? She is my daughter and don't forget it; that is what I am doing and I will hear no more about the matter."

Sam laughed. "You sure have changed from a pussycat to a tiger overnight."

"I am empowered Sam, thanks to you, for the first time in my life."

Monica phoned Celia and told her they had arrived home safely. She and Brendan seemed keen to come and inspect the property having put Brendan's house on the market that day.

Celia informed her mother that she was anxious to leave her past life behind and was looking forward to living in close proximity to her and Sam.

Victoria and Mary phoned, glad to hear they had arrived home safely and promised to come up in a couple of days when they gained back some strength after the recent ordeals.

No-one was happier to be back in the comfort of their own bedroom than Sam and Monica. They lay in each others arms, not talking but soaking up the moment, Jacky contentedly sleeping on the rug next to Sam. The following morning Sam checked on the cattle and walked over to look at the hay paddocks almost ready for bailing. He intended to refill all the hay sheds which was a sensible decision.

Monica sat by the phone calling real estate agents, cleaners, stockbrokers and a boat broker. When Sam returned at lunchtime she was busy preparing lunch, content she had not forgotten anything.

As Sam walked in she told him of her morning and the fact that she also phoned the real estate agent who had the farm for sale opposite. She told Sam she had also phoned Celia and they would be arriving the following morning, excited to see the property Sam had in mind for them.

Felicity had phoned to tell him that she and Tom had decided to visit friends in Bateman's Bay and would be going sailing with them for a couple of days. Looking at Sam Monica said, "I have a funny feeling Sam that your Felicity and Mary's Tom are a bit more than friends."

"Well, if that is the case, no father is happier in his daughters choice. Tom is a top young bloke," Sam replied with a smile.

That afternoon they decided to potter in the garden. After the last week of dramas it was refreshing to bask in each others company amongst the beautiful roses with Jacky watching contentedly.

At three o'clock the phone rang. It was an agent from Sydney calling to speak to Monica. As Monica listened, Sam heard her reply, "Yes that sounds fine, sell both please."

Sam whistled as she hung up the phone. "That was quick."

Monica happily told Sam that because of the boom in housing the agent had buyers waiting. She had sold the house for four and a half million and the townhouse Susan had just vacated for one and a half million. That only left the holiday home in Noosa that Monica knew nothing about and two other townhouses in Sydney. Sam smiled at the way Monica was so casual, seeming happier to unload the properties than concern herself with the money now available; she did not seem to care about it.

"Sam, the farm next door is only eight hundred thousand so after fees and charges I will have enough to pay each three children that much and have a nice sum in balance for the grandchildren. I will make it also that if Felicity and Celia have more children they will receive the same amount," considered Monica carefully as she told Sam of her plans.

"You are unreal. Money means bugger all to you really."

"Learnt that from you Sam. I have never been happier and it is because money is not our god. I've never heard you mention it, in fact, I remember you, Sam, giving an interest free loan to perfect strangers, so you can't go lecturing others."

Sam shook his head. He realised Monica would be glad when everything was finalised. Money matters obviously worried her, being unused to such things, and he noted that she seemed to just want to get rid of the whole financial thing and return to a simple life. She had even forgotten about the money from her villa sold on her departure from the retirement home which he figured was due within days.

The following morning Celia and Brendan arrived, having caught an early flight. They hired a car, eager to also see a bit of the scenery surrounding the farms and did not wish to inconvenience Sam and Monica any more than they felt necessary.

After placing their bags in the room, they looked over Sam's farm and fell in love with it. Celia told her mother she now realised why she loved it so much there.

Sam and Monica accompanied them over the highway to the property for sale. It also had an older homestead and both instantly fell in love with the place, signing the contract on the spot. They realised the house needed some upgrading and both looked forward to the task, even Celia, to Monica's amazement. No longer feeling she had to present her tough façade, Celia became settled and happier in herself, even relishing the thought of motherhood, her past life seemingly forgotten.

Monica instructed Celia that she would pay for the property as it was Celia's inheritance also. Her daughter was grateful and with proceeds from the law firm and the sale of Brendan's property, they had enough money to live comfortably and she would have no reason to work again if she did not want to. In fact, Celia kept talking about her changed circumstances, being unable to believe the happiness the unfortunate chain of events had made to her life.

She even showed an interest in Monica's chooks and vegetable garden, making her mother promise to teach her how to keep the little feathered creatures and how to grow vegetables; with Brendan's help also.

They spent several days staying with Sam and Monica, exploring the area and meeting Victoria, Mary and the intrepid Sandra, who for Monica's sake, forgave Celia and welcomed her to the fold.

By the time Celia and Brendan waved a fond farewell to return to Sydney to finalise matters for the move to their new home, Monica and her daughter had formed a new and loving relationship. Sam liked Brendan. He reminded him of himself, down to earth and easy going, which was just as well with the feisty Celia. Brendan was also keen to get a herd of Herefords like Sam's; he absolutely loved Sam's gentle, red and white cattle.

Sam and Monica were able to settle into marital bliss once again occasional visits from Mary and Victoria, who looked forward to the arrival of Monica's car and the two youngsters they both loved.

Chapter 30

Since arriving home, Monica and Sam's lives remained busy and both improved quickly, owing to the healthy lifestyle and good food; soon returning to as near normal as they were ever likely to get. Wounds healed and bruising faded; their vitality and zest for life never higher.

Sam was busy organising baling contractors and men to cart the hay into his sheds while Monica worked in her vegetable garden, keen to make up for lost time. Victoria and Mary were staying and both helped out eagerly. *The three are like a gaggle of geese talking incessantly*, mused Sam .

Returning home for lunch Sam was surprised to see Felicity drive in the driveway with Tom following in Monica's Volvo. A happy reunion occurred between all six with many hugs and kisses exchanged. Tom had taken Monica's car for a service and detail the previous day and it was sparkling. They had not rang to say they were on the way, wanting to surprise everybody.

It soon became apparent that Monica was right: the two kept nervously exchanging glances at each other and Sam noticed that Tom fidgeted and was nervous. Reading the moment, Sam invited Tom to inspect the farm and he seemed relieved at the invitation. Both had only strolled a short distance when Tom coughing looked at Sam and said, "I hope you don't feel angry with me Sam but will you agree to let me marry your lovely daughter."

Sam laughed. "Angry with you? Of all the young men I

know Tom you would be the best I have ever met as a potential son-in-law. Of course I give my permission. Not many would have the decency to ask these days. Welcome to our family. In fact, bugger the tour, lets go back and celebrate."

It was quite obvious by the laughing and giggling coming from the kitchen that Felicity had already sprung the news on the women. It was Mary who felt the greatest happiness and she could not contain herself, tears streamed down her face in uncontrolled emotion.

At once, Victoria inquired about the wedding plans. Felicity and Tom informed them that Tom was returning home to sell his unit and resign from the police force and that they intended to live in Tasmania with his grandmother.

"Someone has to keep an eye on you lot," he said.

Sam immediately offered to hold the wedding and reception at the homestead. He would erect a marquee and get caterers in; such an important occasion had to be held at the farm, he told everyone. Felicity agreed and said she was going to suggest that this be the case. She and Tom had talked the event over and both agreed to ask Sam and Monica.

Felicity then said she wanted Sandra to be her only attendant and Tom had asked his best friend who had already agreed. Sam and Tom enjoyed a beer while they watched the women-folk, now in overdrive, planning the special day.

Tom informed Sam that he and Felicity had decided to take a break and if Sam would not mind lending them the caravan, they wanted to take a leisurely tour around Australia after the wedding. The trip down had whetted their appetites. Sam insisted they also take the land cruiser as it was not used much and Sam wanted to buy a ute now that Sandra was leaving and he would need one on the farm; the shed space would be handy too, he told Tom.

The ladies informed them that the wedding date was planned for two months ahead, time for Tom to return and resign and also to put the unit he owned on the market.

That evening as they all sat around enjoying a barbecue, Sandra made her usual entrance to everyone's delight. Immediately she was approached by Felicity and asked to be her attendant. The unflappable Sandra was overcome with emotion that Felicity thought so much of her that she would ask her to perform such an honorable task.

Everyone drank so much that at midnight Tom suggested everybody had better stay overnight, somewhere. Much giggling and laughing took place as sleeping arrangements were made. Victoria and Mary would sleep in one room, Tom and Felicity in another and Sandra could make up a comfortable bed on the sofa in front of the fire.

Having finally gotten to bed, Sam looked at Monica and said, "It's strange how a chain of events occurred simply because of your mad decision to go for a nude swim in Broome. I can't comprehend the changes in our lives because of one simple event."

"I never thought of it that way. Hell Sam, I just don't want to think about where I'd still be if I hadn't got half-pissed and thought up such a stupid idea."

"I suppose, actually, it was Victoria who set the whole ball rolling; her decision triggered the lot really," said Sam.

"Felicity found Tom, Sandra has a great new career and I've found happiness along with Celia. I've never seen Victoria and Mary so excited and happy, all because of one simple desire on Victoria's part."

"My only hope is that now we will all spend many happy years together. You know Monica the only one who doesn't have a home is Sandra. One day, when all has settled, perhaps we can do something for her," sighed Same.

Monica sat upright in bed. "Good god Sam she is family. After the wedding and after Celia has moved in we will both look for a small farm for Sandra. You know, out of all of us, that girl deserves the most help."

Settling back into bed Monica's thoughts went into overdrive. In her own blissful happiness she had forgotten about Sandra and felt ashamed; never would she forget her hurtling down the Matilda to save Sam.

Over a late breakfast the following morning Monica suggested Victoria and Mary stay for a few days to help clean up Celia's new home, which was to be settled the following week. The absentee owners had agreed to give Monica the keys early fully aware that the matter would be finalised and both knew Sam well.

As she was leaving, Sandra approached Monica. "Monica would you like to look after old Bella, my favorite kelpie bitch when I go north? I'm worried the heat might play up with her. She's in pup and needs a bit of extra care though. You and Sam are the only ones I would leave my old girl with."

"Sure, absolute pleasure Sandra. I'm happy to give her a loving home for as long as you need me to. Sam can build a nice shelter on the front porch for her to have the pups," said Monica warmly.

Sandra seemed contented with her most worrying problem solved. She loaded her kelpies and drove back to her small worker's cottage.

Sam watched as the others drove off in Monica's car to check out the new home for Celia and Brendan. Felicity and Tom bid farewell and the happy couple returned to Hobart.

Sam found the quiet a little unsettling as he drove his four wheeler over to the hay paddocks as the contractors had started for the day. The dew was long gone and the baling now in progress. Sam's barns were already starting to fill. He had decided to fill one of Brendan and Celia's sheds as it might be too late for them to bale by the time they arrived. The property had been leased out prior to sale and was pretty much eaten out.

Stopping by the gravesite, Sam looked at the resting place of Carol and said out loud, "I wonder what you would think of what has happened to my life in the last few months old girl. What a laugh it would give you. Felicity wants to show you her wedding dress the day she marries. I know you'd be proud of her and Tom is a great young man."

Sam tried but failed to stop the tears in his eyes as he drove off. Although he loved Monica, but Carol would always have a special place in his heart.

It seemed like no time had passed before Celia and Brendan arrived and moved into their new home to begin their new life.

Monica and Celia drove to Hobart visiting the Salamanca Markets, shopping and having coffee with Felicity, Victoria and Mary. Sam noticed how happy she was. Never again did he hear Celia mention her past life; she seemed to be too busy and involved in the change of direction and events in her life.

Sam helped Brendan with the fencing and both worked tractors, cultivating some of Brendan's older pastures for re-sowing and winter feed. Under Sam's guidance they attended cattle sales and purchased sixty heifers to stock the farm.

They were all so busy that time seemed to slip by quickly and next thing they knew, it was time for Felicity and Tom's wedding and the farewell of Sandra to head north for the muster season.

Christmas soon came and passed by. Allen and his family stayed for two weeks and it was the happiest festive season Monica had ever had. Sam noticed her absolutely glowing, bursting with pride as she busily made sure, with the help of Victoria and Mary, that all present had more than enough to eat and drink.

Presents were exchanged and Monica and Sam gave Allen and Felicity an envelope each for Christmas. Monica had already alerted Celia of her plan to give both the same amount as she had received. Celia agreed, more than happy with her new life. For once, money seemed to be unimportant as Brendan fussed over her growing pregnancy.

Both Allen and Felicity were shocked on opening their envelopes as they looked at the bank cheques for eight hundred thousand dollars each. They wanted Monica to keep and enjoy her money but she sternly rebuked both, informing them that money never held much interest for her, or Sam; she had more than was sufficient, and that they both were to enjoy it. "Use it for fuel to come and visit us more often," she smiled as she hugged them both.

Sam took Monica's two grandsons for a couple of days on the Matilda, it was a boys trip only with Allen, Brendan and Tom going also. It was to be the last trip on the vessel as Sam had leased it to Joe and Wayne. They had already added a brine tank and put her back at work fishing lobster.

The wedding day approached and to Sam's amusement, Monica, and her entourage, worked furiously making sure everything was accounted for and in its right place. Victoria had transformed into a general rallying her troops and relishing the excitement; she and Mary quite forgetting their ages.

Mary's entire family had accepted invitations and with the many friends of the couple and AJ's family, over two hundred people would be attending.

Sam was marched off to Hobart to be fitted with a new suit. As the father of the bride Monica had insisted on the shopping trip and Sam, defeated by the onslaught of so many women, had no choice but to agree.

Tom, who had moved to Hobart, was busy helping Sam and Brendan, as well as outfitting the caravan, servicing the land cruiser and preparing for the trip they planned to take after the wedding.

As the day approached and the marquee was erected the homestead became a hive of activity. Monica and her babble of ladies shot into overdrive and Sam was relieved to take Jacky for a quiet walk along the river, contemplating life.

It was on one of many quiet walks, as he crossed the boundary fence to continue along the river, that he met his aged, next-door neighbor. Stopping for a chat she told Sam that her little farm and cottage was on the market; having no family, she had decided to move into town to a unit.

Sam knew the block was only thirty acres but it boasted good buildings and a beautiful colonial cottage. The owner had carefully maintained the property and it was in excellent order.

Sam was sorry that his old neighbor was to leave. Since her husband's death the quiet and gracious woman had kept pretty much to herself. Sam told her of his wish to buy something for Sandra to have when she was home, a place of her own. She told Sam that the agent had put three hundred and twenty thousand on the property. Sam shook hands and the deal was done; he had purchased a small farm for Sandra. Walking home, he felt thoroughly satisfied. All the ones he loved were now taken care of; this was his last deed and he felt a sense of fulfillment, feeling that all his debts had now been paid.

When he returned, Felicity, Celia, and the three sisters in arms, sat finalising the wedding plans. Sitting down with them he told them of his purchase. They wholeheartedly approved, never surprised at Sam's benevolence and sense of honor. Felicity insisted on putting in a third and Monica sternly told Sam she would do the same. A small fight erupted as everybody wanted to contribute. Victoria said it was not fair unless they all gave so much. The gift is from all of us and should therefore include everyone; after all, she insisted, it is a family matter.

In the end Felicity worked out a compromise and each person gave an amount they were happy with. Sam reluctantly agreed, thanking them all for being such good and generous friends.

"Sandra is family Sam," Monica said. "I feel ashamed we never thought of her before."

"Well," Sam said, "now for the first time in her life she will have a home to always come back to. I'll put a few heifers on it for her."

Celia sat pondering her new life while looking around at the happy group. She thought to herself *all these people love each other, it's hard to believe we just tossed away a large sum of money to another person, and then they just go on discussing the wedding as if nothing has happened.* In her past life people schemed to sue and take as much of each other as they possibly could; *a dog eat dog world of greed and shameless people with no conscience or life.*

Chapter 31

The morning of the wedding finally arrived. The preceeding day had been one of furious activity with people coming and going. Sam had hardly slept and Monica had been restless, absolutely swept up in the excitement of the occasion. *Perhaps,* she thought, *it reminds me of my wedding to Sam, the happiest day of my life.*

Tom had stayed overnight and he and Sam had talked well into the night. Tom thanked Sam for all he had done for he and Felicity; both consumed far too much wine. Monica, Victoria and Mary kept bringing both food and drinks, trying to be helpful, but in fact, unknowingly, contributing to the two men becoming intoxicated.

The wedding celebrant was to arrive early. Felicity wanted an unconventional wedding at eleven o'clock stating that evening weddings she had previously attended made it a long wait for everyone.

After lunch, she and Tom would leave to catch the ferry to Melbourne to begin their big adventure, visiting all the places her mother and father had lived and worked in.

Monica had been up since daylight and Sam slept until eight. Dressing, he was shocked to see a mass of people already arriving. The kitchen was jammed with people, food strewn everywhere as Monica, Celia, Mary and Victoria passed food and drinks around.

Catering vans had already arrived, setting up portable kitchens and placing white table cloths, flowers and cutlery on all the tables. Sam had employed the football club that Joe had sternly insisted would do the bar work and maintain order.

The time flew by and soon Sam was dressing, along with Tom; his best man had arrived early and the girls were already dressed. The hairdresser was working overtime. Brendan was fussing about the pregnant Celia, a large bump now showing, and she in turn lapped up the attention.

Five minutes before the wedding Tom and his best man, with the guests, sat quietly in the huge marquee waiting for the arrival of the bride. Sam waited patiently in the driveway, unable to believe the sight of the paddock that was full of cars along the river. Felicity, absolutely radiant, arrived and with the help of Sandra, stepped out of the limo. Sam was unable to control his emotions, he felt so proud. Sandra even looked outstanding; never had he seen her in a dress and with her hair done, she looked completely different to the Sandra he had always known.

Sam proudly walked up the isle with Felicity on his arm, the clapping of the crowd filling his ears. Few times in his life had he felt so proud; his daughter looked stunningly beautiful. Tom turned and smiled at them and Sam was sure he detected a tear welling in Tom's eye.

On instructions from the celebrant, Sam offered his beloved daughter's hand to Tom and stepped back sitting down with Monica, grabbing her hand and holding on tightly, fighting the emotion he felt.

The wedding was poignantly simple and soon Felicity and Tom kissed as husband and wife. After they had signed the papers, they informed guests that one last task remained: the master of ceremonies. AJ told the guests to enjoy a few drinks while the bride and groom visited the grave of Felicity's mother.

Felicity stood before her mother's resting place with Tom and gently placed her bouquet on the grave. This being

Felicity's most emotional time, she broke down and Tom held her as she trembled with great, heaving sobs. Both stood there, still, for a few minutes before turning and making their way back to the celebrations.

The band was playing with wine and food flowed freely as friends celebrated the wedding.

Mary, in her glee, instructed the photographer to take a photo of the entire family; the first time they had all had been together for years. Victoria mingled with the guests having the time of her life, telling all of the meeting with Sam and causing many a laugh.

Sam mingled with friends he had not caught up with for months. Monica was thrilled to catch up with Phillip, the pilot, who had come with Billy from the Kimberlys, not wanting to miss 'Sam's daughter's marriage'.

Wayne Bond and his wife were there. Sam was amused when Wayne told him that Joe was sitting on the ground drunk, unable to attend to his bar duties. Joe was apparently singing away happily, caught up in the moment, telling everyone that Sam saved his life.

Felicity approached Sam after the speeches and toasts which were kept brief. "I think it is time to surprise Sandra Dad. I want to watch her face when we tell her about her new farm,"

Sam signaled to all the family who were involved in the purchase to gather. He then found Sandra singing with Joe and dragged her away from the bar and sat her down at the table amongst the family.

Sam held her hand and said, "Sandra, you have been a wonderful and loyal friend to us for years. We want to give you a small gift in appreciation of your loyalty and courage. We hope this will always bring you back home to stay amongst us. You are a big part of our now extended family and we give you this as a small appreciation of your valued friendship."

Felicity handed Sandra the envelope. "This is from the heart Sandra; you are my most treasured family member."

With a look of surprise Sandra tore the envelope open, staring at the copy of a title deed, it took her a while to notice that her name was on it. Bursting into tears she pulled Felicity to her. "What can I say? I bet Sam was the main instigator of this, the generous old bugger," she wailed.

Sandra hugged everyone. "This will always be my home," she said. "You are my family. I'll come home every wet season to help you Sam."

"Well before you take off, pick out ten heifers to stock your block, a gift from us also."

"You deserve it Sandra. Now drinks and food await, lets mingle. What a celebration," cried Victoria.

The impact of what had just happened slowed Sandra down a bit. It had just hit her how much those around her actually thought of her, it made her feel part of the family and she loved them all, especially old Sam.

Felicity and Tom changed early in the afternoon and all the guests lined the driveway as the happy couple, cans rattling behind the caravan, drove off to catch the ferry at Devonport on the start of an extended honeymoon.

Sam remembers collapsing into bed sometime late that evening, exhaustion and the emotion of the day had taken its toll and Sam was sound asleep within minutes. He never even heard Monica as she later got into bed.

Sam woke the following morning unaware of the time. He looked at the slumped figure of Monica, still dressed, laying on top of the bed, her breathing heavy. As he got out, she stirred and looking with glazed eyes at Sam and said, "Broke my bloody rule Sam; I need water and aspirin fast and take your eyes of my arse. I am too weak to even pee."

Sam smiled as he headed downstairs to get the aspirin and

water. Sandra, with her bridesmaid's dress still on, shoes exchanged for blundstone boots, lay snoring on the couch. Jacky lay next to her, both dead to the world. The little dog had spent the day vacuuming food off the floor of the marquee and looked decidedly unwell.

Returning upstairs, Sam gave the tablets to a suffering Monica and as he washed, he looked out at the carnage below: several cars and vans still remained in the paddock and Joe had the barbecue going, feeding the bedraggled looking stragglers. Deciding that it was a wasted effort to start cleaning up yet, Sam went back to bed next to a groaning Monica. *One thing,* he thought, *Monica is not very alcohol tolerant, that is for sure.*

Later in the day as most people packed and left, the catering company removed the marquee and Joe and Sandra pitched in, filling the tractor trailer full of rubbish, causing Sam to wonder at their staying power. Brendan and Celia turned up, both looking worse for wear as the last of the rubbish was collected and normality started to appear.

That evening, after everyone had gone, Celia and Brendan sat on the verandah with Monica who still looked unwell, while Sam organised a small serving of food for the foursome.

"I will never have another drink ever, I swear," Monica said. "Well perhaps just one when the next big event happens; the birth of Celia's baby."

"Can't wait to I see my daughter come into the world Monica."

"If you think Brendan, you are going to watch me, legs apart, my fanny bursting giving birth, you have another thing coming. For hell sakes it would put you off sex forever."

"Come on Celia, he wants to see his daughter come into the world," said Monica.

"I will probably go berserk and swear and curse him mum. I have no pain tolerance whatsoever."

"Well, poor Brendan is probably used to you abusing him Celia, so what? As for seeing you in an uncompromising situation, he would see nothing that he hasn't already."

"All right you two. For hell sakes if you insist but I'm warning you Brendan, it will not be pretty."

Sam and Monica were glad for life to settle once again. Every Tuesday, Monica would pick up Celia to go shopping and join Victoria and Mary for lunch. It became a routine that they all looked forward to. Every second weekend the routine included Victoria and Mary staying over with Monica and Sam, relaxing and enjoying the tranquility of their home.

Sandra dropped off her old kelpie bitch, now heavily pregnant, and the old dog immediately settled into her new surrounds to be pampered by everyone, apart from Jacky who steadfastly refused her entry to his home.

Sandra bid farewell to her family and with high expectations left for the ferry trip to Melbourne and the long drive to the Kimberlys and her new life. She promised to be home by November to mark the calves and stay over Christmas in her new house. She had offered the previous owner the chance to stay as long as she wanted to but the elderly lady said she felt it was time to move closer to town. Sam promised to keep an eye on her little farm while she was away. Everyone remarked that things seemed a little dull without Sandra bursting into their lives weekly; they all missed her bright smile and lovely outlook on life.

True to her word, Monica fussed over the old kelpie, taking her for vet checks and lining her kennel with woollen blankets. The old dog responded by following Monica everywhere and even Jacky started to accept that his world now involved another dog.

Felicity and Tom kept in touch weekly. They were having a great time and had arranged to meet and stay with Sandra to experience station life for a few weeks. The next few months sailed past until one morning, Sam and Monica awakened to a phone call from Celia.

"Did not want to wake you earlier," she said, "but I gave birth to a beautiful baby daughter this morning at one o'clock. Brendan, the useless shit, fainted during the birth and is still not too good. He is on his way home and will call in. Can you feed him mum? Poor bugger broke down, it was too much for him, and he is so proud of being a father."

Monica sprung out of bed. "Poor Brendan, he'll be starving. I'll get some food on Sam. Isn't this all wonderful?" Sam looked at Monica. "Be better if you got that cute arse back in bed,"said Sam feeling a little aroused.

Monica looked at the time. "Bugger," she said jumping back into bed. "At my age I will never miss out on a good bang so make it quick lover, we have twenty minutes."

The pair had just rolled apart after a wild and lustful encounter when Monica heard Brendan pull up in the driveway.

Sam pulled on his dressing gown and went downstairs to meet Brendan and make him a coffee. Monica showered and dressed, feeling elated that her life seemed to be one big happy journey.

Brendan looked completely exhausted and drained. "I made a fool of myself," he said. "Bloody fainted at the last moment. Never saw my daughter enter the world. God Celia was magnificent, she was so brave."

Monica felt sorry for Brendan as she knew he had been looking forward to the birth for so long. Everyone who heard about it found it highly amusing, much to Monica's frustration, and laughed, including Sam, who seemed more than a bit amused. Brendan went home to bed for a rest as Monica and Sam drove to Hobart to see their new grand daughter.

Even Sam had never seen Celia looking so radiant.

Motherhood indeed suited her and she was so proud of her achievement. "The best thing I have ever done in my life," she kept repeating. "Mum, now I can appreciate what you went through for Allen and me."

Celia came home two days later and once again life seemed to return to normal with the routine of visiting and shopping trips resuming.

Monica and Sam, surrounded by old friends and family, enjoyed marital bliss. Winter approached, the leaves fell off the trees and chilling winds gripped the land. Sam and Brendan fed the cows on all three properties in Sam's new ute and spent many happy hours by the fire with Victoria and Mary talking about the happy times past.

Monica and Celia never discussed their past lives. It seemed they had both erased the memories from their minds; new loves and new directions consumed them, and now both doted on Celia's daughter. Even Sam and Brendan concluded their lives were blessed by Monica and her daughter. Life sure was good concluded Sam.

All looked forward to the return of Tom and Felicity in the spring with the news of their adventures since departing months ago, and Sandra was due to return from the Kimberleys as well.

Celia and Brendan both wished to wait until the entire extended family were home to christen their daughter who they named Emily. Monica was surprised at just how much Celia had completely changed, now truly relishing the family atmosphere. She had even become more loving towards Brendan, realising that he was the only one who had ever truly loved her and she secretly tried to make it up to him for his loyalty and waiting patiently for her for all those years.

Chapter 32

Sam woke early. He loved to lie in bed with Monica listening to the sound of rain smattering on the roof; it had calming effect. Suddenly he realised Monica was not in bed, in fact, Jacky was gone too. Pulling on his dressing gown he made his way down to the kitchen. Monica was nowhere to be seen. Alarmed, he went out onto the porch looking across the paddocks. It was cold and rain belted down. About to go back in and dress in order to search for her, he looked at Bella's kennel and to his surprise, two human feet poked out of it. Walking forward, he bent down, and there inside, he saw Monica with a towel, helping Bella dry several whimpering pups.

Staring into the dim light he also recognised Jacky squeezed in next to Monica staring at the new pups, mesmerized at the new dogs he would share his empire with.

"Nice bum, best bitch I have ever seen," remarked Sam.

"Oh Sam, we have five of the most gorgeous pups and I'll bitch you one day Sam Stewart if you don't help me out of here," laughed Monica.

Sam gently pulled Monica out backwards. She held up a little whimpering kelpie for Sam to see. No-one was more interested than Jacky, staring up at the little ball that would grow into a sleek red kelpie.

Gently placing the pup back with its mother they went into the kitchen to prepare breakfast. Monica insisted on phoning Sandra even though it would only be four thirty in the morning in Western Australia. Monica was surprised when a male voice answered the phone. "Billy speaking," he yawned.

"Sorry I must have the wrong number. I was after Sandra Young."

"No problems," the male voice replied.

"Hello," a sleepy Sandra answered.

"Hi Sandra, Monica here. You are the mother of five of the most gorgeous pups ever," a confused Monica said.

"Gee thanks Monica but they are your pups too, whatever you sell them for, you keep. They're well bred and easy to sell," Sandra replied.

"Have you seen Felicity and Tom yet? They phoned last week and I thought they would be with you by now," Monica asked.

"Yep they are here, arrived day before yesterday. Tom is going in the helicopter with Billy today actually, on the muster," Sandra cheerfully informed the inquisitive Monica.

"Well give them our love. Sam sends his regards and looks forward to you coming home later. Will you be on your own?" asked Monica.

Sandra knew Monica and Sam would be in absolute misery if she left them hanging so went on."No, I will be bringing my fiancee Billy North home. We're going to be married. Was going to tell you guys soon anyway, wanted to ask Sam if he would give me away?"

Passing the phone to Sam, Monica pointed at it excitedly.

"How is my favorite girl Sandra?"

"Fine Sam. In love, isn't it great? Bringing home my fiancee. Billy. We want to be married at your place and will you give me away?" Sandra asked.

"Not only that,' Sam replied, "we'll give you the best wedding ever. I'll book the marquee again and ring the caterers today, just give us a date."

"Gee thanks Sam. Better tell you the full story, no pill here so got carried away and already pregnant. Sam, he is a wonderful young man, you will love him. He is the ancestor of the famous Billy of the North and Lily," Sandra excitedly told him.

Sam and Sandra chatted for a time before Sam hung up the phone. "Well I hope he is a nice young man for Sandra's sake, she seems so happy. Felicity will tell us what he is like next time she phones," said Sam .

"Any other details Sam?" Monica pumped.

"Well, she is pregnant and Billy's ancestor was Billy of the North and Lily," Sam replied.

"We will be swamped by children soon Sam if all the family keeps breeding," Monica laughed. "And who the hell is Billy of the North and Lily?"

"Well, he's a famous legend of the north. Billy was a Scottish sailor who jumped ship to save his mate who was a convict. They ran riot ahead of the law for two decades. Billy married an aboriginal girl, Lily, and had eight children. A true and rather remarkable story."

"Billy must be part aboriginal then. Must be skilled to fly a helicopter."

"Some of them are very skilled stockmen. I look forward to meeting him," Sam replied.

With breakfast over they decided to go back to bed for a while, the weather was foul and Monica had been up most of the night checking on Bella; even Jacky seemed tired and shivered against the chill.

Climbing into the warm bed Monica snuggled up to Sam, her hand wandering down to his penis in a playful mood. She started stroking it and Sam, as usual, was unable to control his desire. Soon Monica was sitting astride Sam rising and falling in ecstasy.

Celia wanted to dash into new Norfolk to purchase disposable nappies and pulled up in the driveway to see if her mother wanted to go for the ride. Because of the rain and wind neither heard her enter the house. Thinking both must still be asleep she went up to tap on the bedroom door.

She found the bedroom door ajar and looking in, took a deep breath as she saw her mother riding up and down on Sam's cock, oblivious to anything around her. Sam had her by the buttocks, slamming into her, both pleasuring each other in absolute abandonment.

Quickly turning, she felt faint as she raced down to the kitchen, needing a cup of strong coffee. She sat on a bar stool sipping the hot drink when she realised her hands were shaking. Never did she consider her mother would still be sexually active. The thought never crossed her mind. Thinking back, her father never even slept with her mother in all the time she remembered. Never had she, even in her wildest dreams, thought of her mother as a sexual being.

While in deep thought, she heard her mother happily singing, coming down the stairs. Monica was absolutely naked and Celia could not help but notice her shaven and shining vagina. Seeing Celia, Monica, looking surprised and said, "Oops, wait dear and I'll throw on a dressing gown."

Monica returned, smiling happily and sat down next to Celia. "What brings you over so early dear?"

"Well, we're out of nappies so I decided to call over to see if you wanted to go into town."

"Well no, I don't think I will if you don't mind. We are going to have a lay in, a good chance in this rain."

"Mum I just saw you and Sam screwing upstairs. Sorry the door was open. Good lord were you into it; he is as big as a bloody horse."

"You won't believe this Celia but we have been caught twice bonking, and yes, he sure is a good lover," Monica cheerily replied.

"Hell Mum I never thought of you that way. I suppose it

was a shock to see you enjoying screwing so much."

"Being honest with you I can say that I am making up for lost time. I was sexually starved for decades and now I intend to make love to Sam whenever the opportunity arises."

Celia looked at her mother. *She is a bloody sex machine* she thought, *never did I consider mum as sexual. Dad always stayed clear of her and I thought she was frigid.*

"Mum, do you still... are you capable of an orgasm?" asked Celia.

"Had my first orgasm with Sam in a small donga at Cape Leveque nearly a year ago and I've had many since. It's a wonder you have never heard me upstairs, he drives me sexually insane."

"How about the lack of pubic hair? Do you shave or what?" asked an inquisitive and still shocked Celia.

"Yes I shave, it's a bit of a nuisance but Sam likes it and it does heighten the sexual act."

"Hell you're honest Mum. It was just a shock, I never dreamt of you having sex and silly really, I've seen the way Sam looks at you. I thought people your age were incapable of sex, but you two out do me, for hell sakes, talk about a pair of goers," said Celia, attempting to regain her composure.

"I don't really know what the accepted age is that people are supposed to be able to maintain a sexual relationship, that is why I intend to enjoy it as long as possible. I'll still love Sam when our sex life ends, but to be frank, I really am enjoying it."

Celia stood up feeling completely at ease. "Well I had better get going. Back to bed you old sex maniac. I will certainly look at you in a different light, hell it is amazing."

Monica waved Celia goodbye wondering what all the fuss was about and made her way back up the stairs and into bed with Sam.

The next few months flew by and Sam and Monica looked

forward to the return home of Felicity and Tom who had decided to purchase a small business so they could work together and requested that Sam look for something suitable for them in Hobart as neither had any ideas.

Allen phoned saying that he and Margaret felt they were missing out on the family life happening in Tasmania and had decided that Allen would leave the army and buy a motel in Hobart that had been recently advertised. The news came as a shock to Monica but she was thrilled at the idea of the whole family being together for the first time ever.

In the next few weeks Allen and his family arrived to take over their motel. Felicity and Tom arrived home to great celebrations and the news that Felicity was pregnant.

"It must be you two sex maniacs. Everyone associated with you is having, or has had babies," commented Celia.

Both Mary and Victoria told Sam and Monica many times of the great thrill life now gave them. Every day seemed exciting with loving family around with wonderful news of pregnancies and each day becoming a new adventure.

Sandra and her fiancee Billy arrived and immediately Sam found Billy to be a fine young man. They seemed hopelessly in love. The empty house of Sandra's had been cleaned up and the garden tidied in readiness for their arrival

Monica and her two old friends purchased a double bed and table and chairs to make do for the first few days until the couple had time to settle in and fully furnish the charming cottage.

Billy said he was sold. He loved the place and told Sam he looked forward to returning each year to stay for a few months when the station was landlocked by the wet season.

It had only been a matter of days since Sandra's return when all the calves on the three properties were marked and tagged; old cows culled and the balance of the steers marketed.

As the wedding day approached excitement mounted as Sam, amused, watched the women in his life go into overdrive yet again.

"Seems to make women happy, either arranging weddings or having babies," he said to Billy and Tom as they sat on the verandah. Both men laughed with old Sam. He was a favorite and many times they had bet with Felicity as to when Sam would say 'a man's gotta do what a man's gotta do' again. It also became a favorite game of the youngsters in an endearing way.

On the day of the wedding the same procedure as for Felicity's wedding took place: Joe again, with the help of his local football team set up early, and Sam noted Joe was well underway before the guests even started to arrive.

Sam proudly escorted Sandra up the isle giving her away to Billy. Monica made sure she only had two drinks and it was Celia who seemed to over indulge, caught up in the excitement. To Monica's delight Celia and Allen seemed to be starting to get on together and the two boys obviously liked Auntie Celia because she made them laugh with her sarcastic comments. Felicity and Tom looked radiant as attendants even though Felicity had started to show a small bump.

Three days after the wedding Sam was shattered to find Jacky dead on the little bed he had next to Sam's; it appeared he died peacefully in his sleep, The whole family attended Jacky's funeral, shedding many tears for Sam's old companion who had shared so much happiness and grief with him. Sam made a small coffin and laid Jacky in front of Carol in the family plot; no one thought this strange as Jacky was a highly respected family member.

With the wedding over and after Jacky's burial, things seemed to settle down once again. Tom and Felicity purchased a printing business and although it made no fortune it gave them a good living and with the investments they lived happily.

Felicity gave birth to a boy calling him Samuel Thomas after two of the most cherished men in her life. Sandra returned to the Kimberlys. Billy phoned just before they were due to return south again with the news that Sandra had given birth to twin girls. She named one Carol and the other Monica after the loves of her mentor and friend Sam.

Life settled into family visits, great Sunday barbacues and watching the children grow like mushrooms, always doted on by Grandma Monica, Pop Sam, Auntie Victoria and Mary.

Sam and the crew of the Matilda eventually received bravery awards for the daring rescue of Wayne and Joe in the fury of that westerly gale on the rocks of Maatsuyker Island. The story of Sam and Monica lasted for years and many spoke of the incident years later; it became a story of love and passion repeated many times.

Victoria and Mary became feeble and just wanted to live quietly, visited by Sam and Monica weekly, imploring both to allow them to die free and not in a old age facility. On one visit Victoria sat next to Sam looking at him, at her old friend. She said, "Sam, I know this is asking a lot of our friendship but Mary and I have one last wish to ask you."

"What ever I can do in my power for you both I will. I thank you both for the many years of happiness that my daughter and I have had through meeting both of you."

Victoria looked anxiously at Sam. "Well Sam, since our first meeting both of us have had a magnificent life. My late husband, who now I only just remember god forgive me, in the mists of time, was cremated and his ashes cast to sea. Both Mary and I wish to be buried, if you will allow it, in your family plot. We can think of no finer people to lay beside than you and Monica."

Sam was a bit shaken by the request but felt honored. "It would be my greatest honor to have you rest in our small family plot Victoria; it has always been my greatest pleasure to class both you ladies as special and loving friends. I'll never forget you both for helping me and possibly sacrificing your freedom to rescue Monica."

Both looked lovingly at Sam and Monica who had a tear in her eye. *Time,* she thought, *was catching up with us all.*

"Since we met you my dear Sam, what a magnificent life you have delivered to us. I am sorry that two old women, even in death, wish to still tag along with you," said Mary.

"You'll both live yet for many happy years. How about coming home with us for a few days."

They graciously accepted, loving the house and company of Sam and Monica, who looked after them, fussing over their every need. Monica helped pack a few clothes and all four drove back to the farm that had given them so much pleasure, happy in the knowledge it would also be their last resting place.

Chapter 33

Two more years had passed by when Monica and Sam drove towards Hobart to visit Victoria and Mary. It had been ten years since the day Monica and her two friends had jumped into Sam's vehicle naked on Cable Beach.

Victoria had felt unwell the previous evening and Mary phoned Sam and Monica to come first thing in the morning. Tom and Felicity were worried and wanted to place her into hospital but the feisty Victoria had refused telling all she would be 'okay' in the morning. She had agreed to go with Sam and Monica to the hospital if she still felt ill the following day.

It seemed she wanted to see Sam and Monica so Mary had phoned. On arrival, they became alarmed to see an ambulance parked out front. They were horrified to learn that Victoria had died peacefully in her sleep; the last thing she uttered to Mary before going to sleep was to make sure Sam and Monica were coming the following morning.

Tom and Felicity were visibly upset. Both Victoria and Mary had been a big part of their lives, baby sitting young Sam and helping in any way they could. Sam and Monica also felt shattered; the trio of sisters in arms was broken.

Mary sat quietly, vacantly staring at the ambulance and her old friend who had changed her life, unable to comprehend living on without her dear friend.

Sam insisted that Mary go home with them, at least until the funeral, if not longer. Mary agreed, anxious to be near the two people she loved and who had made her later years exciting and happy. Victoria was buried surrounded by all her adopted family in a quiet ceremony in Sam's private cemetery.

Mary seemed to lose all interest in living after the death of her close friend and sat for hours on Monica's verandah looking out at her old friend's grave.

Six months later Mary passed away. The family had been worried for some time about her mental condition, she seemed to drift into a world of her own after Victoria's death and refused to go back to the unit they had shared.

Once again, a family funeral was held, this time for Mary, and she was placed next to her old friend Victoria.

Although Sam and Monica missed their old friends they relished the company of each other. Monica had confided to Celia that their sex life had slowed down considerably but she had enjoyed it while it lasted. Monica had joked that at least she experienced nirvana with Sam; he had shown her true intimacy.

Another year of family visits and Christmas passed. Sandra and Billy were home with the girls, both growing like mushrooms, wild and free, just like their mother. Felicity had begun to drop young Sam off to stay nights with his grandfather when she and Tom went to functions. Sam loved to have young Sam stay and they became very close.

Both Felicity and Celia gave notice that once was enough in the child birth stakes and neither felt like a repeat performance.

Celia had not heard from her mother for two days and called her. She became worried when the phone was not answered and after trying several more times, she hopped into her car and drove over to the farm.

Finding the house empty she ran across the paddocks, a feeling of fear making her break into a sweat. The weather was freezing and the ground wet; it had been snowing for two days.

Her heart leapt in her mouth as she saw the bodies of Sam and her mother lying on the ground.

The previous evening, Sam had gone to feed the cows and on the way back had suffered a severe stroke. Police worked out he had tried to crawl to get help by the look of the flattened grass but had died while trying. Monica, alarmed, had gone looking and on finding him had collapsed in grief, trying to cover and protect him with her body from the falling snow. She was still sprawled over him, frozen, having tried to keep him warm, refusing to leave him.

During the long night, grief stricken, she had died not wanting to live without her beloved Sam A look of complete peace was frozen on her face; even in death, she would not leave Sam. He had given her many years of love and tenderness, a new life and the kind of love she had only ever imagined. Without him her reason to live no longer existed.

The funeral was held, and as planned, Sam lay between the two women he had lived with and loved. He had often remarked how lucky his life had been, unable to believe such passion and love would be experienced twice in his life.

It was a sad occasion for the family. The very two people who had brought them all together now lay before them, two amazing people who had always shown true love and friendship, compassion and had wanted always to please and nurture those around them.

Years passed by and Felicity and Tom sold out and retired to the farm. One beautiful spring day two middle-aged women stood before the graves site, it was Sandra and Felicity.

"I often think about the lives of these beautiful souls who lay here. No-one will remember them after we have gone," said Felicity.

"They sure showed us how to love and live. I can still see Sam and both your mother and Monica. He was so happy with them."

"Yes. In many ways, dad was a simple man; he loved life and people loved him."

"One day, these graves will be gone and all traces of their lives gone forever and the story of their lives gone, sadly forever," said Sandra.

"Well, I am going to be buried here and so is Tom with his grandmother Mary so the story will survive another generation," said Felicity.

"I'm being buried here also," Sandra said. "You are my family too. Sam is the closest thing I ever had to a father. I loved him unconditionally and always will."

The two turned and walked slowly back to the homestead where husbands and family waited; it was the barbecue evening, another family get together.